Pauline

Praise for Anne Grant's
MULTIPLE LISTING

DELL BOOKS BY ANNE UNDERWOOD GRANT

Multiple Listing
Smoke Screen

SMOKE SCREEN

ANNE UNDERWOOD GRANT

A Dell Book

Published by
Dell Publishing
a division of
Bantam Doubleday Dell Publishing Group, Inc.
1540 Broadway
New York, New York 10036

ISBN: 0-440-22552-3

Printed in the United States of America

Published simultaneously in Canada

September 1998

10 9 8 7 6 5 4 3 2 1

OPM

ACKNOWLEDGMENTS

Bill Ducket over in Big Sandy Mush let me roam his tobacco acreage. That experience, more than any other, set the tone for this story. I thank him for his hospitality and generosity of spirit. Many other people also contributed to the development of this story: Judith Riven through her enthusiasm for it; Jacquie Miller through her editorial insights and probing questions; AC Hunter, Frances Hawthorne, Ann Mallard Fielding, Craig Fielding, and Mary Anne Riley through their efforts as the best EditGroup the world has ever known; Bobbe Deason through her horticultural sleuthing; Bill Underwood through his knowledge of the law; Sergeant Rick Sanders of the Charlotte-Mecklenburg Police Department through his knowledge of being the law; and, finally, Leighton Kyle Grant through his automotive reenactment of Paul Revere's midnight ride.

1

Over ten years in advertising have made a cynic out of me. I can predict with frightening regularity exactly what prospective clients will tell me about their products. They all tell me they put their customers first, of course. Nobody believes that line anymore, but companies insist on it anyway. Companies all say the same things, so the challenge for me is to say it differently, somehow uniquely.

"Mr. Bolick should be here shortly," the young assistant said. "He's quite busy," she added as she readjusted the pierced hoop hanging from her ear.

Seth Bolick was thirty minutes late for our nine o'clock meeting. If he had been a typical client and his product like most of the others I build campaigns for, I would have left by twenty after. That I was sitting here too excited about Bolick's account to leave said a whole lot about Bolick the man and the product he insisted on calling Snake.

On November 3, Seth had walked into Allen Teague unannounced. Allen Teague is my ad agency. Allen for my birth family and Teague for the long-gone father of my two children. Two weeks earlier I'd never even heard of Seth Bolick, although Bill's law firm was handling Snake's patent work. Bill's my brother, and his purely corporate law firm is Todd, Rains, Allen, Dresser and Ellsworth, PC. I call them the TRADE group, although the only thing this collection of hidebound southern WASPs trade for is buckets of money. Even when my secretary, Sally, suggested he make an appointment through her, Seth Bolick insisted on sitting in the reception room until he could speak with me in person. Sally told me later how, in the two hours he sat with her, he could have charmed the wings off an angel. Of course, my Sally's no angel, and any man who says hello in just the right way has her in his pocket for at least a day.

I'm not so easy though. In fact, my first reaction to most prospects is disbelief. I find it useful. If I can be sold on a product, I figure I can sell others. But Seth Bolick got to me too. On a much deeper level than where he touched Sally. He touched feelings in me I thought I'd dealt with and overcome decades ago. I respected his keen intellect, his inventor's scientific imagination; mostly, though, I envied his dogged determination to right what he saw as a great wrong. And, yes, I guess he was charming on top of everything else.

The assistant shifted uncomfortably on the small red swivel chair. She tugged at her short skirt with both hands, her heels spiking themselves into the hardwood floor to keep the chair from shooting out from under her.

The concentrated determination she brought to this task showed in her wrinkled forehead, reminding me of Chris Evert during her heyday. I couldn't help chuckling.

"What's wrong?" she asked. "Did I say something?"

"You'd think Seth would give you a real chair," I said, pointing toward her seat.

She smiled. "Arms would help." She looked more closely at me. "You called Mr. Bolick Seth. Is he a friend of yours or is this a business appointment?"

"Both. With Seth, I think business is personal and vice versa."

Her expression revealed a confusion I wouldn't have expected in someone who worked with Seth Bolick.

"You're bound to know that," I continued. "You work with him."

She held on to the edge of her metal desk and pulled her chair forward. Once she felt secured between the flanking drawers, she held up both hands, palms up, fingers splayed outwards.

"This all's new," she said. "Last week, I think. They were delivering furniture during my interview. Today's my first day." She looked at me and smiled again, an eager-working-girl, mid-twenties smile. "I just met Mr. Bolick at my interview."

I was curious. "Do you even know what his business is?"

She blushed slightly, cocked her head, then shook it. "Should I? He told me his work was somewhere else, that this office space was for investors and for marketing." She seemed embarrassed, uncomfortable. "Are you an investor?"

"I'm the other. Marketing." I smiled, hoping to

undo the tension I'd obviously built with my last question. "Any other employees here?"

"Mr. Little came in at eight thirty for about five minutes, then left. I believe he's a financial officer. But no one was here at eight, when I got here, and I haven't heard from Mr. Bolick." She reached inside the desk drawer and pulled out a key. "Good thing he gave me this."

The phone startled us both. She looked at her watch and said, "I'll bet that's Mr. Bolick."

I glanced at my own watch as she took the call. Nine forty-five. No matter how excited I was about Snake, I needed to be doing something more productive than sitting in Seth Bolick's recently created reception room.

"Did you say your name is Sydney Teague?" She held the phone away from her ear and motioned for me to come over and take it.

I didn't recognize the voice on the phone. I'd expected Seth, so the clipped tones of a woman I didn't know jarred me for a second.

"Yes, of course I know Sally Ball," I said. "She works for me. Who is this?"

The woman didn't identify herself. Instead she told me Sally was in the emergency room of Wade Community Hospital in Bredon and that my name was the emergency contact found in her wallet.

"Your office gave us this number," she added.

"Are you calling from the hospital?" I asked in disbelief.

"Wade Community Hospital," she repeated.

"What happened? What's wrong with Sally?"

"All I know is she was in a wreck on Highway 29." I could hear a lot of noise in the background. "They just brought her in and had us go through her things to find a contact."

"Wait a minute," I screamed. "Does this mean she can't talk? I want to speak to Sally."

The woman didn't answer. I gripped the phone so tightly I watched my fingers drain of blood.

"Is she conscious? Please answer me."

In the same clipped, noncommittal, reserved voice, she said, "I'm not at liberty to tell you anything, only to request that you come to the emergency room."

I must have dropped that phone. The next thing I remember, I was in the elevator in the middle of the long, slow descent to the bottom of the NationsBank building.

Bredon is twenty-five miles north of Charlotte. My old black Trooper and I were bumper-to-bumper on I-85 before I realized I had no idea where the hospital was.

Her wreck was my fault, dammit. I'd asked Sally to drive up to Wade County before going to work and pick up the video equipment I'd left at Seth Bolick's farm yesterday. I should have driven back there myself. Or called Seth and had him bring it all to town today for our meeting.

My mind flipped back to the sterile reception room I'd just left. How in hell could he have stood me up for such an important meeting? A meeting he called "the official launch of the most important product since the polio vaccine."

"We're not launching it tomorrow," I'd said to him as I was getting ready to leave his farm. "We're beginning a process that's going to take months. Besides, I don't think Salk would have appreciated such a comparison."

But you couldn't have convinced Seth Bolick of that. His new product was his obsession, his life. His enthusiasm was so contagious I had rearranged my schedule and subbed out some small campaigns to create the chunk of time Snake would require.

If I'd been honest with myself and Seth, I would have told him Allen Teague was too small, too geographically off-center to handle the introduction of such a major product. But I hadn't been honest. I'd been selfish and eager and flattered and caught up in Seth Bolick and his cause.

And because of my dishonesty, Sally was probably near death in a Podunk little hospital in the middle of a county known only for its turkeys, its hogs, and its historic tobacco allotments. My speedometer hit eighty-five before I saw the green hospital sign directing me off the interstate.

Wade Community Hospital is all one story, laid out in the shape of a capital E, with its emergency entrance at the end of the top horizontal wing. The winding road leading to this entrance is flanked by waves of Bradford pears, which at this time of year were a deep, mottled crimson. Surprisingly, these leaves hadn't fallen yet.

I screeched to a stop in the almost empty lot, taking the first visitor's space next to an idle EMS van. I steeled myself for what I might possibly find inside. Why hadn't that woman had the decency to tell me what shape I'd find Sally in? It certainly couldn't have been worse than what I'd imagined during the drive up here.

Two sets of automatic double doors swung open ahead of me. The second one emptied me into a room so garishly lighted by fluorescence that I squinted in reflex. On my left, rows of orange plastic chairs were connected to each other by aluminum tubes. An elderly man sat slouched in the middle of the back row, his white hair disheveled and his rumpled raincoat barely covering striped pajamas. His chin lay propped upon his chest. He bobbed to the rhythm of his own snoring.

In front of me two nurses sat in a station the shape of a horseshoe. Neither looked up as I approached. Paperwork consumed them both.

"I'm Sydney Teague. Someone called me about Sally Ball."

The woman closest to me, in fact one foot from me, didn't look up. Instead she said, "Judy, did you call someone about Ball?"

The woman to her right, whom I presumed to be Judy, didn't greet me immediately either. She was writing in what looked like some kind of log.

I moved around to her side of the horseshoe and leaned forward to where my head was just above her curly crown. I cleared my throat.

She stuck up her right forefinger as if bidding at an auction; her head stayed down.

"Just a sec," she said, then looked at her watch before making a final entry.

When she did look up at me, I was surprised to see her eyes were kind.

"I'm—" I began again.

"Mrs. Teague, right?" She leaned to her right and picked up a folder while holding my anxious stare. "Are you a relative of Miss Ball's?"

"I'm her employer. You called me, remember?" I admit to defensiveness. Medical settings bring it out in me. I quickly glanced toward a wide hall behind her, hoping to hear or see Sally so I could get her out of here quickly. Hospitals, in my opinion, aren't healthy no matter how sick you are.

The woman named Judy touched my hand briefly and smiled even more so. She must have seen my type before. "Of course I remember," she said. "There wasn't time to wait for family anyway. Miss Ball's in surgery. She was having some swelling, and they went in to relieve the pressure."

"Swelling of what? You didn't tell me anything on the phone." My throat closed in on itself as I waited for some kind of explanation.

She was holding a black and silver mechanical pencil with one of those hard, useless erasers. She tapped it into her thick salt-and-pepper curls.

I held my breath and waited for the words.

She almost whispered it: "Her brain."

I tried to say "What?" But my throat closed completely, leaving my lips to move silently. A flash of intense heat ran up my neck and exploded in tears. My hands began to shake even though they were propped on the high counter in front of me.

She stood quickly, folding both her hands over mine, her eyes piercing through the unfocused gelatin that my eyes had become.

"She'll be okay, Mrs. Teague. Don't you worry. A wonderful surgeon's taking care of her."

Through my tears I saw her name tag: *Judy Bernstein, LPN*. She looked to be in her mid-fifties, a decade or so ahead of me. Nurse Bernstein told me that Sally had hit her head in the wreck and that swelling like this was to be expected. Meanwhile I should let her family know where she was. She finished her speech by plopping a large box of generic tissue on the counter. It occurred to me she had played this scene before. This woman was a pro. She hadn't told me anything concrete to make me believe Sally would be okay really, but I felt better anyway.

The public telephone was on a light green cinderblock wall behind the sleeping old man. I didn't know Sally's parents, just knew that they were divorced and lived in different states. Her brother Fred lived in Charlotte, but I didn't know his phone number. I opted for calling my office and having my art director, Hart Johnson, find Sally's family.

If human personality were theorized to have three distinct sides, a triangle of opposites, then Sally, Hart, and I could serve as its models. In any given situation, it's a sure bet we will produce three different reactions. We are nothing so simple as earth, fire, and water, but I can count on Hart and Sally to have two opposing takes from me on almost every experience we share. I think it's why we can get at the heart of a product so well. It's also why we three don't socialize much outside of work. Most of the time, though, I feel good about our differences.

Even knowing him as well as I did, Hart's cool

reaction to my news of Sally's wreck confused me. His first words were "So that's why Wade Community Hospital was looking for you. They called here."

"You didn't ask the woman why they were looking for me?"

"I figured they wouldn't tell me, so I didn't ask." His practical conservatism was always at counterpoint to my sometimes unpredictable emotions.

"Hart," I said in exasperation, "as we speak, someone is drilling into Sally's brain."

That comment finally got a pregnant silence out of the man.

"Why didn't you tell me it was that serious?" he said.

"I was trying to," I said. "You made your assumptions before I could finish."

Then he asked me exactly what they were doing to Sally and exactly who was doing it. Now, that was more like it, although I couldn't tell him any more than Nurse Bernstein had told me. "I'll find out though. I'll wait here until she's out of surgery so I can talk to her surgeon. I'll call you then, okay?"

I heard him take a deep breath.

"Meanwhile, call Fred and get him to call their parents."

Hart hesitated, then said, "Don't you want to be the one to tell her brother?"

"Of course not," I said loudly and couldn't believe he was goading me at a time like this. Hart knows I feel less than friendly toward Fred Ball.

The old man jerked, and the entire row of orange plastic seats wobbled as one. He coughed, a rumble like a slowly moving summer storm, and settled his chin back onto his chest. I turned to face the wall so I wouldn't bother him again. A distant siren wailed softly.

I whispered to Hart, "Has Seth Bolick called?"

When he told me he hadn't, I looked at my watch. Past eleven. Damn Seth. What kind of game was he playing with me? Hype me up to let me down. I was sifting the seeds of a major resentment. The siren grew louder and something inside me registered its destination as here.

"Get his number off Sally's desk, please. It's under Bolick Enterprises—the Charlotte number, not the one in Wade County."

While I waited for Hart to get me Seth's number, I rummaged through my pocketbook for something to write on, the siren's approaching shrieks playing havoc with my already frayed nerves. I tore off a deposit slip as I clamped my teeth on the pen I keep hooked onto my checkbook. Juggling the pen, the deposit slip, the closed checkbook to press on, and my big old leather pocketbook was impossible while attempting to cradle the phone between my shoulder and my ear. I put the pocketbook on the carpeted floor just as Hart returned and as the ambulance arrived outside the double doors on my left.

"There's a damn ruckus here, Hart," I said. "You're going to have to speak up." The siren had stopped, but people were yelling instructions, and mechanical devices were clanging against each other, against the cement, and against the doors. The old man even woke up and was turning his head in the direction of the double doors.

I still wasn't sure I'd heard Hart correctly, so I was

repeating the digits back to him when the hospital doors finally opened. Someone in obvious distress was on the stretcher, although I could barely see his body because of the large attendant who was leaning over him to adjust a portable oxygen supply. In fact, two attendants blocked my view, the second one adjusting straps on the patient, who was having some kind of seizure.

"Hang on a sec," I said to Hart, since I couldn't yet hear him well enough to get the number straight.

The straps secured, the second ambulance attendant moved to the other side of the gurney to resume the frantic push into the heart of the emergency room. When he did, the man convulsed again and his distorted face turned in my direction.

If I hadn't just spent the weekend with him, I might not have recognized Seth Bolick. Even under the oxygen mask, though, his jawline was firm and seemed determined still. His thick sandy hair was sweaty and limp; yesterday its amber highlights had sparkled in my camera's viewfinder. His skin had no more of the farmer's ruddiness; it was very pale with strange streaks of blue in the hollows of his cheeks. He had on a business suit, so I guessed he'd planned to meet me in his office after all. Only someone had ripped off his shirt buttons and untied his tie to get to his chest.

For the second time that day, I think, I dropped the phone.

2

S ally was still in surgery. Seth had been taken down
the long hallway on the other side of Nurse Bernstein's horseshoe. I was overwhelmed and was totally
helpless to do anything about what was happening.
This hospital felt like a death chamber. I think if I had
known at that moment exactly where they were operating on Sally, I would have single-handedly wheeled her
out of there. No matter what I said to Judy Bernstein,
she wouldn't let me follow Seth's gurney down the hall.
She kept directing me back to the orange chairs and the
old man. The receiver still dangled from the wall phone
where I'd abruptly walked away from my conversation
with Hart. I picked it up and spoke into it, expecting
Hart to still be there. All I heard was a dial tone. I
gulped back my tears when I heard it. I don't know why,
but something about that sound is so damn final.

I didn't have the presence of mind to call him back.
What could he have done other than what he was
already doing? Sally's family still needed to be called.
And besides, Hart couldn't know how important Seth

had become to me in two short weeks. He couldn't understand my devastation at seeing him like this. No one could.

I did what I've done all my life in a crisis I have no control over. I went outside to smoke. I've been trying to quit for five years now, ever since I showed up at work one morning to find that Sally and Hart had erected Thank You for Not Smoking plaques on their desks. My efforts were halfhearted at first, until the day my then ten-year-old son, George junior, came home from school two years ago, after a day of modern, practical education, and asked me point-blank if I knew that I'd been hurting him and his sister Joan with second-hand smoke.

My efforts at quitting began in earnest that day. I went to the doctor, who prescribed a patch, but I found myself smoking while on it and almost passed out from the reaction. Then I began the maze of courses and classes geared to scaring me into stopping. Unfortunately, I found that I don't scare very easily, and the cynic in me was always rewriting their curricula. I even tried using a hypnotist who'd had success with some hard-core smokers I'd known from my twelve years sober in Alcoholics Anonymous. He asked me to think about the times I didn't want to smoke. After two or three sessions we determined that I didn't want a cigarette while I was standing on the actual threshold of a door, between the jams. We didn't get around to any other locations, because by then I had joined what I truly thought would be my salvation from the monster. Smokers Anonymous sounded like my kind of organization. Like a passel of other self-help programs, it had been modeled after AA, and AA had miraculously freed me from my addiction to Scotch. The group began each meeting with the Serenity Prayer, and everybody shared their personal triumphs and tragedies of the past week. So far, so good.

My problem arose, and it was a big one, when they would read the Twelve Steps of AA and substitute nicotine for alcohol. Even at Step One I froze. The phrase "my life had become unmanageable" kept me from hearing beyond it. No honest alcoholic, and we all become honest eventually if we stop, could pretend that her life is manageable. But for the closet smoker, the one who no longer inflicts the addiction on others but continues to feed it in private, "unmanageable" was not the word. The hard, cold fact of smoking addiction is quite simply that I was slowly killing myself. No one else was involved. I also knew instinctively that everything else about the addiction was life enhancing, or so it seemed. My life was manageable, truly manageable, and that was the problem.

I sat on the hood of the Trooper while I smoked the cigarette. I inhaled deeply in the crisp November air and felt my nerve endings obediently align themselves. A gust of cool wind caught my brown corduroy jacket and pulled it away from my lightweight cotton turtleneck. I shivered briefly and pulled the lapels together. A pile of pin oak leaves followed the invisible air current across the asphalt.

Leading off the far end of the parking lot was an asphalt path that appeared to wind around the entire hospital grounds. I thought about walking it but was afraid to leave my view of the emergency room door. In the distance I could hear the traffic on the interstate. It was whooshing and rhythmical, not mechanical at all. I tried breathing to that rhythm but couldn't get it right. I watched two robins pecking among the hodgepodge of dried leaves at the path's edge only to be warned away by a lone black crow who lit between them. I slid off the car and lunged at the crow until he flew off; I don't like bullies, feathered or otherwise. The robins didn't return. Hordes of squirrels gathered acorns and nipped at each other in a frantic display of last-minute grocery shopping.

I stubbed out the cigarette on one of the Trooper's rusted-out spots, turning the dime-size slice of orange to gray. I slipped the butt inside my jacket's pocket and felt the stone when I did. Seth's stone. I pulled it out and looked at it. He'd called it a lapillus. Again I saw the swirling patterns of dark gray that appeared to me as veins seeking the stone's heart. Seth had said those veins were merely an illusion.

"Feel it though," he had said, and grinned when I did.

The lapillus was as smooth as the finest polished marble, maybe smoother. It was the smoothest object I've ever felt, smoother even than glass. It wasn't much bigger, though, than the nuts these squirrels were carrying around in their mouths. I couldn't even imagine a fire so intense as to forge this tiny thing.

"Will it bring me luck?" I remembered asking Seth when he gave it to me.

"If luck's what you need, I suppose so," he had answered. "It's brought me what I needed at just the moment I needed it." I'm sure he was talking about scientific inspiration at the time, and since his inspiration had come from his father, it made sense. His father had given him the stone. Seth had given it to me.

I stroked it now and the sweat from my palms streaked its surface just as if it were glass. You need something this moment, Seth, I said to myself. Luck and something more. I closed my palm around the stone as I closed my eyes. I asked God for whatever He might be able to give as well.

When I opened my eyes, I saw the backs of a woman and a boy who was barely a teenager. They were going into the emergency room. I dropped the lapillus back into my pocket and followed them inside.

They were talking with the nurse who was not Judy Bernstein, and even with the boy's back to me and as young as he was, I recognized the broad shoulders, stocky build, and sandy hair as a Bolick. I had seen his photograph at the farm this weekend and had remarked to Seth at the time how much the boy favored him.

"I don't want him to go through anything approaching what I went through as a teenager," Seth had said to me.

By the time he'd said this, he didn't have to explain. I knew the demons Seth had faced, just as he knew mine. We had spent as much time talking about the moments that had shaped us as we had his product. What had happened to him had taken the life he might have had and altered it in ways impossible to measure. I had had those defining moments as well. I guess we all do. Just not as defining as Seth's.

Once they had moved to the orange chairs, I took my turn with the same nurse.

"Is that Seth Bolick's son?" I asked.

She nodded. "Johnny. And his mother. Mr. Bolick's ex." Her voice lowered to a whisper. "But not technically; they just don't live together. Name's Sara. She was a Hutchins."

I smiled. "How do you know all that from a two-minute conversation?"

"Bredon's small," she said. "Everybody knows just about everybody else in Wade County. Unless, of course, they're one of those Northerners who've come here in the last ten years."

"Overrun, are you?"

She shook her head. "The more Charlotte fills up, the more people keep coming to Wade County. They drive forty-five minutes in there to work every day and think it's just dandy. I don't know any of those people."

She said this sarcastically with a tinge of pity in her voice. Then, as if remembering something critical, she held her head back and studied me for an instant.

"You're not one, are you? One of those northern commuters?"

I held both hands up, palms facing her, proclaiming my innocence. "Do I sound like one of them?" I did my best drawl. "Don't worry. I actually live in Charlotte."

She relaxed. "And you know Seth Bolick?"

"I've been working closely with him for the past two weeks. He hasn't been sick. At least he hasn't let on to me."

She continued to give me her attention. "And the woman from the wreck is your secretary?" Her expression was now solicitous. "Judy told me that."

"Yes," I said. "I wish you could give me some good

news about both of them." I wanted to say "help me get them out of here."

She stared evenly at me, no expression on her face now at all. "We don't know any more than you do. We'll come get you when the surgeon tells us something about your secretary." Then she stared—in that same blank manner—in the direction of Johnny Bolick and his mother. She said, "Seth looked bad."

There was no place to go but back to the orange chairs. It seemed silly to me to sit away from them but somehow intrusive to sit next to them, so I opted for the same row, with two chairs between us. I decided to introduce myself.

"Dad mentioned you." The boy smiled nervously at me.

I smiled nervously in return. I didn't know what else to say.

Sara Bolick extended her hand. "I'm Sara Bolick. You're working with Seth on Snake?"

I nodded. "I had a meeting with him this morning. He didn't show up." I looked into her eyes. "What happened to him?"

She frowned at me, looked away quickly. I didn't think the question had been rude under the circumstances.

All three of us were silent.

"Chemist or investor?" she asked after a full minute of strained quiet.

"Neither," I said. "I'm working with him on a marketing campaign." I felt apologetic but didn't know why.

She sighed. "There've been so many people coming in and out recently. The state agriculture people, the FDA, all those health organizations."

The boy said, "The National Institutes of Health and the National Cancer Institute." There was a distinct pride in his voice. He couldn't have been older than thirteen.

Nurse Bernstein called out my name and motioned me to her desk, where I saw a man in white coming from that long back hallway. I guessed he was Sally's surgeon. The man whispered something to Judy, who then nodded in my direction.

"You're here for Miss Bull?" he said, looking at the paperwork in his hand.

"Ball," I corrected him, then nodded, although he didn't see me.

"Follow me." He turned around and began walking toward that hallway.

I followed. We ended up in a tiny office off the very beginning of the hallway. This was, I supposed, where they inevitably gave family members either the good news or the bad news.

He closed the door, making the room seem even smaller. He took a seat on one side of the little round table and laid a clipboard and manila file folder onto it. He didn't ask me to take one of the other two chairs, but I did anyway. So far this doctor had not looked at me, and that made me nervous.

"My name is Dr. Fritz, and I'm Miss—" He stopped and looked at the top of the clipboard. "Miss Ball's surgeon."

I opened my mouth to give my name, but he didn't look up from his paperwork. He continued: "She suffered a fractured skull from a sharp blow to her head. A hematoma developed very quickly, and by the time she had reached us, it was apparent an extradural hemorrhage had occurred."

"Extradural?" The information was coming too fast. I had to interrupt him.

He looked at me for the first time. I saw impatience in his eyes. "Between the dura mater and the inner surface of her skull."

I nodded as if that explanation had satisfied me.

"A CT scan confirmed it," he continued. "We opened her up, drained the clot, and clamped the ruptured vessel." He flipped to the next page on his clipboard. "Her vitals are coming along. She probably won't wake up until tomorrow. Can go home the first of next week with no complications." It was as if someone had given him the list of most commonly asked questions and the answers to memorize. He restacked his clipboard and file, then pulled them to his edge of the table as if he was getting ready to stand up.

He said, "Mrs. Ball, your daughter should be fine."

I didn't know whether to laugh or cry. Sally is a mere five years younger than I am. No one's ever mistaken me for her mother—at least, to my face.

"Sally is my secretary, not my daughter." I was trying to keep the hurt out of my voice. "Can I see her?"

"I don't think you want to. She looks pretty bad."

"What do you mean by 'bad'?"

"Swollen, bruised. Brain surgery does that to people. Besides, she won't wake up until tomorrow. Why don't you come back then?" He was standing again now, looking very impatient with me. His shoulders had actually turned toward the door.

"Wait a minute," I said. "I might want to have her

transferred to Carolinas Medical Center in Charlotte. I want her to have the best care." I bit my lip. I knew better than to tell a doctor his care might not be the best. His shoulders had turned back to face me. "The most appropriate care," I added quickly. "I meant to say the most appropriate care."

I shouldn't have worried about hurting his feelings. If anything, he became haughtier. "Wade Community Hospital is her most appropriate care, Mrs. Ball—"

"Teague," I said. "My name's Teague."

"Wade Community is now part of Carolinas Medical. Soon we'll be known as Carolinas Medical North. Besides, you don't have the authority to call for a transfer. She's fine here."

When he left the room, he didn't close the door. I could hear his footsteps moving deeper into the bowels of the hospital. When I felt he was safely distant, I didn't stick my tongue out, but I did say "Oh my God" rather loudly.

Then I heard a woman cry. One loud "Seth, no" seemed to drag on for a full minute, followed by sobs and the scraping of chairs. I stood at the door and looked into the hall. I could barely see Johnny and Sara Bolick across the hall, one room down. Over my shoulder I heard the padded shoes of both nurses as they rushed toward the sounds of people in pain.

Confusion completely overwhelmed me. I didn't want to believe what I was witnessing, what my mind had known the second I heard Sara Bolick scream. Seth was dead.

3

Some people get off on other people's pain. I've noticed that all my life. When human tragedy strikes, many of us turn into voyeurs.

My reaction is the opposite. Maybe it's the alcoholic in me, this instinct to run from pain, but it's so strong at times that my memory of an event is almost lost. A stranger probably wouldn't notice it, though, because the flight is a mental thing. I've been told I appear calm, even helping those in pain should I need to.

But that day my flight was physical. I found myself outside the building, running as fast as I could with no destination but away from that hospital. I didn't stop in the parking lot but continued to the asphalt path. As if the building itself had exploded and survival meant distance between it and me.

Only when I thought my lungs would burst did I slow down. I stumbled and fell against a large, hundred-year-old oak. Its roots were gnarled and bulging, its striated bark so firm that I compulsively ran my hand up and down its surface. Over and over I repeated the stroking, until the strength of the tree seemed to pull me back into reality. When it did, I began to hit that big, old oak with the side of my fist. I finally let my own tears flow. For Seth. And for me.

I remembered the day we met, when he finally made his way into my office after winning Sally over. He was not the most charming man I've ever met, but still, he was charming enough. I'm not immune to such qualities. But I've never altered my life for charm. I did alter it for Seth's dream.

Seth knew he couldn't hook me with charm alone. He knew he would need more than a standard advertising commitment out of me. His bait would have to be stronger. He'd done his homework, although I didn't know it at the time. It all seemed to unfold so naturally.

He had inhaled the air inside my office dramatically, even holding up an index finger as if to gauge a nonexistent wind. "Ms. Teague, you smoke cigarettes." Just as dramatically, he had leaned across my desk to within a foot of my startled face. "Surely you know how bad they are for you." Then he sat in my blue client chair and waited for me to react.

"Get out of my office," I said.

He turned up both palms as if to show pure innocence. "Why?" he said. "What have I done to offend you?"

"That's personal," I said, remaining firm.

He scratched his head. He really did look innocent.

"You don't walk into someone's office and start criticizing her personal habits. And, if you're another snake oil salesman with a stop-smoking pitch, save your breath—not mine. Sally shouldn't have let you in." I glanced toward the door leading from my room to Sally's reception area.

He seemed amused at my irritation. "Your secretary has no idea why I'm here. She was loyal, brave, and true," he said mocking my displeasure. "She said I'd have to wait until you were free. So now you are, Sydney, so here I am."

I was shocked he'd used my first name. I'd been so convinced until now that he was an off-the-street solicitor. I looked closely at this man, wondering if I was supposed to know him already. Nope, never seen him before. I would have remembered.

I sighed. "Okay, just who are you and what do you want out of me?"

He settled back into the chair, sometimes a sign of long-windedness to come. Just in case, I added, "Twenty words or less."

First he counted on his fingers, then he said, "My name is Seth Bolick and I'm a chemical engineer and a farmer. I want to be your favorite client." He raised bushy eyebrows in anticipation of my approval. "Twenty words exactly. Engineers are precise."

I swallowed hard. Prospects come looking for me about as often as gold shows up in my rock garden. I shot up out of my swivel chair and reached to shake his hand.

"I'm so sorry, Mr. Bolick," I said. "I'm Sydney Teague, but of course you know that already."

He was grinning.

I kept on. "The cigarette thing struck a nerve, I'm

afraid. Every time I turn around, someone is trying to make a buck off us poor hard-cores."

"I understand," he said. "When I was younger, I cherished the leaf myself. Had to where I grew up."

I nodded at his admission. "Oh boy, so now you're out to reform the world. All because you had the power to quit."

His laugh was self-deprecating. "No, actually I got asthma when I hit thirty." He reached into his shirt pocket and retrieved one of those little submarine-looking nebulizers—complete with periscope.

"Maybe we all need a little asthma," I said. "Just a little bit," I added when I saw he wasn't amused.

"You don't want asthma," he said quite seriously now. "I'm luckier than most. Only get attacks on cold mornings or when I go running." He opened his mouth and pretended to squeeze the inhaler. "A squirt or two of this acts as a preventative. Other people aren't so lucky."

I wanted to change the subject. I asked him how he'd heard about Allen Teague.

"Your brother's handling some patents of mine," he began. "When the subject of marketing came up, I asked him who he could recommend."

I was both surprised and pleased. Bill and I don't, as a matter of business, refer clients to each other very often. "That was nice of Bill," I said and smiled.

Seth laughed. "He recommended two larger firms, one in New York; the other in Atlanta. Your name only came up after I gave him my criteria."

"And what were your criteria?" I asked but wasn't sure I wanted to know.

He leaned forward and began to count on his fingers again. "An agency that was small. So people wouldn't mind rolling up their sleeves to do the work. Just as important though was the creativity. I wanted a highly creative group. I read up on you so I know about all your awards. And, third—this is the most important of all—I wanted an agency whose principal smokes." He grinned and sat back.

I made a mental note to recommend my dear brother the next time someone wanted a corporate attorney who commits adultery on a regular basis. What I said to Seth though was, "That's a first. Don't expect me to be flattered."

He raised his eyebrows again and looked at me sheepishly. "I'm honest," he said. "Surely, that counts for something."

I sighed. "Strangely enough, for me, it does. So, tell me about yourself and your product." I stared at him and waited.

He stood slowly, pulling up his slouchy khaki pants at the belt as he did. He lumbered over to my office door, his tan leather work boots looking out of place against my old oriental rugs. He leaned into the open door, waved and winked at Sally, then closed the door before returning to face me. He ran a hand through his thick, unkempt sandy hair as if the motion would stimulate his mind.

"I'm not important," he said when he finally spoke. "Neither is Bolick Enterprises."

He let his words sink in.

"Okay," I said.

"The product's all that matters. I need your help to

get it on the market." He had walked to the window and turned to face me.

"Okay," I said again. "So tell me about your product." I took out a fresh legal pad, just as I always do with a new client.

Seth paused and gazed out the window at the cars traveling East Boulevard in front of my office. His shoulders rose, then slumped quickly as if releasing some built-up pressure. I noticed how broad his shoulders were and registered his strength.

He turned toward me again and smiled. Even though I didn't know him, I could see that he was tired. His eyes were bloodshot and puffy. I decided it was probably a combination of overwork and his asthma.

"I don't know where to begin," he said, then laughed as if surprised at himself. "I've spent so many years not talking about it that I feel I'm doing something wrong now."

I scratched my Pilot V Ball pen against the top yellow sheet to keep the pen's fluids active.

"Just tell me what it is," I said, trying to hide impatience. I stuck the bottom of my pen into the side of my mouth and sucked briefly.

Seth walked over to my desk and pushed around my stacks of paperwork. "Where are they?" he said.

"What?" I restacked a pile of Chamber of Commerce work his rifling had sent sliding across some other files.

"Your cigarettes. Where are they?"

I reached into my middle desk drawer but hesitated before I brought out my pack of Vantage. "Come on, now," I said. "If your product's snake oil, I warned you. Selling or inventing makes no difference. I'm not buying."

He wasn't listening to me. When he saw the cigarettes, he grabbed them and held the pack in front of my face.

"Don't you wonder why they've never made these safe?" There was urgency in his voice.

The question was a shock, I admit. Assuming it had been mere rhetorical windup, however, I chose to sit there waiting for him to continue.

He didn't. Instead he wanted me to answer.

"Well, I don't guess I have. Wondered, that is."

"Why not?" He was still standing beside my desk.

"What do you mean by 'safe'?"

He looked dumbfounded by the question.

I rushed to clarify myself. "Are you talking about secondhand smoke? Because tobacco companies have tried reducing the smoke, and so far nobody's liked what they've come up with."

He said, "Safe is a very simple concept. It means something which doesn't kill those exposed to it."

I shrugged.

"Did you think they didn't know how? Did you think they didn't have the technology?" He stared so intently I had to look away.

I was beginning to feel uncomfortable. The truth was, the less I had to think about my habit, the better. Seth Bolick's probing was making my skin crawl.

"For almost thirty-five years," he said, "the official government position has been that it kills." The anger in his voice was unmistakable. "During those years, we've been to the moon and sent back pictures from

Mars. We've learned how to transplant human body parts. We've invented and mastered the computer, and our drug therapies for chronic illness are unmatched in the history of chemical engineering. We can genetically alter anything that has genes. Animal or vegetable." He paused to take a breath, then carefully placed the pack of Vantage on my blank legal pad. As he did, he said, "Don't you think, after all these years and all these miraculous inventions, that someone, somewhere, would have invented the truly safe cigarette?"

We stared at each other. I felt it was clearly my turn to say something, at least ask a question. But I didn't. I just continued to stare at him.

Seth Bolick exhaled through his nose, a clear sign of his frustration with me. He looked at the big, black-rimmed school clock on my wall, then back at me.

"It's twelve thirty. You have any lunch plans?" He put both hands in his pants pockets. In spite of his stockiness, there was almost an impish quality to the way he gestured and moved. It showed mostly in his facial expressions though. Especially when he smiled. His mouth, smooth and rounded when serious, dipped to a V when he smiled.

Oh yes, he had piqued my interest. And he was a new client, after all. So I climbed into his pre-1990 full-sized Bronco. But not before picking up my cigarettes and putting them safely in my pocketbook.

Sally sent us off with much fanfare, actually telling me to take my time over lunch. There wasn't anything pressing at the agency, she'd said, as if she were in charge of doling out the labor. I could see right through her. It was Seth Bolick. Sally wanted to be sure I took the time to sell him properly, and if that meant she'd have to cover for me because of a long lunch, it was certainly worth her while. The world is short on his kind of charm, she'd say later.

Excitement and fear are an agitating combination, but I felt them both as I left for lunch that day. I understood the excitement, because his enthusiasm was catching. I felt I'd been invited on an adventure, a Yellow Brick Road. But I'd felt that before with new clients. What I wasn't used to was the feeling of dread that danced in the back of my head as we left. I thought at the time it was probably the whole subject of cigarettes and that what I felt was nerves. Now I wonder. Maybe it was something he carried in his presence, something that was simply a part of Seth Bolick, something I couldn't possibly understand at the time.

Normally I'd have spent a new client lunch like that selling the prospect on our creative resources. What Sally would call "locking in," a term she'd used since dating a Gulf War pilot. This lunch was a veritable opposite, with Seth Bolick selling me, instead, on his considerable inventive powers.

The day had started out cold with a slight spray of frost covering low areas. By lunch the day had turned into what I always dream summer in Charlotte will be but never is: seventy-five degrees, blue sky, and no humidity. For November 3, it was unseasonably warm.

Seth had insisted on eating outside, so I had him drive two short blocks up to South Boulevard and the Pewter Rose, where the second-story balcony renders an exquisite view of power lines and a brickyard. I've attended many a boring lunch on this particular balcony, one memorable one having yielded via napkin the design of a brick patio that graces my backyard today.

The lunch with Seth was anything but boring. Before I'd even taken a good look at the specials, he had a ballpoint pen in his hand and was drawing lines and circles all over his napkin. I ordered the salade niçoise and he the cold salmon and "several extra napkins, if you don't mind."

"What's the doodling?" I asked him.

He chuckled without looking up at me, then quickly finished his drawing. "This isn't 'doodling,' Ms. Teague." He then held it up for me to see. "This is your brain after a hit of nicotine."

What I saw were merely the lines and the circles, to which he'd added letters and a few numbers to indicate, I supposed, some kind of chain reaction. Looking at it made me nervous. In fact, I wondered at that moment why I was sitting there with a person determined to make me feel bad about my one remaining addiction.

So I decided to speak up. "Look, you're not going to get what you want out of this."

He looked as if he might be concerned. "What do I want?" he said.

"You said you wanted to be my favorite client, remember? If you keep picking at me like this, you won't be my client at all." I made a point of staring at him steadily so he wouldn't think I was kidding him.

Relief cleared his eyes, then he rolled them skyward— toward the power lines. After that little bit of drama, he folded the napkin he'd been drawing on and handed it to me.

"Here," he said, "put this in that big purse of yours. It's the basis for your 'favorite client's' new product."

I took the napkin and put it in my pocketbook.

He started to say more, then grabbed my napkin instead and began the same type of scribbling on it. I opened my mouth to speak, but he held up his hand in protest. When he was through, he showed me this napkin as well. It looked just like the first one in terms of the circles and the lines. He'd written across the top of it all the word "Snake." I wondered what a snakebite and nicotine had to do with each other, but I was sure it was some kind of poisoning reaction. Every article I'd read on nicotine in the last twenty years liked to draw the comparison. I stuffed it into my pocketbook along with the other napkin.

Seth stared at me. "Why'd you put that in your purse?"

"Why not?" I said. "You told me to put the first napkin in there. I figured I should put the second one in there as well."

Exasperation showed in the drop of his jaw. If he thought I'd be an easy convert to whatever "miracle cure" he was selling, he was now discovering his misconception. I held firm. I wasn't about to listen to another lecture on cigarettes.

Our food arrived. Neither of us said a word. The young waiter filled the table with plates, bowls, glasses, and pitchers. I looked at Seth as the table was transformed from his personal desk to something resembling a full tic-tac-toe board. I picked up my fork and put a piece of tuna into my mouth. Before I could even return the fork to my plate, Seth took both that plate and my butter plate and placed them on the empty table beside us.

"Take those napkins out of your purse," he said matter-of-factly and with an authority I hadn't heard before.

I chewed, then swallowed the tuna slowly. Seth removed the fork from my hand and placed it on my plate. I was beginning to feel bullied.

"Go on," he said impatiently. "You need to compare the two structures."

"Please don't lecture me," I said evenly as I bent over to retrieve my pocketbook. I waited for him to answer before taking out the napkins.

His eyes narrowed. His heavy brows looked like fur. "I have no intention of lecturing you. I don't know where you've gotten the idea that I would." He nodded at my pocketbook.

"Yeah, like comparing nicotine and a snakebite's not the basis for a lecture." I removed the two napkins and put them on the table where my food was supposed to be but wasn't. I was glad what I'd ordered was cold to start with. I looked at the drawings on the two napkins. Everything about the two drawings was identical excerpt that one said "Snake" and the other, he'd said, was nicotine.

He tapped his finger on the napkin labeled "Snake" and said, "That's not a snakebite reaction, Sydney."

"What is it, then?"

"My product. I call my product Snake."

I looked at the napkins again, then back at him.

"It's synthetic nicotine," he whispered, although no

one was sitting close enough to hear him. "The first truly safe, but fully addictive, cigarette."

It took me a minute or so to even know what I should ask him first. Hundreds of questions rammed into each other inside my head. He waited patiently as I sorted my thoughts.

"God," I said while I was still thinking.

"Not quite, but thank you for the compliment." He grinned and gave me back my lunch plates.

I finally said, "Why did you make it addictive?"

"Hallelujah," he said as he put both hands on the table. "That's the most important question you could ask."

"You've created a drug. Won't you have to go through FDA trials?"

"Begun." He put his hands back in his lap. "I'm dealing with every regulatory agency the bureaucracy can throw at me."

"And?" I said. He hadn't answered the first question.

"You want to know why it's addictive when everyone screams how bad that is, right?"

I nodded. "It seems you're creating yourself a problem. How're you going to sell something you admit is addictive?"

He grinned. "You're going to help me figure that part out. We'll be selling doctors as much as the public. Snake will be prescribed."

I shook my head. "You think doctors will knowingly prescribe an addictive product?"

He laughed. "They already do. The positive addictions they call 'dependencies.' Do you know anybody who's insulin dependent?"

Now I laughed. "That's not the same thing. Diabetics need insulin to live. I can live without cigarettes."

"Why don't you, then?" He tapped his index finger on the edge of his plate and waited for my answer.

"It's hard," I said evenly.

"You won't have to," he said and smiled. "Nobody's into cigarettes for the burning paper and dried leaves, Sydney. You're not, are you?" I didn't have to answer. He knew. "If you were, you'd be smoking those herbal blends right now, wouldn't you? Have you tried them?"

I nodded. I felt mesmerized.

"Why do smokers have to choose between death and addiction when the technology's out there to make a cigarette safe? Addiction itself isn't deadly; it's not even negative."

"Seth, addiction takes your control away. I know. I've lived with it."

He chuckled, the way I do sometimes when my kids show their naïveté. "Control's a myth. None of us have the control we think we do. And addiction? It's simply part of the human genetic makeup is all."

He leaned forward. "It all depends on what you're addicted to. Nicotine doesn't alter behavior—not like the drugs it's compared to. Not like cocaine . . . or even alcohol. Unhealthy drugs, unhealthy behavior—those are the problems. Remember. We can alter behavior positively now, and we do. I bet half the people you know take Prozac, Sydney." He looked closely at me, the cool passion of his eyes paralyzing me. "You have to really get that distinction, Sydney, if we're going to be partners in launching Snake. Do you? Do you understand what I've said?"

"I do," I said, and the words felt almost like a wedding vow.

In retrospect, I'm not sure I heard everything he told me. At some point, though, he had me as surely as if he owned me. Not in the proverbial palm of his hands. I have defenses against that. No, it was his eyes. His bloodshot, puffy eyes pulled me in. Like a deep mountain lake on an August afternoon, the promise I found there was more tempting than the dangers I knew were there too.

I never returned to my office that day. We didn't leave the Pewter Rose until five thirty, when people were starting to show up for early suppers. I remember being shocked at my loss of time. And every day since November 3 had been the same as I gradually let Seth Bolick's obsession take over my life.

4

Once Fred Ball arrived, I took the surgeon's advice and left the hospital. If Sally wasn't going to wake up until tomorrow, there was nothing useful I could accomplish by remaining. I hadn't exactly won the affection of her doctor, and, unfortunately, just being in Fred's self-centered presence irritates me.

On top of all that, I had watched Sara and Johnny Bolick leave the hospital. A large man I recognized as Ian Bolick, Seth's brother, met them at the nurses' station and took them outside. They walked right past me but didn't see me. I wanted to reach out to them, but I knew I'd be no comfort. They didn't really know me. I was nothing more to this family than a late-coming business associate. Besides, I needed comforting myself. The boy was totally silent, but his body was shaking with grief. Tears had flooded his face, even down to his lips. Yet no sobs, no cries. My guess was he was trying to act like a man for his father. My heart broke for him.

Before I left, I cornered Nurse Bernstein and gave her a business card with my home number scribbled on the back of it. I made her promise to call me if anything out of the expected happened with Sally before tomorrow.

The drive back to Charlotte took only thirty minutes, not the forty-five the other nurse had said. The Allen Teague building is on East Boulevard in the heart of Dilworth, a late-nineteenth-century "suburb" of Charlotte that's now referred to as "in town." The building is actually a pre-1920s Craftsman house with some gingerbread molding and interesting roof angles left over from the strong Victorian influences of this neighborhood's earliest days.

My children and I live a couple of blocks behind my office on a street called Kingston, which is convenient and helpful since I'm a single parent and have been since Joan was six and George junior was only two. I found myself wanting to go home. The kids would be back from school soon, and I wanted to be with them, to hug them and feel them hug me back. Johnny Bolick was not much older than George junior.

I drove past my house, satisfied myself that George junior and Joan were still at school, turned around at my street's dead end, and went to my office. I found the front door locked and the lights all off in Sally's reception room. I looked at my watch. It wasn't yet three.

The small business owner in me jumped up, and I said aloud, "Well, it's a good thing business is slow. We're not exactly a welcome wagon for prospects."

"Somebody down there?" Hart's soft voice barely made its way down the steep staircase.

"It's just me," I yelled back while I stared at the blinking answering machine. I hit the button and saw that there were twenty-seven messages. A whole damn day just to answer them.

I could hear the rustle of the papers he was carrying before I saw Hart himself descending the stairs. He is so slim and moves with such grace that I alternate between jealousy and concern. That day I merely wondered how anyone, particularly a man, could be that delicate.

"Well?" he said as he reached the room.

"She's going to be okay."

"Thank God." I could hear the pent-up breath flowing out of him as he said it.

"She should wake up tomorrow. They don't expect anything permanent."

"Whew!" He began walking toward me with both hands holding oversized art layout paper.

I was looking at little hot-pink sticky notes with Hart's handwriting. He'd stuck them all over Sally's desk. These notes too were about phone calls or drop-ins to get in touch with. And a missed two o'clock appointment I'd completely forgotten.

"I didn't know so much activity took place at Sally's desk," I said lightly, then looked up at Hart and chuckled. "I think she has the hardest job among us."

"I'm sorry," he said. "I couldn't get this work done and answer the phone too. I sat here an hour, then put the machine on." He looked embarrassed.

"What's so pressing?" I asked as I glanced toward the papers in his hands.

"Snake." He put a layout on the desk in front of me.

It was a logo treatment showing a caduceus, a stylized snake wrapping itself around a cigarette in such a way as to make it similar to the AMA's logo. Really quite brilliant.

I burst into tears. All the need that had built in me since Sara Bolick's scream poured out onto Hart. I grabbed his thin shoulders with such violence that we both rocked precariously.

"Seth is dead," I cried. "Oh God, Hart, Seth is dead."

In spite of his natural reserve, he put his arms around me. To say that Hart is not demonstrative is an understatement. In the almost eight years we've worked together, we had never hugged before now.

My emotional onslaught took a lot out of him. After he'd finished helping me to one of the room's two burgundy love seats, he plopped onto the other one. There he sat silently waiting for me to talk. Once I started talking, I couldn't seem to stop. I told him about Seth not showing up for our meeting this morning, about his desperate fight for breath on that gurney and the inhuman convulsion that brought home to me who that dying person was.

"God, Sydney, that's awful. I wondered what was going on. You were talking to me, then you were gone."

I smiled at him weakly, then ran my fingers across my eyelids to dissipate the excess moisture that was still in my eyes. The salt stung. "When I came back to the phone, you'd hung up."

"Asthma?" Hart asked me.

"What?" I said.

"Was it Seth's asthma?" Hart repeated. "Did his

asthma kill him? From what you said about his not being able to breathe, I thought—"

"God, I didn't even ask what killed him. When it hit me that he was dead, my mind sort of snapped. I lost it for a few minutes. I thought I had myself together again before I got in the car to drive back. But it never entered my mind to ask the nurses what happened to him. They might not have known themselves. It all happened so fast." I shook my head while staring into Hart's pale blue eyes. "It couldn't have been his asthma though. He didn't have it that bad."

"Sounds like you were in shock," he said with the tone of a cool clinician. He looked closer at me and his tone softened. "No wonder. First Sally, then to see Seth like that."

Listening to him, I began to unwind. Not to a point of relaxation, but straight to bone tired. I found it very odd to be so tired, and on top of that, I felt somehow disloyal to Seth for my exhaustion. All of a sudden, though, I was overwhelmed by a desire for sleep.

"See. Now you're sleepy," Hart said. "That's what happens after shock."

Hart scratched his jaw absentmindedly. His eyes wandered to Sally's desk and the layouts that were covering it. He looked back at me, and he didn't have to say it. I knew what he was thinking: Did we still have a client? Was Snake going to come on the market anyway in spite of its inventor's death?

I shook my head. "I don't know what happens now," I said in anticipation. "Bolick Enterprises is a corporation. It holds the Snake patent, I assume." Emotion began to well up in me again. "Oh, Hart, he was so close. This is so unfair."

"You okay, Sydney?" Hart touched my arm. My eyes had started to fill again.

"It was his life, Hart." I squinted as I spoke, hoping to hold back the threatening spill. "I mean really his life. His whole life. Everything he's thought, planned, studied, and done since he was sixteen years old was for Snake. How cruel this is to happen now . . . just when the dream was becoming reality."

"I know," he said softly and looked at me closely. "Don't get angry with me, Sydney, but I watched you while you were with him. I've never seen you so involved with a product. Or with a client, for that matter." He hesitated.

I stared at him and waited.

He looked at the floor rather than at my gaze. "Sally thought you were in love with Seth. I thought it was the product." He didn't look up.

I snickered. "Come on, Hart. You know Sally. She casts every man she meets in a romantic lead."

He looked up at me finally. "But she usually casts herself opposite. Not you." His mouth turned up slightly.

I nodded and smiled too. Sally's foibles all seemed sweetly eccentric at this moment. "Did I ever tell you about Seth's father?"

"That he was a scientist too? Yes, you told me that."

"Did I tell you he killed himself?"

Hart shook his head and looked dismayed the way people always do when suicide is mentioned.

"He killed himself after years of trying to create

what Seth finally accomplished. Seth's whole life was about his father. About finishing his work. About proving to his father that his work hadn't been in vain."

"That's sad, Sydney."

"Sad? I think it's heroic. To carry on, to fix a wrong, to believe in someone and speak for him when he can no longer speak for himself. Why's that sad?"

His expression told me he thought the answer was obvious, but I kept staring at him, so he had to answer. "Didn't give Seth much of a life, did it? What about his own dreams?"

"That's the part that's sad. He would have seen them come true now. Don't you see? Snake would have evened that score. What's sad is that he'll never have the chance now." Something caught in my throat. I cleared it and coughed. "I think Seth would want us to go ahead with Snake, don't you?"

The phone started ringing before Hart could answer me. "Let the machine pick up," I said. "I don't want to talk to anybody." We listened to my bland outgoing message, then my brother Bill began to talk.

In spite of my exhaustion, I jumped off the love seat and grabbed the phone at Sally's desk. "Bill . . . Bill. Don't hang up. This is Sydney. I'm here." I held the phone cord up high, leaned my upper body over the desk, and maneuvered around it to sit in Sally's chair.

"Why are you screening calls? Where's Sally?" he asked.

I exhaled breath I didn't know had built up. "It's too complicated," I said. "To both of your questions."

He was silent for a couple of seconds, then said,

"Have it your way, Sydney." His tone challenged me. An old familiar undercurrent.

"I'm not withholding, Bill. I'm just tired." I took a deep breath again. "If you want me to tell you everything that's happened today, I will. But it's not pleasant."

"You sound stressed, Syd. I'm sorry. I'm afraid I have something to add to it."

"About Seth?"

"How'd you know so quickly?" he asked.

"That's complicated too, but I was at the hospital up in Bredon this morning when he was brought in. I was still there when he died." My voice sounded to me like it belonged to someone else. I added, "I'm heartbroken. I don't know what he'd want me to do. Hart and I were sitting here trying to figure that out."

"Ian Bolick just called me. I told him I'd call you." Bill sighed. "I don't understand it, do you? Seth had everything in the world to live for. Why'd he go do something like this?"

"What are you talking about?" Something snagged high in my stomach. My hand pressed at the spot in reflex.

He hesitated. "You said you were there when he died."

"I was at the hospital like I told you. EMTs brought him in. He was having some kind of seizure. . . ."

I pushed my thumb as deep into the pain as I could stand while I waited for Bill to explain. He didn't.

"Dammit, Bill. Tell me what you're talking about." I said it so loudly that Hart squirmed, then stood up nervously.

"Ian told me Seth killed himself."

I heard him well enough. I asked him to repeat it anyway. It wasn't my ears that were having difficulty.

"I don't believe it," I said after he'd said it again.

"I know how you feel, Syd. I've handled his legal work, but you got much closer to him. He told me the other day how much he thought of you."

"I mean I really don't believe it. It's not true."

"Aw, come on now, Syd."

"He couldn't kill himself, Bill. Not in a million years."

The small sound he made carried his years of frustration with me. "You have a hard time with reality. You know that? Sometimes you have to just accept things as they come. Whether you like them or not."

"I do," I said slowly. "Accept things. But only when they're true."

His smirk sounded like one of those honks circus clowns make with their noses. "I'm your brother, remember? I've known you a long time."

"This isn't about me. It's about Seth, and if you think I'll believe garbage about him because you got a phone call, you've got another think coming."

"The phone call was from his own brother." His words had a measured cadence.

"So?" I said, knowing I sounded just like I did when we were kids.

"I can't take any more of this," he said and hung up without saying good-bye.

I continued to stare at the phone even after Bill was gone. He'd never learned to fight fair. No wonder he spent his days dotting i's instead of fighting court cases.

I stared at Hart's back as he straightened the award plaques on the wall.

"Did you hear that?" I asked. He didn't turn around. "Hart?"

He jumped slightly as he turned to face me. "Oh, I thought you were still on the phone."

Only then did I hang up the receiver. He walked to Sally's desk, stopping about three feet from me. His light brown eyebrows were furrowed the way they get when he's worried.

"Do you feel okay, Sydney?" he asked.

I realized I still had my thumb jammed into my rib cage. I pulled it away and mumbled something even I didn't understand.

"Are you sick?"

I shook my head. "I think it's nerves. Did you hear what we were talking about? Did you hear what Seth's brother is saying about him?" I sought some confirmation in his eyes but didn't find any. "He's telling people Seth killed himself. Why would he do that?"

He didn't answer me. Maybe he thought my question rhetorical, but it wasn't. The idea of Seth Bolick committing suicide was right up there with Mother Teresa doing the same. People with causes don't call it off voluntarily. Hart merely shook his head. It was a noncommittal action on his part. At best. I didn't want to ask him what he was thinking.

I looked down at the Snake logo sketches covering the desk, then flipped through them all. "Let's go up there in the morning," I said without looking up at him.

"Where?" His voice cracked slightly because he knew the answer already.

I stood and handed him the logo work. "Those are nice logos, Hart. Seth would love them. I just know he would. If I have to grovel to get his brother to let us continue Seth's work, I will do just that. Otherwise his life will have been in vain."

"You make it sound as if he died in battle, Sydney." He studied his art rather than making eye contact with me.

"Maybe he did" was all I said.

I returned one phone call, then called Patrick Gallagher to apologize for missing our two o'clock. Hart busied himself mounting his art onto boards for presentation.

"Can you pick us up some flowers on the way in tomorrow?" I asked when I was through. "Or do you think little Bredon might have a florist?"

"For Sally? Will she be alert enough for flowers?"

"How alert does one have to be for flowers, Hart? It's just to show we care."

"I just thought she might appreciate them later in the week."

"Then we'll take her some more at the end of the week, okay?" My exhaustion returned suddenly. I began to pack up to go on home.

"Hospital first, then the Bolick farm to find Ian. Okay, Hart?" I gazed out the window to see how hard the wind was blowing. A purple-leafed spirea brushed against the pane.

"Who's Ian?" he asked.

"Seth's brother and the only board member I know. Other than Seth, of course." I stood and put my corduroy jacket back on.

"I don't know about this, Sydney," he said as I was at the door to leave. "How can you be thinking about Snake when Seth's dead and Sally's just had brain surgery?"

My shoulders sagged. I took my hand off the doorknob. "That's a low blow, don't you think? If there were something I could be doing for Sally right this minute, I wouldn't be standing here. You know that. If her mother weren't coming, I'd probably figure out a way to spend the night at the hospital."

"I'm sorry," he said. "I know that."

"And for the record, the last thing I want to be thinking about right now is product marketing." My eyes sought his and held them. He needed to understand what I had to say. "Except for one reason. It's exactly what Seth would want me to do. I'm sure of that."

He looked down at the floor again. "Go on home," he said. "You look beat."

I didn't go straight home. Instead I drove out Sharon Amity Road to the cemetery to have a talk with Dad. I had come out here for the first time in years a couple of days after getting to know Seth, after understanding why he had really developed Snake. Snake was his gift to his father. It was all about being loyal to him, about speaking the truth and standing up for the man—even at great cost to himself.

And I knew how difficult that could be, because I didn't stand up for my dad the only time it ever really mattered. Seth's the one person I've ever shared this with, although sometimes I think Mother and Bill must have always known how much it bothered me.

Of the two of us, my dad was the one who stood for causes. He was one of those increasingly rare lawyers who loved the law and the rule of law. People still stop me on the street to tell me how very good he was. As a lawyer and as a man. When I was growing up, I don't believe I gave two seconds of thought to what he did for a living. Not until it affected me and my little, insulated world. When I was sixteen, he defended a man named Samson Hall who was accused of beating up and raping a girl at my high school. All of Charlotte had convicted Hall before my dad took the case—including me. After he took on Hall, I was embarrassed to be Will Allen's daughter. People were angry at him. Some people avoided me. I lost some friends during the year and a half it went on. I blamed their loss on Dad too.

Many times Dad tried talking to me about the trial, about why he took the case, about issues like justice and innocence. Every single time he did, I turned away.

Dad got Samson Hall off, but it didn't matter. It didn't even matter when another man was caught and confessed. All the damage between Dad and me had been done by then. I'd grown distant. I said only what was expected, even kissed him perfunctorily. But I no longer shared my feelings or my fears. My dad had made me vulnerable. I know now that something always breaks down that big mirage of safety we live in as children. The loss of that feeling is part of growing up. It could just as easily have been the betrayal of a false friend or the death of a dog. It's too bad for me and my dad that his defense of Samson Hall was the catalyst that so abruptly ended my perfect little world. Charlotte forgave and rewarded my dad. I punished him.

When I went off to college, I slowly began to realize the problem between us was mine and not his. Dad came up to Chapel Hill for a football game my freshman year. He came alone without Mother. I think he was reaching out again. When I'm being honest with myself, I have to admit I know he was. We talked about Kant and Proust, about the end of the war, the taking of political hostages. We even talked about my crazy roommate and some of the men I was dating. But we never discussed what had happened to us. After he left for Charlotte, I decided it was time to mend our fence and tell him I was sorry. Thanksgiving break was two weeks away, and I would talk with him honestly over that long weekend. Looking back on my attitude at that time now, I still can't believe my own arrogance. Who did I think I was deciding exactly when and where I would give up my righteousness? Like some distant goddess who doles out her blessing only at the altar of her choosing.

Dad died two days before that Thanksgiving break. He was in court defending a client against perjury charges. His heart simply stopped. Mine broke.

I don't believe death to be the big separator most people crack it up to be. So I believed Dad knew this minute how I felt; he knew I was sorry. When I was drinking a lot, Scotch dissolved some of my memories, kept this gnawing at bay. Sobriety is funny though. It leaves your wounds raw and open to heal in clean air, yet tells you to bury the past. Supposedly, we cannot change our pasts. I believed that too, but the piece of barbed wire inside me jabbed away as I said it. Seth Bolick was doing for his dad what I wished I had done while my dad was alive. He was simply standing up for him.

I wiped the tears away with an old tissue I found in my pocketbook and looked around the large cemetery. An elderly woman walked a path some distance from me. She carried potted pink mums. I sighed, then blew my nose. I wasn't even sure whom I was crying for. I knew I needed to forgive myself. It was long overdue. Helping Seth had seemed to me the best way to do it. Strangely enough, it still did.

I gathered a dogwood limb knocked down by the wind. Although its leaves were gone, it still had fat, red berries. Beside Dad's grave is an overgrown hedge of speckled aucuba. I snapped off a couple of branches. It wasn't much, but I lay the bouquet beside his stone, kissed my fingers, then rubbed my hand against the recessed letters of his name. For what I hoped was the last time, I said aloud, "I'm so sorry, Dad."

5

I had stayed at the cemetery just long enough to give rush hour a chance to start in earnest. It now spans four until seven, another world-class indicator for Charlotte, North Carolina.

By the time I pulled into my driveway, it was, at most, thirty minutes earlier than I usually arrive. The kids weren't going to start asking me what was wrong that I was home so early. For all Joan and George junior knew, I'd been sitting two blocks from home all day writing ad copy. I didn't see any reason for them to know otherwise. I share the broad strokes of my life with the two of them. I want the details of theirs. George junior, I feel sure, still gives me his, but I'm not so certain of his sixteen-year-old sister. Joan was now about the same age I was when my problems started with Dad. I wondered how she would react if I turned principled on her as Dad had me. I didn't even need to think about it, as I was certain of the answer. Joan's more mature than I was at her age. She knows more about all kinds of things too, people included. I think she's a better person than I was.

The calendar my kids and I live by is a sports calendar. For instance, if you say April to me, I don't think spring clothes or quick trips to the beach; I think baseball, softball, and tennis. Regional tournaments ended the soccer and volleyball seasons last week. In early December, basketball practice begins. I've always liked this second half of November. We get a break from all those sports. Don't read me wrong here. I love every one of those sports. I'm the one who encouraged their play in the first place. But I'd almost forgotten how nice it could be to just come home in the afternoon. No hard bleachers in hot gyms on the other side of town.

Joan was on the phone and George junior on the computer. I got a nod from her and a "Hi, Mom" from him. I wrote the word "nap" on a sheet of yellow legal paper and put it in front of each of their faces before going to my bedroom.

I dreamed one of those jumbled, nonsensical dreams that happen just on the other side of consciousness. Dad was in it, as he often is. He was where I always see him: in court defending his client. The client's back was to me; the judge sat high on an exaggerated podium that oddly resembled a series of graduated fireplace mantels. I couldn't understand what Dad was saying, but his gestures were passionate as he walked from the judge to his client, then pointed at his client and shook his head dramatically. The back of the accused's head was familiar to me. Thick neck, sandy hair. He turned toward Dad and I saw his profile. It was Seth. I tried to get his attention, then Dad's. I yelled out from the back of the courtroom, but neither of them turned toward me. The judge heard me, though, and called me out of order. She began to bang her gavel at all three of us, one at a time. I looked more closely at her angled jaw, her straight nose, her thick hair streaked by the sun. Good God, what was this scene? The judge was me. But I remained in the back of that courtroom watching myself be that judge, watching me disdain us, listening to the death-knell rhythm of my still-pounding gavel.

I heard George junior yell, "Wake up, Mom." I automatically jerked upward to a sitting position. I was awake. The gavel finally stopped pounding. I shook my head, trying to reorient myself. It had been George junior's fist on my bedroom door.

"Okay, sweetie," I said. "What's up? Come on in." I propped myself against two down pillows, one a large bolster. He opened the door and held out the cordless phone.

"It's Detective Thurgood. Want to talk to him?"

I nodded and smiled as he handed me the phone and left my bedroom. "Just a minute, Tom," I said into the phone. "Hang on a sec and let me get situated." I didn't wait for him to answer. I was already situated, but I wanted a cigarette. I lit it quickly, put the ashtray on my lap, and eased back onto the pillows as I exhaled the smoke.

Tom Thurgood is a homicide detective with the Charlotte-Mecklenburg Police Department. A few years back we were a couple, and a pretty serious couple the more I remember of that relationship. In fact, we would probably have married if I'd been up for that sort of thing. Tom was looking for a wife, but I was looking for my sanity instead. I couldn't be what he wanted from me. We both got what we needed somewhere else. Funny how these things happen. I'd all but forgotten about Tom Thurgood until I saw him at the Law Enforcement Center a couple of months ago. In the years since we'd been together, he'd found a wonderful wife, then lost her to cancer. I'd learned to be comfortable both sober and alone. We were enjoying each other's company more this time. At least I was. Neither one of us was looking for answers in the other.

So the pressure was off. All the pressure, that is, except tennis. The man is obsessed with our partnership on the court. He's even tried to put me on one of his nutrition training programs, the very program he puts his young police recruits on. I try to minimize our doubles play every time he builds it up. I even tried to blow our championship match in the city tournament last month. But Tom pulled us out. I knew at the time it'd be hell to pay if we won, and I'd been right. He'd found a USTA tournament schedule and was calling me almost nightly, it seemed, with suggestions on other tournaments we could play. Tonight it was Savannah and a tournament coinciding with their St. Patrick's Day festivities.

"You might even want to wear green," Tom said. I couldn't believe he thought I might think like that.

"Do I seem like someone who'd do theme tennis, Tom?"

He backtracked. "Green's not a theme, Sydney. It's just a color. It's no more a theme than red at Christmas."

"Just my opinion, but I think that's thematic too." I

paused so he could think about it. "I don't wear red during the whole month of December."

I admit I was pushing. It's always tempting with
Tom because he tries so hard to anticipate me. A lot like
our tennis together.

"Well," he said cautiously, then went mute for a full
ten seconds before continuing. "Sydney, I've got the
whole USTA tournament schedule for all of 1998 here.
Why don't I give it to you and you decide where and
when we should play."

I stubbed the Vantage out in the ashtray, put it on
my bedside table, then sighed. "Tom, Sally was in a
wreck this morning, and on top of that, my favorite
client died." There. I had said it. Seth had gotten what
he wanted out of me: he was my favorite client. By far.

"Is she okay?" His first thoughts were for Sally, of
course.

"Not really. But she's going to be if the asshole surgeon in Bredon knows what he's doing. He had to go in
and relieve the pressure on her brain."

"Jeez," he said softly. "Bredon? What was she doing
up there on a Monday morning?"

"Helping me." My voice cracked slightly. I cleared
my throat. "Remember I spent all yesterday up there?"

"Yeah, it's why you couldn't play."

"I forgot my video equipment and the tapes I'd
filled to make investment videos for Seth Bolick."

"The cigarette guy you've spent so much time
with?" Tom's priorities were coming through loud and
clear. He understands my life in terms of time away
from him and tennis. There may have been some slight
jealousy in his voice too, a jealousy apart from time.

"Snake isn't really a cigarette," I said, the publicist in me coming out even though what Snake was or wasn't had nothing at all to do with this conversation. "He died today." My throat closed up just as it had in the emergency room this morning.

Tom's response was a low guttural sound in his throat. I could tell he was genuinely sorry. He waited for me to say more.

When I didn't, he finally said, "How?"

"I don't know. There's rumor it was suicide, but that's ridiculous. I would have known."

"How would you know something like that?" he said cautiously.

"I knew him as well as I've ever known anyone in my life." I said this with so much conviction I surprised even myself.

"In two weeks of knowing the man?"

"Yes," I said matter-of-factly. Now I knew I heard jealousy coming from him. I wasn't going to try to explain, nor was I going to argue the point.

I could hear him breathing. He didn't talk.

"Hart and I are going up there tomorrow."

"To where?" Tom's mind was still on my feelings for Seth.

"First to Wade Community Hospital in the hope Sally is better." I sighed. "Then we're going to try to find Seth's brother."

He whistled softly through his teeth. "Let me know if I can do something, okay?" I knew he meant that, but in this case, like most situations in which that statement is made, there was nothing he could do. "I don't suppose you want to hit some before work in the morning."

"Nope. Sorry. We're leaving from the office. I have to look decent, Tom." I was irritated he thought I might want to hit tennis balls at a time like this. Tom could squeeze tennis into a ten-minute coffee break if I let him.

Then he said, "Hey, Sydney. I'm really sorry about your client."

Joan appeared at my bedroom door with a big steaming pizza on an aluminum pan. One hand was inside a quilted mitt painted to look like a shark. Its mouth was firmly clamped on a piece of pepperoni. She motioned with her other hand for me to get off the phone.

We were hanging up anyway. I joined my two children in the kitchen. George junior had washed and dried the lettuce like I'd taught him. He'd rolled the portion we were to eat inside a doubled-over paper towel and squeezed it to transfer the excess water to the towel. Then he'd shredded the lettuce with his hands so it wouldn't bruise, as it would have with knife cutting.

I complimented him on his skill as I pulled a large piece of paper towel out of my mouth.

"How did that happen?" he asked.

"You're sloppy," his sister offered.

"No, he's not," I said. "I've done it myself." I looked straight at Joan, then added, "It's easy to do."

"Sorry," they both said at the same time.

My kids are good kids. Sometimes I worry about them because their father has chosen to keep his distance, not be involved in their lives. But that worry is rare. As nice as it would feel to think otherwise, I know there's nothing I can do about him. All any of us can do is live the lives we're in. We can't change people. We can't change the baggage we've carried this far either. And we surely can't change relationships we had with people who are no longer around. It doesn't matter whether those people left us through divorce or death. I wish Seth hadn't planted the seed in my head that I could change those things. Thinking I might have that power made me nervous. Besides, I really believed that I couldn't change the past. Even more importantly, I believed it didn't matter that I couldn't.

Seth kept everything simultaneous: the present, the past, and the future. That kind of juggling act would have led me to the closest bar. I envied his ability to do it though.

He told me he had no choice, that the course of his life was set the day his father, Jonathan Bolick, literally fumigated himself with a solution of nicotine so strong it would have killed an elephant. If the Wade County coroner had ever heard Seth talk about his father's suicide, he would never classify his death the same thing. He really couldn't. Seth was marked by suicide the way Depression children are marked by poverty. He would have gone to any length to avoid it. And that's what he was doing—going to any length. Hell, Seth was re-enacting his father's mission in order to change its ending, not duplicate it.

The Bolicks have farmed six thousand acres in Wade County since before the Civil War. In the beginning, half that acreage yielded cotton and the other half bright leaf tobacco. After the war, when the demand for cotton decreased without uniforms to manufacture and the popularity of chewing tobacco, or plug, as it was known, was on the rise, the Bolicks converted all six thousand acres to tobacco production. The log factory where that plug was processed is still there today.

Seth's great-grandfather, a college-educated man, took a keen interest in the notion of branded packaged goods. It was the early 1890s. A little north of Wade County a family named Green had begun to mass-produce and mass-market a brand of smoking tobacco called Bull Durham. When the Bonsack cigarette machine became available, the Bolicks bought one and began to churn out their own brand, which the elder Bolick called Snake.

The early Bolick brand was not the only reason Seth had insisted on calling his new product Snake, but he did admit the name gave family efforts some continuity. The first Snake's tenure as a product lasted only fifteen years, but it gained enough market share to be attractive to the Reynolds brothers a couple of miles down the road in Winston-Salem. Seth's grandfather was the Bolick who actually sold Snake to R. J. Reynolds, amassing enough money to automate the farm's harvesting operation in the deal. Then Reynolds squashed the brand a mere year later.

"Why?" I'd asked.

"Father told me ladies had started smoking by then. They didn't like the image of a Snake."

"See?" I'd said. "Women are going to react the same way again. It's still not too late to reconsider that name."

"They'll grow to like it," he said, refusing to discuss it again. God, but Seth could be stubborn.

Seth's father was a born do-gooder. As a boy he

wanted to be a clergyman, then a doctor. He was smart enough, but his emotions got in the way. At Duke Medical School, he fainted at the sight of blood. He couldn't overcome it, so Jonathan Bolick switched to biochemistry instead. He taught some at the state university branch in Charlotte, but mostly he took research grants to study anything having to do with tobacco. With the family money, he built what was probably considered at that time a state-of-the-art facility with a well-equipped lab. Seth used the same facility, but it was no longer up-to-date. Most of Jonathan's research concentrated on the insecticidal use of tobacco and its combination with other "natural" substances.

Meanwhile the family continued to farm its lucrative cash crop, tobacco. Seth's grandfather and then his older brother, Ian, were basically in charge of the mainstay. Jonathan loved the land always but was never involved in its operation.

After the Surgeon General's Report in 1964 that first attacked cigarettes, Jonathan changed drastically. Although Seth couldn't have been older than four at the time, he remembered his father's first clinical depression, how the elder Bolick would sit for hours and stare out the window at the family's land. Between the ages of six and thirteen, Seth remembered his father being hospitalized four times. Once for an entire year.

When Seth was thirteen, his father's dark mood lifted. In fact, Seth recalled, he became downright jubilant. The federal government and the tobacco companies joined forces. Together they would develop a safe cigarette. Jonathan Bolick was one of the first research chemists approached to join this massive effort. His education, his experience as a researcher, and his intimate knowledge of tobacco put Jonathan in a unique position with the Safe Cigarette Committee, as the coalition was called. He became their poster boy. In 1973 he was on the cover of *Time* magazine: the man who forsook his family's heritage to do good.

Seth talked to me for hours about his father's eighteen-hour workdays during that time, how intensely happy he'd been. He remembered his father traveling a lot, sometimes to the Far East, mostly to Washington for meetings.

"He didn't make a single football game when I was in junior high," Seth told me. "You know what? I didn't care. My father was happy at last, and that was all that mattered to me."

From what we know about tobacco today, the stated goal of the committee was impossible. Researchers like Seth's father were told they could alter anything in a cigarette but tobacco itself. Additives were fair game, as were all kinds of filtering devices. If they could develop a new strain of tobacco or find an existing strain better than traditional bright leaf, they were encouraged to do so. Hundreds of experiments in the alteration of primary processing itself or methods of leaf curing were going on simultaneously. But they were being asked to turn a lion into a kitten, a tank into a tricycle. Tobacco itself was the culprit. Tobacco companies knew it even then. The millions of dollars doled out for research in the seventies is one of the biggest shams ever perpetrated. One by one, the independent researchers figured it out. Some didn't care as long as the money kept coming.

"A friend of my father's clued him in," Seth told me. "It wasn't just the tobacco companies that were lying to them. Father's friend told him the NIH was going along too, its top brass having decided the quest for a safe cigarette was great politics—no matter what research was finding. An NIH official told the friend he didn't want to see a 'safer' cigarette, which was the best most researchers were hoping for at the time. The official said such a cigarette would be a 'one-fanged rattler.' "

"A one-fanged rattler," I repeated. "So that's where Snake comes from?" I asked. "That and the family's old brand?"

Seth nodded. "I want to hit them in the face with it," he said angrily. For the one and only time I heard vengeance in his voice as well as vindication. "Father was devastated. He'd been naive, that's true. Maybe all people who want to make a real difference are a little naive."

"You're not, Seth."

"No, no I'm not," he said, although later, much later, I realized that he had been. So was I. I believed we were making a significant contribution and people would honor Seth for his lifelong work. I didn't know what some people are willing to do when they feel threatened.

"But I'm not out to save the world either," he continued. "I'm not my father. I just want to right the wrong done to him."

I noticed his chin started to quiver. But Seth's voice got even stronger. "I found him the next week. He'd mixed a solution of 50 percent nicotine and run it through the fumigation line in the greenhouse. That's where he was when I got home from school."

"And now you have a chance to finish what your father started," I said. There were tears in my eyes as I said it.

He nodded, composed himself, then said, "I don't mind telling you profit is a motive too. My son's future is another. I don't want him farming tobacco."

That was the day Seth gave me the lapillus. His father had found it near an old volcano on an island off Mainland China. He'd been looking for new leaf, for a "safe" new blend.

Within a year of his father's suicide, most researchers had soured on the search for the safe cigarette. And pretty soon the money dried up.

"The technology's been out there awhile though," Seth said. "Once we learned how to manipulate the areas of the brain that produce these dependent pleasures, we opened the door for Snake."

I didn't know science had done that, but then I'm not very scientific either. "Is that common knowledge?" I asked, afraid he'd laugh at me.

He didn't laugh. Instead he explained how Prozac and similar drugs work. "With that drug technology came the ability to artificially bind receptors in the brain. It's the same area where nicotine produces its effect. All addiction researchers know that. All mood manipulation researchers know that too."

"Then why hasn't somebody invented something like Snake before you?" I asked. "If the technology's been out there, why not use it?"

"You're as naive about these things as I was, Sydney," he said then. "Tobacco companies won't fund the destruction of their industry. That one's easy to understand. Politics is the hard one. Politicians have too much invested in getting rid of anything resembling a cigarette. That's the public posture anyway. On the practical side, a lot of them owe their jobs to tobacco money."

"But Snake will save lives," I said.

He had laughed. "So what? Minor point, I'm afraid. Anything caught between profit and politics is destined to lose. Even human life."

When I'd looked as depressed as I felt, he said, "But we're fixing that, aren't we? We tapped the technology for Snake."

From then on, Seth had said "we" when discussing the product. I was part of his team. To be honest, I'd never felt so useful. It was the closest someone like me would ever get to saving a bunch of lives.

"Your part's the hardest now, Sydney," he continued. "Convincing the public, that'll be hard."

I knew that. I'd understood how hard it'd be that first day at lunch. To most people, Snake would seem an oxymoron. Safety and addiction cancel each other. Biochemically, however, that's not true. At some evolutionary point, something akin to addiction helps us survive. Otherwise, we wouldn't do things that make no sense intellectually. Like running to a point of cellular breakdown and calling it a high. Or drinking Scotch to a point of oblivion and calling it relaxation. Or working eighteen-hour days in the name of achievement, then collapsing from the grind. Or sucking burning leaves into our lungs and calling it pleasure.

I didn't know if Allen Teague would be able to convince the general public of Snake's benefit. I honestly had my doubts. But I knew smokers would storm us en masse. Synthetic nicotine was the basis for Snake, but underneath it was the technology for synthetic addiction of all kinds. The implications for that technology were both exhilarating and frightening. In some form, we'd not only be able to smoke it, but also imbibe it, whiff it, even dab it behind our ears. All in order to keep our receptors bound. It could be used for good or ill. In fact, there was a negative side I didn't like to contemplate.

Not a very popular notion, I admit. I've never seen addiction as a moral issue though. How could I and live with myself? However, we all like to think the choices we make are intellectually or, at least, ethically based. Even an alcoholic feels this way. God help us if our "choice" is a chemical reaction occurring in our brains.

Yes, Allen Teague had its work cut out.

After supper I called the hospital to check on Sally. Her mother answered, and I was relieved. Sally was still unconscious. Mrs. Ball said the nurses told her not to worry, though, that the coma was part of her brain's plan for healing itself. I thought that was a nice way of wording it, so I told her so. She said they still expected Sally to come out of it sometime tomorrow. I told her both Hart and I would be visiting in the morning. In case she needed anything, I gave her my number as well as the number at Allen Teague.

I didn't smoke anymore that night. Instead I went to bed when the kids did, seeking the comfort of routine.

6

Tuesday morning I listened to at least the beginnings of all those messages at Sally's desk. Only two had been clients, so they were the ones I returned. Several were either prospects or referrals, though, and I panicked that I didn't have the time to follow up right now. If Sally had been here, she could have at least called these people and set up appointments for later in the week.

"Why don't we hire a temp?" Hart said while I was biting on one of Sally's nice Allen Teague pencils.

I'd actually been thinking the same thing. We'd hired them on occasion before, when we were snowed under from work or when Sally was out sick. Then there was the time she thought she was going to get married and took off for Las Vegas with a guy she'd known only a week. She came back two days later, broke and disillusioned, and I had a two-hundred-dollar temp bill to show for it.

"We should," I said to Hart. "Fact is, whether we still have Snake or not, we're going to be busy either doing it or trying to replace it." I pulled out Sally's media tickler file drawer. "And somebody's got to be sure these ads get to the magazines on time."

As I was closing the drawer, I remembered the girl in Seth's office yesterday. I wondered what would happen to her.

"I've got an idea, Hart. Seth had a brand-new secretary all eager and ready to go to work." I found Bolick Enterprises in Sally's Rolodex. "Maybe she needs someplace else to work right now."

"Not if they're going ahead with Snake," he said.

"We'll see," I said as I dialed.

I didn't even know the young woman's name. As we talked, she told me it was Leslie, and that she, in fact, had been on the verge of looking up Allen Teague and calling me. She'd found out Seth was dead late yesterday afternoon. People had started calling, asking if it was true Mr. Bolick had died.

"Then Mr. Little came back this morning and told me I wouldn't be needed anymore. Ms. Teague, I just started this job, and Mr. Bolick had been so nice."

"Is Mr. Little there now, Leslie?" I wondered what authority this man had to do such a thing. I wanted to ask him myself.

"Nope. In and out just like yesterday. I'm packing up now, not that I have much to pack. Mr. Little said he'd send me a check."

Why hadn't Seth ever mentioned this Mr. Little?

"What am I going to do, Ms. Teague?" Her voice

had a whine to it then, telling me she was closer to my daughter's age than my own.

"I'll tell you what you're going to do. You're going to come to work for Allen Teague for a couple of weeks."

Hart was standing in front of me with art in his hands. Grinning.

"That's if you want to," I added.

Her response was overly enthusiastic, so enthusiastic that I hoped she'd calm down a bit before getting here. My clients weren't used to such exuberance, although Sally had more than Hart and me combined. But Leslie's exuberance made even Sally Ball pale.

While we waited for her to drive the ten minutes from downtown to Dilworth, I wrote some notes for her. If she could just answer the phone today and give us the messages rather than my having to punch that damned button, Leslie would be worth it. Besides, I felt as if I was doing a good deed in rescuing her.

Hart had packaged the art he'd been holding between cardboard and was going out the back door with it.

I stopped him. "Are we going to be able to meet the deadlines we worked out with Seth?"

Hart put his free hand on his hip to indicate an attitude. "If his brother cooperates," he said cynically.

"You sound as if you don't think he will," I said. My chin itched. I picked up a pencil, rubbed the eraser against it.

"I don't think I would," he said as he opened the door.

"Well, thank God you're not his brother. You just

don't get how important this product was to Seth, Hart."

"It's messy," he said.

"Doesn't have to be," I countered. I looked at Hart. "We've got a huge retainer. We'll do all the work. He can live his life the way he always has."

Hart let go of the doorknob and put his hand on his chin. "Your chin," he said. "That's what I meant. Something's on it. It's messy."

I looked closely at the eraser. What should have been pink was a splotchy black. I realized I'd tried to erase ink, then had transferred it to my face.

While Hart put the artwork in the Trooper, I washed my face in the bathroom. The little bit of blush-on I'd applied this morning left with the ink. I could tell already this was going to be a difficult day.

Leslie was thrilled with both Hart and me, thrilled with our office, and even thrilled with Sally's chair, which has arms. I prayed to the god of moderation that she would settle down while we were gone.

Outside, the air was damp and the brilliant blue of yesterday was gone. It had been replaced by several shades of gray, the darkest in some distant clouds which were charcoal if not black. The wind that had begun in gusts yesterday was a steady fifteen miles an hour today. As I pulled the Trooper off the interstate at the hospital exit, I noticed a grove of tall oak and maple trees in the distance. More than half their leaves had fallen.

"If it rains today," I said to Hart as I nodded in the direction of those trees, "the rest of those leaves will go."

"Yuck," he said. The word sounded funny coming

from his mouth. It was a Joan word. "Then they'll be on our shoes and all over the floor."

Hart is meticulous, a trait I find essential in a traditional mechanical artist. I don't suppose it's so important since computers have largely replaced our boards, but it's nice to know that coffee, dog hairs, and random smudges will never turn up while I'm showing art to clients.

Hart has had the same pair of suede Hush Puppies since coming to work for me back in 1989. The kind with those dark pink rubbery soles. So I was mildly surprised he had on boots, those standard-issue fake-leather boots from Sears or Wal-Mart.

I commented on them.

"Seth always wore boots," he said. "I thought there must have been a reason. Stuff to step on, I guess."

I laughed. "Hart, it's a tobacco farm, not a cattle ranch. Besides, I have no plans to walk the fields. Unless that's where Ian is."

Then I noticed the suede patches on the elbows of Hart's tweed jacket. If I hadn't known Hart so well, I would have thought he was doing a city guy's version of landed gentry. But I remembered years ago when this same tweed jacket had frayed elbows. Hart was actually trying to prolong its life. It had probably belonged to his father before him.

The overall effect of Hart's wardrobe, however, was gentrified. Yes, I'd even have to say he looked thematic.

I'd failed to wear boots, actually had on two-inch heels instead and a charcoal gray jumper to blend with the sky. I did remember to bring a raincoat, George senior's rubberized army coat. He'd forgotten to take it when he moved out ten years ago; I've made it my own ever since.

Judy Bernstein, LPN, sat in the same spot on her horseshoe as she had yesterday. She smiled when she saw me. When she spoke, I understood why.

"Your Miss Ball is awake," she said to Hart and me. "I heard when I came on my shift."

Hart and I both beamed. Hart held a bright orange ceramic pumpkin, potted with a Christmas cactus that would clash with the orange when it faded. Today, though, the combination was perfect.

Wade Community Hospital is a rectangular maze that would be unnavigable if it weren't for color-coordinated signs at each intersection. The Intensive Care Unit was in the absolute center, the gut it seemed, of the building. It took Hart and me ten minutes to walk there at a full trot, and, I imagined, it would take us another ten to get out no matter which green exit sign we followed. I'm not claustrophobic that I know of, but the deeper we went into that hospital, the more I began to pop out in little beads of sweat all over my forehead.

"Hold it, Hart," I said as I stopped and removed my rubberized army jacket.

"Are you having a hot flash, Sydney?" I detected a smirk in the angle of his smiling mouth.

"Hot flash? What do you mean 'hot flash'? I'm not old enough to have a hot flash." I pulled the raincoat off my neck. "This raincoat is rubber. No wonder."

We began walking again.

"My mother has started to get them," Hart said casually. "You looked just like she does when that heat creeps up her neck."

"Well, I'm not your mother," I mumbled under my breath. I remembered Dr. Fritz's comment to me yesterday, and I added, "I'm not Sally's mother either."

Sally's mother, Lenora Ball, was in the tiny glass-enclosed room with her daughter. Only two people were allowed in at a time, so Hart waited in the visitors' room while I took myself and the trans-seasonal floral gift into the room.

"Awake" is not the word I would have used for the condition Sally was in. Dr. Fritz had been right: she looked horrible. As if she'd been the loser in a heavyweight bout. Her head had been shaved and was wrapped heavily in tape. Electrodes were taped to both her chest and the sides of her head behind her ears, where they fed vital information to wires, which, in turn, fed it to the computer monitors in the nursing station on the other side of the glass walls. I didn't want Sally to truly wake up in here like this.

Mrs. Ball was sitting in the one chair reading a *People* magazine. I whispered hello to her, then stood beside the bed, cradled the pumpkin, and reached gently for Sally's hand. Her eyes fluttered like a sputtering car engine, then closed again. Twenty seconds later she tried again and slowly lifted one swollen eyelid in my direction.

Sally's effort was so determined I found myself focusing all my own concentration on her struggling eyes. When a nurse tapped me on the shoulder, I jumped.

"The pumpkin will have to go," she whispered, pointing to the planter perched on my hip. "No plants in Intensive Care."

Before turning it over, I swiped it across poor Sally's limited line of vision and said softly, "Pumpkin," as if I was teaching a toddler her first word. I asked the nurse to give it to the man in the hall. I looked down at Sally again and the moment had disappeared. Her eyes were closed again.

I leaned down. "Sally," I said, "don't open your eyes. Hart's outside. We just want you to know we're here."

A smile struggled across the lower half of her face.

"You're doing great, Sally," I whispered. "The doctor says you'll be fine."

Her lips then moved. She was trying to talk, but no sound came out. She gripped my hand, pulled at it.

I leaned down as close to her mouth as I could get without disrupting the wiring.

"Got . . . the . . . video." The effort took all the energy she had plus more, from what I could see. Her face was now motionless. Not even the twitching I'd noticed at her eyelids.

Lenora Ball stood and motioned me out to the hallway. "This happens," she said when we were outside the room. "She comes to briefly, then goes back again. The nurses say it's to be expected, that consciousness doesn't come all at once."

"I'm sure the nurses know what they're talking about," I said. "They're the ones who see this sort of thing."

"Yes, dear, but still I'm waiting for her doctor, a Dr. Fritz. He should be by here shortly."

I knew I should leave then or I would say something stupid or sarcastic about Dr. Fritz. I didn't want to prejudice Lenora against the good doctor or against me, the wise employer.

Hart handed me the pumpkin and went into the room to stand by Sally's bed. While he was gone, I asked Lenora if she knew what had been done with Sally's car and if she knew whether or not it had been totaled.

She told me she had no idea. Her son, Fred, was taking care of the car.

Hart and I followed the little green signs. Then I saw a red one and switched to it. I wanted to get back to the emergency room. Hart didn't protest, not even about having to tote the pumpkin.

"Do you have any information on Sally Ball's car?" I asked Nurse Bernstein when we were back in the emergency room.

"Like what kind of information?" she asked.

"Like where the police may have had it towed," I said.

She scratched her curly gray head. "I'm not sure. The only auto shop in town is a Ford dealership." She pointed north. "Just take a right out of the parking lot and you're on Main Street in three minutes. Ford dealership's about six blocks down Main."

I thanked her and started to leave.

"Sad about Seth Bolick," she said as if it were an afterthought. She stood to retrieve a stack of folders from the curving counter. She shook her head, then looked into my eyes. "Just like his father."

Her words coursed through my brain like random

jolts of electricity. "What did you say about Seth's father?" The perspiration was starting to pop out on my face again. I could feel the heat on my neck. I knew my tone was challenging, that aggression on my part wasn't going to change her words. But I had to stop this rumor.

Judy Bernstein looked embarrassed all of a sudden. She didn't want to answer me. She opened a file and leaned into it as if it was difficult to read.

"Please . . ." I put my hand on the paperwork she was staring at. "Tell me what you know. I've heard the rumors." My voice was a hoarse whisper.

She whispered in return, "I thought you were a family friend. I shouldn't have—"

I grabbed both her hands. "I was," I began. "I am. I know all about Seth's father and his sui—" I couldn't get the whole word out. "Why are people saying Seth did the same thing?"

She removed her hands slowly. She shook her head. "I think it makes sense," she said softly, so softly she must have thought I'd break. "He died of respiratory arrest. Nicotine concentrate was in his blood and in the inhaler his family brought in." She let her hand slip over mine and squeezed gently before releasing it. "I'm sorry."

7

"Seth wouldn't do that, Hart. Not in a million years."

Hart was driving the Trooper. I couldn't trust myself to concentrate after what Judy Bernstein had told us. I felt as if someone had stolen something from me in broad daylight. How on earth did nicotine get into Seth's inhaler? And if someone were going to kill himself—which, of course, Seth wasn't—why go to so much trouble? Why not take out a hunting rifle or, the more obvious, stand under the fumigation lines like his father?

"You never know what's eating a person," he said. Hart was chewing on his bottom lip, a symptom I'd grown to know as a sign of stress. I think my adrenaline was frightening him.

"Usually I'd agree with that . . . but not this time." I hit my open palm against the glove compartment and felt a surge of adrenaline. "Hell, no. You were around him, Hart. Did he act depressed to you?" I didn't want an answer. "Hell, no, he wasn't depressed."

"Depression shows up in strange ways sometimes." His words came in measured beats as if he were subconsciously counteracting my rising pace and pitch. He leaned a bit in my direction, then said, "Is that Keeter Ford down the street there, Sydney?"

I could barely see a portable marquee two or three blocks ahead of us. "Looks like it," I said and settled back in the seat. When I did, I noticed a dark green Cherokee behind us by two car lengths.

Hart pulled into Keeter Ford.

I twisted in my seat, ripping at my harness like a bull awaiting his turn at the matador. "Like how, Hart?" I asked sarcastically.

His eyes grew small, and his mouth opened when his chin jutted out. "Huh?" he said. "Are you still talking about Seth?"

"Depression. Ever seen it show up as sheer joy? 'Cause that's what Seth was, you know. Sheer joy!" I struggled with the dangling seat belt as I mumbled under my breath.

Hart shook his head, put the Trooper in park, turned off the ignition, and looked at me with what I can only describe as sad anxiety. "I'll wait here," he said softly.

I stomped into the aluminum trailer draped in a banner saying Top Dollar for Your Clunker.

"The Ball car," I said, clipping each word as if I was announcing a military assault. Only then did I take in my surroundings. The ten-by-fifteen trailer held two metal desks at right angles to each other. The walls were flanked with rows of metal file cabinets and above them automobile posters from the Model T through the Expedition. The floor was littered with fat vinyl ring binders, about half of them open with pages ripped or ripping.

A morbidly obese man leaned back precariously in a straight-leg wooden chair on casters. It was hard for me to tell if he was trying to sit at one of the desks.

"Yep?" he said. He bounced forward, and I marveled at the strength of good hardwood. "What can I do for you today?"

"My friend was in a wreck," I began in a soft tone that surprised me. "I was told her car would probably be here." I gave him Sally's name and my own, then told him I was her employer. I didn't know if the relationship was enough to get me a look inside the car or not.

The man squinted at me, rubbed his nose before scratching his neck, then scooted himself in his chair back to a tall metal filing cabinet where he pulled out a file that appeared to be lying flat along the tops of the others.

"Just had this out," he said as he scooted back toward me. He removed a piece of paper from the folder, turned it sideways, and squinted at it the same way he'd squinted at me.

"Her brother's already been here," he said, still squinting at the paper. "A Fred Ball. Gave me the insurance information. You don't need to do anything."

"Actually, I'd like to see the car, if I may. She had some company equipment with her when she had the wreck."

He rolled himself again to a hook with a large

circular brass key chain dangling ten or more keys, pulled the chain off the wall, and braced his hands on the chair's arms in preparation for standing up. I looked away because I knew he would find it difficult. I studied his posters again and noticed no Edsel. No Ford history is complete without the infamous Edsel.

Sally's car was a disaster. The Civic hatchback looked like a golf cart. The front was entirely gone right up to the dashboard. It amazed me Sally hadn't broken both legs in addition to taking the jolt on her head.

"God, this is awful," I said. "Do you know what happened?"

"Single car. Ran off the road. Hit an old pine tree. Good thing it wasn't no oak. Your friend would have gone the way of this car."

I wondered what could have caused Sally to run off Highway 29. The road was mostly straight. And yesterday had been beautiful. No slick leaves on the road. No puddles. No way to hydroplane. I might not ever know, because she most likely would never remember. And it really didn't matter as long as she was going to be okay.

The video camera was in the hatchback area, remarkably unscathed. It was as if the back portion of the car hadn't even been in a wreck. But I couldn't find the three tapes I'd filled anywhere. They couldn't have been thrown out during the course of the wreck, because the windows and doors, although bent and cracked, were intact. Maybe the wrecking crew had stolen them.

"My tapes are missing," I finally said. "Who towed the car here?"

"That'd be me. Keeter Wrecking." He scratched his

neck again. His fingernails left white lines on the loose, flowing red skin. "Didn't see any tapes."

"I'm not accusing you, but somebody has taken my tapes."

He shifted, placing his forearm on the hood of an old wrecked Fairlane for balance. It occurred to me how lucky he was his products were so sturdy. "Why would somebody take tapes and leave the machine here?" He was referring to the camera.

"I don't know, but they're gone and they didn't just walk away. Who has jurisdiction here? The sheriff?"

"Yep."

"Where can I find him?"

"That'd be me. Sheriff Keeter." He took his arm off that old Fairlane and extended his hand to me. The Fairlane's axles creaked, then hit the gravel with a cacophony of metals in various stages of rusting out.

I sighed heavily. Clearly I'd get no help here. Without knowing exactly why, I thanked the sheriff and headed back to the Trooper to fill Hart in on these developments.

I needed to feel control over something, so I asked Hart to move over. I held on to the steering wheel and pulled myself up into the driver's seat. The old Trooper beneath me felt good—like a trusted old horse whose rhythms create your own.

"Who knows," Hart said. "Maybe the tapes will turn up in Sally's handbag."

I had my doubts about that. Hart seemed determined to voice the opposite side of every opinion I shared with him that day though. So I didn't tell him I thought they were stolen. I also chose not to mention Seth again, as a creeping sense of ownership had begun to come over me. As if Seth's honor belonged to me. As if exposing that honor to any more innuendos or accusations was disloyal. I knew he hadn't taken his own life. At least not intentionally. The assumption that he had would be straightened out before these rumors went much further. I was sure of that. The whole notion was too stupid to argue about anyway.

Bredon is a ghost town on weekdays. With the exception of housewives with their small children in minivans and farmers in old trucks, everyone else is in Charlotte. So I thought it strange to see the same green Cherokee I'd noticed earlier as I pulled out of Keeter Ford. Now I watched it pull out of a metered spot just down the street as we passed it heading east toward the Bolicks' farm. I passed close enough to register that the two men in the front seat both were wearing suits. Those suits were the real oddity; at least, they're what I would remember. Nobody wore suits in Wade County.

The Bolick farm flanks Highway 29. Long-leaf pines, several rows of them, screen the land from view. All these pines were the only way I could tell the entrance was near. The unassuming white sign looks more like a secondary road sign than one announcing entrance to a six-thousand-acre farming operation and laboratory. Just as understated are the small hand-lettered words "Bright Snake Farm" and underneath them the name Bolick. The name had been another bow to the early Bolick's pride in his product. The family had never changed it back.

"Why didn't you change it when your grandfather died?" I'd asked Seth.

He laughed. "Two hundred years of Bolick men are buried on the land. If we even thought about changing it, they'd roll over in unison."

I wondered where Seth would be buried.

Once Hart and I passed the pines, we could see without obstruction. The long, straight gravel road ran about a mile to Seth's lab and, just across from it, his house. I wondered if anybody would be at either place. Ian's house was somewhere on the farm, as was Sara and Johnny's, although I'd seen neither of them, only Seth's.

"I've never seen so much land," Hart said as I drove.

"When's the last time you were on a farm, Hart?" I asked.

"I think my class took a field trip in the mid-seventies."

"You were a baby," I said.

"Second grade, I think. But I remember it. I saw a cow being milked and decided I never wanted to see anything like that again." He wasn't laughing.

"Well, so farming's not your thing." I looked over at him. "But you've got to admit the land is beautiful."

"If you like grass," he said, pointing. "I thought this was a tobacco farm. All I see is thousands of acres of grass."

"It's for winter cover. Tobacco's gone for the year."

We were silent for the rest of the drive to the lab. I thought about my first trip out here with Seth and when we drove down this road. Ian had been planting the last of the rye that day.

I'd asked Seth what his brother thought of the synthetic nicotine. His answer wasn't direct. Something like "He's on the board." I didn't think much about it at the time. Maybe it was Seth's way of telling me Ian approved; maybe it was something else. I wondered now, though, since so much depended on him. Whatever Ian's feelings, we needed to get a handle on the future today. Were he and the rest of the board willing to follow through? For Seth's sake, the answer just had to be yes.

Seth's laboratory was the building his father had built: a two-story concrete block building that probably would have been metal if it had been built today. Strictly utilitarian. Inside here he had developed the compound that could mimic nicotine.

"This is the lab?" Hart asked. "I'd have expected something more impressive."

"It worked great on the video I shot Sunday," I said. "Had sort of an Abe Lincoln quality to it. Abe reading by candlelight in a log cabin; Seth slaving over a test tube in a nondescript concrete building. The humble-beginnings approach."

Hart nodded. "Yes, I can see that." He smiled at me, then quickly lowered his eyes. "Too bad about the tapes."

I stared at him. "Three tapes won't fit inside Sally's pocketbook," I said. "Hers isn't as big as mine."

My pocketbook sat between us. Hart looked down at it, then up at me.

"Who'd want to know that much about what you and Seth did on Sunday?"

I shrugged.

He smiled. "One of our competitors? What's Mickey Sutton up to these days?"

I groaned. Mickey Sutton's my professional nemesis. He watches my every move, trips me up every chance he gets. But I didn't think he'd follow us to Wade County. It's just too country for high-rise Mickey. "Nah," I said. "Mickey doesn't drive two-lane highways."

"What about Seth's competitors?" he asked.

I thought about that question off and on for the next couple of days.

I recognized the lone car. It belonged to Seth's lab assistant. Her first name was Betty, but I couldn't remember her last. She greeted us and took us into an area toward the back of the first floor where a couple of old sofas and a makeshift kitchen served as all-purpose conference room, break room, and home away from home during the long months as Seth came nearer to his breakthrough. Both sofas were made out of a stubby cotton-wool blend in an orange and green plaid. The refrigerator and stove were that yellowy gold color from the seventies that was pushing to make a comeback. This room had obviously not been touched since Jonathan Bolick, before Seth, had set out to develop the safe cigarette.

When I'd met Betty before, I'd noticed the university research look she carried so effectively: the wire-rim glasses, the sharp nose, small dark eyes, short black hair, small stature with rounded, almost hunched, shoulders. She had that look of total concentration. As if standing erect would somehow break the umbilical connection between her and her test tubes. Now her features looked pinched, as if nerves, rather than focus, had wired them together. Her shoulders seemed less intellectual slouch than mere exhaustion. Her small eyes were puffy slits behind the wire and glass.

"I'm just trying to get his work done," she said hoarsely. "I don't know what else to do."

"Nobody's come by to talk with you?" I asked.

She looked at me as if I might be crazy, then turned away and laughed sarcastically. "You mean someone from Bolick Enterprises?" She shook her head. "You tell me, Sydney, who else besides Seth was part of Bolick Enterprises? Huh?" She swept her hand across the side of the room that was all tubes, burners, and computers. As she did, her expression changed from pointed sarcasm to awe, then sadness. Her voice broke when she said, "This was all . . . one man."

"Two," I said.

"Two? You mean his brother?"

"No," I said. "I mean his father."

Betty nodded slowly. "Yeah, you're right. We even worked from his notes in the beginning. His nonburning blends are still part of the delivery device." She smiled.

"Is the FDA going to give you some slack because of Seth?" I still couldn't say the words easily.

She shook her head. "They called first thing this morning. Like every morning. I told them about Seth. Asked them if they couldn't hold off a few days. At least wait until he's buried."

"And they're not going to give you that?"

She shook her head again. I knew the demanding schedule imposed by the Food and Drug Administration before Snake could be even test-marketed. Phase One trials had begun. One patent had been filed; several more were in the process. The actual public launch was more than a year away, and even with that much time everybody involved, including Allen Teague, had something critical to do almost every day. This was a massive and complicated process.

"We were working out optimum delivery for nonstick users when . . . when this happened." Betty was having the same problem I was. We were both avoiding the words.

I envied her though. That same visionary quality Seth carried with him was here with Betty and the work. I realized more than ever I still wanted to see Snake make it. If the work could keep going, then, in a very real way, Seth could keep going too.

"You need some rest," I said. "A day or two in either direction isn't going to mess up the FDA."

"Yeah," she said. Her voice was suddenly low. "You tell them that." She looked as if she might cry.

She turned away from me. Her shoulders rose, then sagged even lower than before. I heard a muffled sound escape her lips. Then she bent down abruptly and retrieved an off-brand soft drink bottle from the old refrigerator. She kept her back to us as if her interest in the refrigerator was all-engrossing.

I didn't know what to do. The woman was upset and was doing a poor job of hiding it. But she was trying so hard to maintain her private grief. I didn't feel I should reach out, but to walk away would be rude. So I stood awkwardly, as did Hart.

Just when I was adjusting to the awkwardness of

her back, she turned around and extended the drink to Hart and me. We shook our heads. She sat down with it, unscrewed its cap, and took a small sip. When she looked up at me again, I could see that a few tears had made their way to her cheeks after all.

Hart had already begun easing himself back toward the entrance. I think he was afraid I'd start crying right along with Betty.

I really felt for her. She'd been working with Seth for well over a year. Her skills and enthusiasm had been vitally important to Seth. He'd told me so.

"Why are you two here, Sydney?" She seemed to have regained her composure.

"To find Ian Bolick," I said. "I know he's on the board. He has to make some decisions for us."

"He doesn't know anything about this work," she said.

"He doesn't need to know to give us the go-ahead. Hart's my art director. We've brought some Snake logo ideas."

She sighed. "Well, I'm going ahead anyway." The thin rim of her glasses cut across the middle of her pupils, but I could still see the determination in her eyes. "I know what I need to do."

Hart shuffled his feet in the silence that followed.

"Have you heard what the coroner's saying?"

I nodded.

"Can you think of anything more ridiculous?" Her words came quickly now, rising in pitch.

Hart stood silently.

"Yes," I said. "I heard. It has to be a mistake. I can't believe anyone who knew him would think such a thing."

I looked over at Hart as I said the words "anyone who knew him." He looked away.

"Who told you?" I asked. "I thought you hadn't talked to anyone?"

"Johnny told me. He's my pal. He said the coroner was at their house early this morning. Johnny tried to tell the man he was wrong, but none of them would listen."

"Who wouldn't listen? Besides the coroner, who was there?"

"The whole family, from what Johnny said. At least a couple of generations of them anyway."

"How can Johnny be so sure?" I said, wanting some hard evidence to file away with my mounting doubts.

She took one last long swig from the bottle in her hand and put it in a recycle bin. "Because Johnny was with him when it happened," she said.

8

We left Seth's research assistant to her work and went looking for Sara and Johnny Bolick. I needed to know what had happened to Seth more than what would happen to his product. Hart didn't have a lot to say about it, since I was driving.

A group of Mexicans were putting in irrigation lines farther down the main road from the lab. I pulled over onto the slight embankment and asked the man closest to the road where I could find Señora Bolick. He took off his hat and leaned in on Hart's side of the car. "Which one?" he asked in very plain Southern-accented English. "There are three Mrs. Bolicks."

"Sara," I said. "Mrs. Seth."

His expression became sad, his mouth downturned. "She is the first side road to your right in this same direction you're heading," he said. "They aren't seeing any visitors though. Mr. Seth Bolick died yesterday."

"I'm a friend," I said and felt a pang of guilt at the

unnecessary lie. I'd never met a single Bolick female until the emergency room yesterday. Now he was telling me there were three.

He tipped his hat to me before I pulled back onto the road.

"Sydney, don't you think our showing up like this is a little on the rude side?" Hart was biting his lower lip again.

"Not if we handle it diplomatically," I said as I pulled into the driveway. "Sara and Johnny are bound to be as upset as I am about the coroner's findings. Maybe they don't know there are ways to fight these things. They can make the coroner look for something else."

Hart just stared at me. "It's none of our business," he said.

I wanted to scream at him. But I breathed deeply, then turned to face him. "Hart, I know some things about Seth's past you don't know. You just know about the work. I know why he was doing it. He would have moved mountains if he could to see it all the way through."

"It really sort of was through. The invention at least." Hart's eyes were full of questions.

"No, it wasn't," I said. "Betty's still working. You saw her. Seth would never abandon Snake." I looked at Sara's front door, then back at Hart. "This has been some terrible mistake. I just can't let it alone."

Hart appeared to be thinking over what I said while I got out of the Trooper. I waited for him at the front walk.

"Bring the pumpkin," I said. "I need something in my hands."

He opened his door but just sat there and stared at me. "The pumpkin's not appropriate," he said while shaking his head.

"And why not? Flowers are always appropriate."

Hart thoughtfully scrunched his features. "It's not flowers, Sydney. It's an orange pumpkin. It's neither a grief color nor a grief symbol."

"Why'd you order it, then?" I was nearing the end of my rope. Hart and I shouldn't go on the road together.

"I chose it for Sally, to cheer her up. And it was on sale." His eyes were steel blue. "I didn't know it would end up at a wake."

"This isn't a wake. It's a house call." I rolled my eyes. "Give it to me. I don't mind being inappropriate." I walked over to him, took the pumpkin out of his hands, and walked back to the front door.

When he finally exited the Trooper, he started to go around to the back of the car, then hesitated and looked at me.

"I don't guess I need the art, then. We're not going to talk about Snake, are we?"

I shook my head. "We'll do that when we find Ian."

He hesitated again.

"What's wrong, Hart?"

"I don't have a reason for going in there. I think I'll wait in the car."

I looked at my watch. It was just after noon. My stomach knew it was somewhere around that time without even checking the watch. "We need to eat something. If you come inside with me, you can make sure we leave quickly to go get lunch."

He opened the passenger door and stepped up into his seat. "Make it as quick as you can," he whined.

It occurred to me, as I stood at Sara Bolick's door, that Hart hides from anything the least bit unpleasant. He does it all the time. At the office he quietly disappears back to his art room. What I had here was merely a different setting.

An older woman wearing an apron over a black knit dress greeted me at the door. She was on the short side, at most five foot one, and had white wavy hair held up in a utilitarian bun in the back. A very diluted golden wash looked like it had been brushed across her hair. She must have been a true blonde in her day. Her eyes were an intense, dark blue edged with lots of short, little lines that radiated from their corners. They appeared to be laugh lines. Her hands were rough with crevices etched a thin beige from the soil. They had obviously worked this land. Although I'd never met her before, I knew instantly she must be Seth's mother. She was a lovely looking woman. Why hadn't Seth ever mentioned her?

Jen Bolick warmly introduced herself, graciously accepted the pumpkin, and asked me to come inside. I was impressed with such hospitality from a mother who'd just lost her son. She led me to a large, high ceilinged family room paneled in warm Honduras mahogany. The furniture was all old leather, those massive, worn kinds of pieces that remind me of western saddles. Quality orientals and kilims were scattered and overlapping on the pine plank floor. I thought about what I'd seen of Seth's small house Sunday in contrast to this. His one living area was a kitchen-dining-den combination with sparse Salvation Army furniture placed awkwardly as if mere annoyances to be maneuvered on his way through the house. From what Seth had told me of his life these past few years, it had become twenty-four-hour work-days, with his home meaning nothing more than the necessary bed.

Sara and Johnny sat on one of the two wine-colored sofas. Jen motioned to me to sit on the other large sofa, and she sat on a wooden straight-back chair, which looked as if it was a match to a dining room suite. The television was on low in the background.

Jen Bolick nodded in Johnny's direction. "Turn the television off, Jonathan dear."

Johnny got that sullen early-teen expression on his face, but he clicked the remote anyway. He was older than my twelve-year-old but younger than my sixteen-year-old. If kids only knew how predictable their be-havior is at each age, they might try changing it. After all, one of their most common characteristics is a bla-tant, uniform belief in individuality.

"Hey, Ms. Teague," he said, and I saw a lot of pain in his eyes. Maybe it hadn't been sullenness I'd just seen, but the pain instead.

"Hey, Johnny. I'm so sorry." Then I turned to Sara and then to Seth's mother and said the same thing.

Both women acknowledged my sympathy, but it was Jen who spoke: "We loved our Seth. Nobody could ever love a son like I did my Seth. He was just like his daddy, my love, my Jonathan." She gazed lovingly, sadly, at Johnny, who, embarrassed, stared at the floor. "And Jonathan here, my Jonathan's namesake, loved his daddy like he was the sun and the moon. And Sara. Sara loved him, but she couldn't live with him. Nobody could've lived with my Seth. I'd be the first to tell you that. But we're all comforted by knowing he's at peace. My boy's finally . . . at peace." What had begun as a stoic speech she'd no doubt practiced for well-wishers broke down at the end just as she did.

Sara jumped off the sofa and rushed to the older woman's side, putting her arms gently around her shoulders. She asked Johnny to retrieve a box of tissues from the bathroom and asked me to get her some water.

The kitchen led off from this room, so finding it wasn't a problem. Finding a glass that didn't look like good crystal was, however. The kitchen was bigger than my family room, with forty cabinets to my ten. Finally I settled on a quilted ice tea glass, poured her cold tap water at the sink, and returned it to her in the den. Johnny and I met at Jen Bolick's knees, I with the glass and he with a square floral box of tissues. Our eyes locked, and I smiled warmly. He looked away quickly. Before he did, though, I detected something in his eyes that threw me for a minute. Embarrassment? Anger? A question? I couldn't figure it out, because I wasn't expecting any of those three things when I caught his eyes. If anything, I suppose I was expecting to see some empathy for his grandmother's feelings.

I sat back on the sofa. While I waited for Sara to finish comforting Mrs. Bolick, I tried to get Johnny's attention. The boy wouldn't look at me, even though, without his television, he had effectively no place else to look. I was beginning to feel as awkward as he was behaving.

Jen Bolick had put the ceramic pumpkin on the

coffee table when we came in. It was the only thing I could think to talk about that wasn't charged emotionally. "Johnny," I began, "I think you can use this pumpkin as a candy container when the cactus dies." I know it was a weak subject, but it was all I had to get us started.

He nodded.

"Do you like candy corn?"

He nodded again. I saw an ounce of interest, maybe less.

"I have a son about your age. His name is George. George loves candy corn."

"Dad told me you had a son," he said. At that moment, and just that moment, he seemed to be pleading with his eyes. He wanted something from me, I felt certain. Maybe it was friendship, a common bond now that Seth was dead. As close as he was to his father, I'm sure he knew how close I'd grown to him as well.

He had brought up his father. I was trying to decide whether to risk asking him about finding his father the day before when Jen Bolick broke our silence. She apologized for breaking down.

"I'm the one who needs to apologize," I said to all three of them. "I probably shouldn't have come here today, but I wanted—no, I needed—to tell you how much I thought of Seth." I decided not to bring up the coroner's ruling right away. I hoped one of them would, and I could simply state my opinion then.

Sara smiled at me, then put her hand on Johnny's knee and turned to him. "See, Johnny, people thought a lot of your father."

Johnny pulled himself out from under her hand

and stood abruptly. "If he was so wonderful, then why couldn't we live with him?" His face was turning red with anger as he screamed at his mother. "You're a hypocrite." He turned to his grandmother. "You're a hypocrite too. If either one of you cared about Daddy, he wouldn't be dead." He ran to the long, winding steps leading to the second floor. Neither woman tried to stop him. I could hear his footsteps on the uncarpeted hardwood as I sat feeling guilty and embarrassed for having caused his outburst.

Sara put her head in her hands and said, "Oh God, what's going to happen to us now?"

The elder Mrs. Bolick was saying, "Now, now, Sara. The boy's upset. He doesn't know what he's saying."

"Oh yes he does," cried Sara. "This isn't anything new because of Seth's death. Johnny's always felt I let Seth down and let him down in the process."

Sara looked up at me. "What could I do? You knew him. You saw the obsession." She laughed sarcastically. "Only imagine it ten times worse than what you've seen. When I met Seth Bolick, we were fifteen years old, and he was the most carefree, wonderful guy in the world." She glanced over at Jen, then back at me before continuing. "Then his father killed himself and Seth changed. He had loved animals and always wanted to be a veterinarian." She turned to Jen and said, "Not a week after his father's death, he told me he'd changed his mind. He was going to be a biochemist, a molecular engineer. He was going to carry on with his father's work. I should have fought him then. Before the obsession took hold. We got married when he was still an undergraduate at Duke. I thought the marriage itself and having me around all the time would jolt him into seeing he had his own life to lead."

Jen Bolick had been picking at the tissue in her hands as Sara talked. She pulled another one out of the box and dabbed at her eyes. Just as Sara was about to say more, Jen interrupted her: "He couldn't, Sara hon. You know that." She looked at me. "Ms. Teague, Seth never did learn to live his life. He was sick that way. Like his father. Neither of those men ever learned there was more to life than that building up the road."

I must have looked confused, because she said, "The laboratory, dear. Both of these Bolick men spent more time in that building every day than poor Ian does in the fields during a harvest." She shook her head. "What they had was like an illness. A real bad illness." She returned her gaze to Sara. "That's how I've always seen it. The men couldn't help themselves. What made their minds sick killed them both in the end." She gazed at Sara. "I warned you about it when you married him, Sara."

Sara cut sharp eyes back at her mother-in-law. "You can handle anything, Mama Bolick." Sara's attitude toward her mother-in-law seemed full of alternating love and hate. I watched the venom dissipate slowly. After a silent minute she turned to me and added, "Mama's naturally in charge. She can handle things. I can't."

She laughed again, and I wondered at what. It was a strangely sad, self-deprecating laugh. "He got worse," she continued, almost as if the elder woman hadn't interrupted her. "He volunteered for research projects whenever there was an opening. He held two at one time, and we didn't even need the money. Then on to MIT just like his father had done. Even when I had Johnny . . . and I had insisted myself on naming him after Seth's father, just knowing that having his own son now would keep him home." She took a deep breath and ran her forefingers along the sides of her nose. "If anything, Seth got worse after Johnny was born."

She stood up and walked over to her mother-in-law's chair. They touched hands briefly, then Sara pulled a tissue out of the box and blew her nose. "Two years ago I couldn't stand it anymore. What was the purpose of our marriage? Johnny had no father anyway. I had no husband. I told him to get out."

Jen Bolick broke in again. "I backed Sara in her decision. As much as it pained me to ask a son of mine to leave, I had to agree with Sara."

"This is your home, Mrs. Bolick?" I asked, finding it hard to believe a mother could do such a thing.

"The home I've always lived in. Since I married my Jonathan anyway. Where I raised both of my boys; where their father was raised and his father before him. It's the Bolick family home." Her voice was prideful, almost haughty.

"What about Ian?"

I caught a quick exchange of expressions between the two women. From my angle on the sofa, I couldn't see enough of their faces to decipher them. The exchange itself said something about this family though. Everything wasn't right on the surface. Some kind of undercurrent was rippling through the politeness I was being shown.

Sara spoke again: "Ian and Bev have too many children to fit in this house with Mama Bolick. Two girls and four boys. Mama's house has only the four bedrooms. It was perfect for us."

"Where's Ian's house?" I needed to know this if Hart and I were going to accomplish anything today.

Sara told me Ian had built a mile down the road, deep into the middle of their land.

"He's the true farmer among us," Jen Bolick said, that note of pride still hanging in her voice. "Ian and his boys all love this land."

"You do too, Mama Bolick. Nobody loves it more than you."

Jen thought about that before answering: "Sara honey, I just do what has to be done. You live off the land, you take care of it." Then she turned back to me and said something I'll never forget. "Tobacco gets in your blood, hon." She had no clue of the irony in her statement.

I couldn't figure out how to move the conversation around to Seth's suicide. Both women were so emotional, and rightly so, that the last thing I wanted to do was upset them all over again. But I couldn't let it go. Somebody had to ask the coroner to reconsider his findings. I didn't know the law in this area, but I'd be willing to bet a request like that had to come from a family member or somebody with proof to the contrary.

Jen Bolick stood and wiped both hands on her pink apron. "Won't you join us for a bite of lunch?" she said to me. "I was just getting ready to serve us all sandwiches when you arrived."

I thanked her, then said, "I wish I could, but my art

director has been waiting for me outside in the car. He and I will just drive down the road to get something."

Sara laughed. "You'll be driving a long way, then, if you're looking for a restaurant."

"Bring the fellow on in," said Jen. "Sara, go out there and get Ms. Teague's artist friend. We'll all have a bite together."

I was grateful she hadn't asked me to go get Hart, because he wouldn't have come inside for me. He's too polite to refuse a stranger, though, so I knew Sara would succeed. Confidently I followed Jen into the kitchen.

Turkey, ham, roast beef, four or five different kinds of cheeses, and every imaginable kind of bread from French to kosher rye were laid out on a large platter.

Jen smiled when I complimented her. "Praise the Lord, not me, for this one. The churchwomen came and went early this morning. They'll be back Thursday after the funeral too, I guarantee you." Jen winked at me. "Now go into the living room and get us that centerpiece you were kind enough to get." She patted the center of the table. "We'll put it right here."

I purposefully avoided eye contact with Hart as Sara dragged him into the house. Well, she wasn't really dragging him, since he was in front of her. She had both hands on one of his elbows as if it were some kind of steering mechanism. They followed me into the kitchen, and we all sat down to lunch.

A bold, blue vein stuck out on Hart's pale forehead as he unfolded his napkin. He looked so uncomfortable. He'd really rather not have to deal with people he doesn't know. For that matter, even people he does.

Sara looked at the pumpkin and then at Jen. "What's

this?" she asked her. She must not have noticed it when
Jen had put it down in the living room. Her tone wasn't
complimentary. I stared hard at the pattern on the plate
in front of me.

"A gift, Sara. Wasn't that kind?"

"A gag gift? Not very appropriate, if you ask me."
She reached for a bowl of mayonnaise, then turned to
Hart. "What kind of upbringing made someone think
an orange pumpkin with a half-dead cactus would be
appropriate for the grieving?" She shook her head in
disbelief. Hart joined her. I prayed that the subject be
closed.

Hart's foot left a slight indentation in my ankle,
however, before he was through driving home his point.
I had a feeling I would hear about the pumpkin for
years to come. Jen had the good sense not to tell Sara it
was from me.

I was quiet while I ate my sandwich. I watched Sara
and Jen work together in coaxing Hart out of his shell.
They mostly succeeded only in making each other feel
better, however, because Hart's shell is harder and deeper
than anything these two women had ever encountered.
But, bless them, they were trying their best.

"What about Johnny?" I said as they were discussing whether *Fargo* was art or gore. He had been
waiting to eat lunch too when I showed up unannounced. Shouldn't one of the women have called him
down to eat?

"I'll take him something when you leave," Sara
said. "He's really too upset to be around anybody but
family."

Jen sipped steaming coffee from a delicate cup, and

as she put it back on its saucer, it rattled and some of the coffee spilled. She dabbed the tablecloth around the saucer with her linen napkin, then she looked up at me.

"He's having a hard time. It's hard on all of us, but Johnny was . . . with his father yesterday . . ."

"How horrible," I said, pretending I hadn't heard already.

Her hands shook as she again brought her napkin to her mouth. She looked at me as if no one else was in the room. At least it felt that way. "I'd give anything . . . everything if that hadn't happened."

She was staring at me already. This was my opening to ask the question I'd come here with. I was afraid I wouldn't get another chance if I didn't speak up now.

"Mrs. Bolick," I said looking directly into Jen's eyes, "I don't see how you of all people could believe Seth would kill himself after what he went through with his father."

She opened her mouth as if she was about to speak, but I'd held it in too long, and I wasn't going to stop now.

"Giving value back to his father's life is what Seth's whole life has been about. He wouldn't do it to his father . . ." I stopped long enough to look across the table at Sara, then added, "and he wouldn't do it to his son."

There was nothing but stunned silence at the table. I looked from Sara to Jen and back Sara again.

"Don't you think there must be some mistake here?" I said to them both.

"Ms. Teague," Jen began, "perhaps you don't know this, but when Seth couldn't be revived, the doctors decided to examine his nebulizer. As the coroner told us, they just knew something wasn't right. The bottle was filled with nicotine concentrate." She looked at Sara before looking back at me. "So he used it in front of his own son."

I shook my head. I couldn't help it. "No," I said firmly. "He wouldn't do that. Not in front of his son."

"He'd obviously poisoned himself, Sydney." It was Sara speaking. Her tone was harsh and challenging. She wanted to believe the worst of her estranged husband. I wondered why.

Jen smiled nervously. "He certainly didn't mean to hurt Johnny, Ms. Teague."

It still didn't make any sense to me. First, that he'd do it at all, and secondly, that he'd put himself through all that agony when he could have just put a bullet through his head. "Something's wrong here," I said with a growing conviction I couldn't silence. "Somebody else must have tampered with his nebulizer."

"I don't think you know the history of this family, Sydney," Sara said. "You wouldn't be saying that if you did." Her voice was suddenly laden with sarcasm, and it shocked me.

I toned my own voice down for fear that I had agitated Sara. "I do know the history, Sara." I was almost whispering, I was trying so hard to remain calm. "It's because of the history as Seth knew it that I don't believe Seth could ever do what his father did."

Although she appeared to calm down, Sara's tone was still sarcastic. "Well, you of all people should take another look at your interpretation of Seth Bolick."

She folded her napkin and slammed it on the table between herself and Hart. Hart began to rearrange his silverware. Nervously.

"What does that mean?" I asked. "Me of all people?" I didn't know what I'd said to upset her so. It was as if I had done something personally to hurt her, and I was being called to task.

I looked at Jen. "Is there any other evidence that Seth took his own life?" I asked this as evenly and sanely as I could, with no hint of the crusader.

Jen Bolick smiled again, only nervously this time. I saw the source of the lines about her beautiful blue eyes. "Well, dear, there's the note he left."

I hadn't been prepared for this. Suicides leave notes. Only people who know they're going to die leave messages for people. "Note?" I asked in disbelief. "What note?"

It was Sara who answered. Like the lines at her mother-in-law's eyes, the source of Sara's anger toward me became clear. "The suicide note he left to you, Sydney."

9

Jen said she hadn't seen this note. Sara said she had, but all she remembered was its brevity and the fact it had my name on it. She and Johnny had found it together when they returned to Seth's house after his death the day before. They had given it to the coroner. I knew that sometime I would need to find this coroner.

To say I was thrown for a loop is a big understatement. I had been so convinced somebody murdered Seth that I hadn't allowed the genuine possibility of his suicide to enter my mind. Now that it had, I found myself wanting to go home, wanting to forget as best I could the emotional investment, not to mention the professional one, I'd made in Seth's cause. But why would he leave me a note? Why not his family? Particularly his son, whom I knew he loved? My emotions were shot. I was on a personal roller-coaster.

"Let's find Ian Bolick and get this over with, Sydney." Hart rolled down his window and stuck his head out as I was backing out of Jen Bolick's driveway. He gazed back at me. "Roll your window down," he said. "Smells great outside. Like it's going to rain."

I didn't touch the window. I just sat there with the rear of the Trooper jutting out on the Bolicks' main road. I couldn't decide whether to leave or do as Hart said and see if we could find Ian Bolick. Hart wasn't used to this kind of behavior from me. He knows I'm a person who believes taking action, any action, is preferable to indecision. To tell the truth, I was having a hard time understanding myself as well.

"The note really shocked you, didn't it?" he said.

I nodded. I was overwhelmed with sadness, and I knew it wasn't just Seth. I was sad for my father and the daughter he had all over again. "Do you believe he wrote me a note?" I asked.

Hart shifted in his seat and rolled his window up. He began to look uncomfortable again. He started to answer me, hesitated, then started again: "Sydney, what happened this weekend? Did he say anything that, when you look back on it, might have told you he'd do this?"

"I don't know," I said without thought. "I showed Seth your storyboards for everything we had planned. Hell, I had nine hours' worth of film. And I still couldn't get him to sit down and do the direct interview with me for the finance on those investor spots. He kept saying he didn't want to be the one to answer the financial questions directly on tape. He relished answering the chemistry questions, but he was fighting me on the financials." My own voice sounded strange to me as I groped for understanding. "Hart, it was the only disagreement we had all day. And it was purely a strategy disagreement like we have with clients all the time. He wanted me to get their accounting group and the brokerage house to go on tape for the financials, so I didn't film that part of your storyboard. Honest to God, Hart, there was no indication he was considering such a thing."

"I got the impression . . ." Hart bit his lip, then turned away from me as he seemed to be summoning the courage to say something he didn't want to say. "When Seth would be in the office these last two weeks, I got the impression there was something between you and Seth. That the whole Snake thing went way beyond the work. I told you what Sally thought about you two. Don't get mad, Sydney. If I'm wrong, I'm sorry. It's just what I noticed."

"You're not wrong," I said. "There was something between us. I could talk to him about things I couldn't share with anyone else." I looked over at Hart. He was staring out the window, not making eye contact—the way he does when talk gets personal. I touched his hand so he'd look at me again. "But what's your point about that, Hart? I really want to know, okay?"

"Just that maybe he said something along the way." He was talking to me calmly now, his anxiety at broaching the subject gone. "If you thought about it, went over everything he said to you, you know, you'd probably come up with it."

He had said what he needed to say, and I was left to ponder it.

Only I didn't want to think about it then. I would think about it when I got home that night. One of AA's many benefits is the choice of when and what to worry about. I have learned to make appointments with myself for stewing over things. Scarlett O'Hara had a point about tomorrow. It is another day, although sometimes I am afraid it will never come, that death will come first. Like it did with Seth.

I couldn't concentrate though. I wondered if Betty knew anything about this mysterious note Seth left. If she did, why didn't she tell me? As I drove, I fumbled for the car phone buried under my pocketbook. I almost had the lab number memorized. Off just one number. Hart read it out to me from the clip-on directory I keep on the visor.

When she answered, I told Betty about our conversation over lunch and asked what Johnny had told her about the note. I pulled the car over to the side of the gravel road. I was afraid I'd be at Ian's house before I wanted to be.

"Oh my God," she said breathlessly. "Are you saying we were wrong? That Seth really did kill himself?"

"I don't know what I'm saying, Betty. Can you remember if Johnny said anything about a note like that?"

I could hear her crying through the static. When she had regained enough control to speak, she said that he hadn't. "Maybe he was trying to spare me," she added. Even at the time, I thought that was an odd comment.

"If he's talking to you already about what happened yesterday, ask him about this note. Don't push him, but this is going to drive me crazy until I find out," I said.

"Stop by here when you're through with Ian. Maybe I'll know something then. Johnny usually stops by in the afternoons." Her voice was almost a monotone now, as if the reality of what must have seemed a betrayal on Seth's part had set in. "How could Seth do it, Sydney? How could he?"

"Maybe I'll find out something from Ian," I said before settling the little phone back in its cradle.

I put the Trooper in first again and eased back onto the makeshift road.

I couldn't worry about Johnny. Not now. Now I needed to clear my head for one purpose. I had to ensure Snake would continue for Seth somehow. If Ian loved the land as much as Jen and Sara, I had my work cut out for me.

I pulled into Ian Bolick's parking area, looked at Hart, and set my jaw. "Let's fight for Snake, okay?"

A thin piece of his hair fell across Hart's face as he leaned over the seat to reach his art. He grabbed his work, pushed his hair back, and put his hand on the door handle.

I touched his shoulder to get him to answer me. "Okay?" I said again.

"It's just work." He wouldn't look at me as he opened the door. "It's not ours to fight for. Stop turning it into something it isn't."

I felt my jaw twitch, then slip. Hart might as well have slapped me in the face. It took me a good minute to recover enough to open my own door.

Ian's house was massive compared with where Seth had been living, large compared to his mother's. I guess it made sense, since he was the Bolick who had all the kids.

One of those kids met us at the door. A pleasant if plain-looking girl, maybe two years Joan's senior. Her light brown hair was pulled straight back. She wore no makeup, had no distinguishing features. Her voice was weak—genetically so, not from illness that I could tell. She told us her father was in the field with her brothers. Then she pointed past the Trooper into the field and said, " 'Bout a half mile is all."

I thanked her and walked back to the Trooper. Hart put his art into the backseat again. I had turned the ignition when I realized he wasn't getting into the car. He was just standing there at the back door.

I waited before putting it in reverse. What was he doing?

Finally Hart walked slowly around to the driver's window.

"Get in," I said. "It's getting late, almost two thirty."

His eyes got small and beady; the corners of his mouth quivered and gradually turned upwards. Then I heard what I've rarely heard from Hart: an out-and-out, hearty laugh. He staggered, literally staggered, to my window, and held on until he could gain control over himself again.

"What?" I said.

He turned and pointed across the field—just as the girl had done. He was still sputtering with glee as he did. "Show me the road, Sydney. You can't drive this monster car through the man's field." He pushed back from my window so I could see all of him. "Guess what?" He bent his knee, twisted it awkwardly, and lifted his foot while he did. "You should have worn these," he said while patting his fake-leather boots.

* * *

I suppose it could have been worse at that moment. It could have been raining. So far it had held off.

After we'd trekked a short distance, I removed my mud-caked heels and let the young rye grass act as carpet to my stocking-clad feet. I actually enjoyed the walk and the opportunity to clear my head. Hart had been right about this air. It was rich and the humidity intensified the smell. The grass was so sweet I could almost taste it. Somebody had spread cow manure, not all completely rotted, I noticed. The mingling of the grass and the manure produced a third smell that was new to me and so robust it both energized me and mellowed me. This was aromatherapy I doubted they'd ever bottle.

One of the Bolick boys was atop a large machine that appeared to be sweeping up the remains of this year's tobacco crop. That rich, musty tobacco smell broke lose with each slice of the blade. Ian was standing with another son, and I noticed another in the same kind of machine in the distance. All his sons were much older than Seth's Johnny; in fact, they seemed to be in their twenties. Then I remembered how much older Ian was than Seth. He'd been a grown man when his father had killed himself. Maybe he'd be able to help Johnny. Somebody sure needed to.

As we approached Ian, the aroma of the tobacco wafted up to us even more powerfully. It was heady, almost like an expensive Havana cigar before lighting. The perfume of it came to me in waves as the machine crushed each massive leaf. I leaned down to pick up a piece of the old tobacco stalk and saw that I was now standing in mud up to my shins. Hart looked over at me as I was leaning down. It was the first smile I'd seen on his face in the thirty minutes we'd been walking.

Ian didn't recognize me at first, and he couldn't hear me at all over the machine. After a few minutes of yelling, he motioned us to follow him. He led us a mere forty feet to a skinny little dirt road where his Chevy truck was parked. The roar of the machine was muffled this far over.

The first question I asked him was if the dirt road ran all the way to his house. When he told me it did, I glared at Hart, who leaned away from me defensively.

At first I went through the same sentiments of sympathy with him I'd done with his mother, sister-in-law, and nephew. Unlike the wild fluctuations in emotion I'd seen at Jen Bolick's house, Ian Bolick was stoic at most. He mumbled and lowered his eyes as I offered my condolences.

Ian was built like Seth. All the Bolicks were stocky. Only Ian was a little over six feet tall, a good couple of inches taller than Seth. He had that beautiful blue intensity to his eyes I'd seen in his mother's, but he had none of Seth's intellectual gaze. He had lines like his mother's too and not only around the eyes. Deep horizontal lines were etched across his forehead. The wind and sun had worked his skin to leather. His hair had probably been sandy like Seth's when he was younger, but the practical crew cut he wore was more salt-and-pepper now than dirty blond. He looked at least fifty years old.

"Can't this wait?" he said as soon as I told him why we were here. "My brother's not even in the ground yet."

At that moment I wished I could sink into mud above my eyes. I should have guessed Ian wasn't part of the Snake crusade. I would have known it, I suppose, if I'd allowed myself.

"What is this? A sales call to make sure you get more business now that your contact's dead?" His eyes were piercing the top of my head.

That statement hurt too badly not to respond to it. "That's not fair," I said. "We're on retainer to you, and we're trying to meet the schedule Bolick Enterprises laid out for us. We simply need you to tell us what to do now." I finally met his accusing eyes with a little confidence. "Ian, I don't even know who else is on the board besides you. If I did, I wouldn't have bothered you."

Something I said, although I'll never know what, changed the expression on his face. He was still angry, but I could tell it wasn't at me. The wind gathered itself and blew steadily at the back of my gray jumper as I waited for him to respond. I tried not to shiver, tried not to alter my gaze from his eyes until he answered me. Hart, of course, had said nothing. For once, I was glad that he hadn't.

The anger slowly dissipated as we stared at each other. He let it go like a balloon that had never been tied quite tight enough.

"You're cold," he said to me. "Let's sit in the truck and talk this over."

He opened the passenger door for me, and I slid inside. Hart stopped short, realizing there was no place for him to sit. Then he turned away abruptly and wandered back into the field as if he had a destination there. From the view I had of him, with his boots and his old tweed jacket, he looked like a second-rate stand-in for Ashley Wilkes in *Gone With the Wind*.

I decided to try for the upper hand. As soon as Ian was behind the wheel, I said, "Is there someone else I should be talking to? I know it's a bad time for you."

He let out a lot of the breath I'd seen him holding in. His light, ironic laugh floated on top of it. He turned to face me.

"I guess I'm it," he said. He saw my immediate confusion and continued, "Seth came to me one day and told me he had to form a board for legal reasons. He said he was going after investors so he could launch his Snake in a big way." He looked me in the eyes, raised both his eyebrows, and said, "So I said, 'Okay, little brother, whatever you need.' The board of Bolick Enterprises is me, my mother, and Sara now. Seth never even called a formal meeting of us. We were just on paper so he could move ahead with his little project." He said those last few words with more than a hint of deprecation.

"You sound like you were humoring him. Is that what you were doing?"

He nodded, watched his sons in the distance for a second or two. "Sure. I always humored my little brother. Seth was full of ideas."

"You didn't think he knew what he was doing?" I asked, reminding myself to cool it and find another way to defend Seth besides offending his brother.

"Oh, I thought he knew. Seth was brilliant." He stopped and took a deep breath again, letting only a small amount out. "Then again, my father was brilliant too. He brought nothing to his family but unhappiness."

We sat silently. I wasn't sure what to say to him.

"Look," he finally said, "I don't want this thing he's made, this drug or agent or device or whatever the technical term for it is, to get to market. I want it stopped, and I guess I'm willing to do whatever it takes to stop it."

"That'll be close to impossible to do. It's already in the loop with the FDA. The NIH, NCI, AMA, and every other acronym in the country have been pouring into that little lab up the road. What makes you think they'll all agree to pretend there was never a Snake?"

"I'll withdraw it from the FDA process."

"And what's to keep somebody else from coming out with it?" I asked.

His stare was one of total resolve. "Bolick Enterprises owns the patent," he said. "That's me now. If I have to, I will sit on it for seventeen years until the patent runs out. Then we'll see."

I'd have to ask Bill about the patent. Could Ian just stop it like that? And how did the farm boy, who supposedly didn't know anything about business, know patent details? My calm expression camouflaged my feelings. I was the one getting angry now. How could he do this to his brother?

Ian spoke again: "Have you given any thought to what this Snake would have done to this family?" He waited.

"It'll make you all rich, for one thing," I said.

He laughed. "Is that all you advertising types think about? Money?" He looked at me again, this time with a passion in his eyes I hadn't noticed before. It startled me because it made him look like Seth. "Tell me what you do with six thousand acres when your crop is no longer viable."

"Seth said you'd be using herbs, a blend of herbs. Can't you change over to his blend?"

He rolled his eyes. "Oh yes, his unique blend. I asked him if he'd ever tried to parallel park an eighteen-wheeler, 'cause that's what it'd be like to try shutting down the tobacco industry. My family's been farming tobacco for a hundred and fifty years. I got boys that want to keep farming it. Over a hundred thousand families just like mine farm tobacco. Most of 'em aren't as big as Bright Snake, but their farms mean as much to them as this land does to us. I can't be a party to destroying so many people."

"Strange you phrase it that way," I said. "Seth thought 'destroying people' is what tobacco's been doing. He wanted to put a stop to it. Just like your father." I hoped the memory of his father would bring Ian around. I was wrong.

"What does my father have to do with this?" Ian's tone was challenging.

"Seth cared so much about your father's quest for the safe cigarette. That's what this was all about, you know. It was a worthy goal . . ." I hesitated, not knowing how he would react to what I wanted to add. I decided I had nothing to lose, so I said it. "You say your heritage is the land and the tobacco. The search for a safe cigarette is part of your heritage too." I watched him as I talked, looking for some understanding of a bigger picture. I couldn't see anything in his face but anger. I decided to end what I had to say by returning to what I thought was safer ground. "Doesn't your father's work, and Seth's after him, deserve your consideration?"

He had his hand on the door handle when he answered: "My father was a total lunatic. In today's politically correct world, he would have been called chemically imbalanced, but back when I had to live with him—back when my mother cried all the time, when my little brother had anxiety no kid should have—back then, my old man destroyed our lives. If it weren't for him, Seth would be here right now." He shook his head. "No, my father's work won't get consideration by me."

I sighed loudly. I fought to hold back tears. Lightning cracked across the sky, followed quickly by rolling thunder. Almost as a reflex, I looked into the sky above us. When I did, I swallowed hard. What now, Seth? How do I fight for you now?

"We owe you some money, then," I said quietly. "Seth paid us an advance to get started. We haven't used that much of it."

"What do I have to do to end our relationship with your agency?"

"You just have," I said.

He opened the door. When he did, I could see the rain had begun. It was a gusty rain, the kind that crawls inside your raincoat if you're lucky enough to have one. I had left mine in the Trooper.

I reached out and put my hand on his shoulder. "Ian, I need to tell you something."

He hesitated and turned back toward me. "I believed in everything Seth was doing. At some point the money didn't matter at all."

He nodded to let me know he believed me. "I'll come to your office to pick up any work you've done. You can give me a check then. When's a good time?"

We agreed on four o'clock the following day, then he got out of the truck and came around to open my door. As he did, the rain blew in with such force that I struggled to get out. Hoping to produce some velocity of my own, I pushed off from the metal glove compartment with my hands inside my shoes. In the process, I knocked free two triangles of mud, one from each shoe where the heel veers from the sole. They fell to the floorboard like two small calf patties. I wasn't about to pick them up.

Standing by the truck, Ian looked around, then yelled over the wind, "Where's your car?"

I held my right hand over the top of my eyes so I could see him. "At your house," I yelled back. "We walked out here."

I wondered where Hart was, then saw him in the distance, a small, lonely looking dark shape leaning away from me into the wind. He was walking back to the Trooper.

"Get in," Ian called out. "I'll take you back to your car."

The deluge sounded like hundreds of rifles shooting at the roof of the Chevy. Ian drove fast down the skinny dirt road, now turned to mud and small pools of rust-colored water.

Hart jumped out of the way in time to avoid being hit by the truck but not the mud that splattered all over his fake-leather boots and heirloom jacket. Ian stopped and motioned for Hart to hop in the back. Reluctantly, very reluctantly, Hart did, pushing his back up against the cab so I couldn't see his face. He pulled his knees to his chest, put his head down, and braced himself.

I was grateful when Ian Bolick let us out of his truck.

I spread George senior's old army raincoat on the passenger side so the mud on Hart wouldn't transfer to the seat. I was so depressed from my talk with Ian that I didn't even feel like teasing Hart. Having meticulous, hygiene-oriented Hart in such disarray right here in my car should have lifted my spirits. It didn't. Neither did the rain's cessation and the hazy yellow sun.

We headed down the road, much worse for our visit to Bright Snake Farm, neither of us talking. I did stop at the lab to tell Betty what I'd just been told. It might have been easier, I thought, coming from me.

I was wrong. Nothing, I quickly discovered, could have made this news anything less than devastating to Betty. Like me, she'd bought into Seth's cause. Only her passion had been a scientist's need, I thought, that life-long dream of significant contribution. Mine had been merely the needs of a child, the need to hear her dad say, "Well done, you are my child after all. Flesh of my flesh, spirit of my spirit."

Tell me, Dad, how do you know when the battle's over?

Betty had more fight in her than I did. "He'll have to tell me himself," she said. "And then I'll make him get a court order. I'm not leaving this project unless I'm removed by the courts."

Betty's anger and frustration were palpable. Her hand motions were jerky as she moved two full test tubes from a container to a burner. She turned to me as if I were now the enemy. "I don't give a damn," she said. "Understand? I'm doing my part."

"But . . . if Snake won't get on the market, what good will your work do?" I asked.

She didn't answer me. Nor did she answer me when I asked if Johnny had come by while we were at Ian's. She just shook her head and stared at me. I could have sworn the anger was directed toward me now, not toward Ian.

I backed off. We each needed to do what our consciences dictated.

I gave her my card in case I could help in some way, although advertising didn't seem to be what anyone needed these days. I liked Betty instinctively but felt I'd fueled her anger somehow. I envied the woman's courage.

As I was opening the lab door to leave, she said, "Why'd he leave you a note?" After she said it, she turned toward me.

I shrugged. She shook her head.

When I climbed back up into the Trooper, Hart said, "We don't have to stop anywhere else, do we?"

"No," I said, and it was the only word I used in conversation with him all the way back to the office.

Traffic on Highway 29 was heavier than I'd seen before out this far from Charlotte. I had to wait a good five minutes for a wide enough break in the cars for the Trooper to get in the flow. As I waited I noticed the green Cherokee we'd seen this morning. It was across the highway from us, just pulled over as people do when they're going to change drivers. I noticed two things.

First, the driver and his passenger were watching us when I first looked at them. When I continued to stare, they both looked away. Secondly, the car had a dent in the right front bumper. In fact, the headlight on that side had been knocked out as well. I don't think Hart noticed the car; he didn't say anything if he did. If the traffic hadn't been so bad and if both Hart and I hadn't been in such bad shape, I think I would have driven over there and asked them if they were lost or something.

Along with my clip-on phonebook, I keep a little pad suspended from my visor with a pencil attached. I decided to get the license plate number of the Cherokee and have Tom Thurgood check it out. So I pulled out to the right, turned into another farm road, and headed back so I'd be behind them. I jotted down the plate number and left the pad hanging there. Hart leaned forward to look at what I'd written, but he didn't say anything and neither did I.

As we hit the Charlotte city limits, Hart groaned in a way that was more for effect than real. He'd tried to uncross his legs and found them stuck to each other. Only slightly, though, so I offered no sympathy.

"I feel like a farm animal," he said.

I didn't respond.

When we had driven into the Allen Teague parking lot and both were gathering ourselves together, Hart opened the car's back door and took out the logo art.

He stopped and gazed in my direction.

"We don't have Snake, do we?"

"No," I said.

10

"Uh-oh, what happened?"

Hart and I were standing at Sally's desk, which now held Leslie. Temporarily, of course. We both looked at her, then at each other and smiled grimly. Hart looked like an equestrian whose horse had taken a shortcut through hell or, perhaps, the Catawba River. I couldn't see myself, thank God, but I must have looked just as bad, since Leslie was staring as much at me as she was at Hart. I touched my hair, which is quite thick and streaked with a varying amount of blond, and found the nice body I was used to had turned to matted clumps.

"Does my hair look as bad as it feels?"

"It's not so bad," said Leslie.

"Seaweed," said Hart.

It was just after four thirty. I told Hart to put the art up and go on home. We'd talk about the Bolick work tomorrow afternoon.

"Are we giving the work to Ian Bolick?"

"He's paid for it. Why not?" I said.

"But he's not going ahead with it?"

"No."

"Then why does he want the work?" Hart was going up the steps with the logo art in his hands.

"I don't know. Something to show for the money, I guess."

Hart disappeared into his large upstairs room. I raised my voice so he could hear me. "By the way, he'll be here at four to get everything, so gather it together. I won't be back from Bredon tomorrow until after lunch."

Hart came back downstairs. He had his car keys. "Going to see Sally?" he said.

"Yeah, and maybe that coroner," I said.

He raised his haughty eyebrows, but, brushed with dried mud as they were, his opinion of my plans didn't have much impact.

Leslie had calmed down and seemed much more confident in herself. I was as grateful for that as I am sure she was. When Hart left, she showed me what she'd done while we were gone. Much to my relief, she'd mailed some time-sensitive magazine insertion orders. And then an amazing feat: She'd figured out Sally's filing system. "Remarkable," I told her. "Absolutely remarkable."

She handed me a list of business calls, then said, "And you had two personal calls. One was a Tom Thurgood. He wants you to have dinner tonight."

I laughed and pulled at a piece of my wadded hair. "I don't see how I can do that one. Where is he? At work or home?"

She handed me the number, and I saw it was the Law Enforcement Center.

"And the other one?" I reached my hand out, assuming she'd give me another piece of paper.

She looked sheepish, tentative, a bit afraid. "He said you couldn't reach him. I didn't know if you'd be in before closing, so I gave him your home number."

"Who?"

"The Wade County coroner."

"Did he say what he wanted?"

"Just that he had something for you." She wore those same loop earrings she'd had on yesterday. I watched her twirl a finger around the inside of one. "I hope it's okay that I gave him your home number. I didn't know what to do." She lowered her eyes. "I thought it might be about Mr. Bolick."

"Thank you," I said with as warm a smile as I could muster considering the shape I was in. "I was going to call if he didn't call me."

"Whew!" she said. "I'm trying to get this right. I wasn't sure about that one."

"You're doing fine, Leslie. In fact, I'm seeing Sally in the morning and I'm going to tell her what a great job you're doing for her." I gave her an okay sign with my fingers, then added, "Speaking of tomorrow, I won't be here until sometime in the afternoon, and you need to gather Bolick Enterprises together for me before four." So I showed her how to take Hart's and my time and expenses off the computer for billing purposes.

"I heard you and Mr. Johnson talking just now. I didn't know there was another Mr. Bolick."

"His brother," I said. "He hasn't been involved.

But he'll be here at four tomorrow expecting a check from us."

"I wonder why Mr. Little isn't representing the company. He acted so in charge."

I hadn't thought about this Mr. Little since talking with Leslie yesterday. "I should have asked Ian Bolick about him for you. Remind me to ask him tomorrow. We want to make sure you get your check."

She swallowed hard. "Ms. Teague, you don't think there's a chance he won't send me my check, do you?"

I thought about it a second. "Don't you worry about your money. We'll talk to Ian Bolick and get some assurance." I was headed back to my office and turned to smile at her. "And if he can't assure us, we'll just tack what they owe you onto what we keep for ourselves. How's that?"

She visibly relaxed, and I told her to go on home. Then I went into my office to call Tom Thurgood.

Once he knew it was me, his first words were "How's Sally?"

I told him what I knew, that her mother was there and that she'd sort of recognized me that morning. I also told him I was going the next morning, to see her and to handle some unfinished business.

"What unfinished business?" he asked.

I took a deep breath. "It's complicated, Tom." Then I remembered the license number I'd written down. I rummaged through my pocketbook until I found it. "Can you check a license plate for me?"

Now he breathed audibly. "Why do you want it, Sydney?"

"I think the car's following me."

"You sure?"

"No, I'm not sure." His idea of "sure" has always been more concrete than mine. "But I also think it may have run Sally off the road. It's got a busted light in the front, and the way Sally's wreck was described to me sounds as if some other car may have been involved."

"Like how?"

Sheesh, talk about cynics. "Like she goes off a straight road into a pine tree," I said. "No rain, no dark, no leaves on the road even. On top of that, the tapes she was getting for me are removed from the car before the wrecker gets there."

"How do you know that?"

"Because the wrecker is the sheriff," I said, trying to keep an edge off my voice.

He laughed. "Small towns," he said. "Gotta love 'em."

So I gave him the number, and he said he'd see what he could do. When he brought up dinner, I told him I wasn't in any shape.

"What about your place?" he said.

"I was rained on," I said. "I wore two-inch heels a fourth mile into a tobacco field that was more mud than anything else. The shoes got so heavy I took them off and walked barefoot another fourth mile. Seth Bolick may have committed suicide after all, and, to make it even worse, he may have left me a note when he did." I felt something gathering in my throat. I fought it back. I jabbed at the continuing pain in my stomach. "I'm not much in the mood for merriment tonight. To tell you the truth, it was a pretty rotten day all the way around."

"Then I'll bring Chinese for all of us," he insisted. "You'll do whatever it is you feel you need to do for yourself tonight, but the kids and you have to eat." He paused. To see if I would object, I guess. When I didn't, he added with a laugh, "I do too."

Sometimes Tom Thurgood is just too nice.

George junior and Joan were both in the kitchen when I got home. They had laid out an assembly line of bread with various combinations of mustard and mayonnaise already attached. They were preparing to install a host of options: lettuce, ham, Swiss cheese, potato chips, and bananas. The bananas are one of Joan's quirks; the chips, an aberration of George junior's taste buds.

I'd remembered to bring in the video camera, so I put it on the tiny bit of remaining counter space. Although both kids had given me an automatic "Hi, Mom" when I opened the door, only when I invaded their factory space did they look up at me.

They giggled, of course. Everyone, I supposed, who could have seen me at this point would get a good laugh.

"I thought you had a 'thinking' job, Mom," Joan said. She grinned at her brother, who was staring at my mud-caked calves. He was probably trying to determine where the calves stopped and my shoes started.

"Don't worry, George junior," I said. "You're seeing correctly. I don't have shoes on." Then I turned to my daughter. "What makes you think I haven't been thinking, Joanie?"

" 'Study, study, study, kids,' " she said, doing a pretty good job of both mimicking me and mocking me, " 'or you'll end up doing manual labor.' "

"I think I'd like manual labor best," George junior said thoughtfully.

I carefully sat on a kitchen stool. A chip of red mud hit the black and white tile floor anyway.

"Georgie, you say that now at twelve," I said. "You'll change your mind when you're forty, believe me."

Neither child asked me where I'd been that day or what I'd been doing to look like I did. They no more had a direct line into my life away from them than I had had into my father's. I wondered if they understood the kinds of issues that motivate us adults. The difficult decisions we have to make in order to live with ourselves. Or if their world was as small as mine had been when I was young like they are now.

"Before you ask," Joan said, "both George and I have studied all afternoon." The two of them were gathering their concoctions, pouring lemonade, assembling it all onto trays. "We're going to watch some TV until supper, okay?"

I nodded. "So that's just a snack? Good. Tom's bringing Chinese for all of us."

"What time?" Joan asked.

"Don't know. Whenever he gets here, I guess."

I looked at them with the trays in hand, like two young waiters in a diner, poised to slink downstairs to our family room. "Hold it, you two. Clean up this mess first." I slid off my stool, leaving a pile of mud underneath it. "Sweep up this little mud here too, if you don't mind."

Joan's face belied minor irritation. George junior said, "Aw, Mom."

"A little favor for your tired mom, okay?"

Joan said, "Not your mud, Mom. That just takes a sec. But can't we clean up the sandwich stuff when we come back upstairs?"

I shook my head. I was on the stairs going up to the third floor of our home, where our bedrooms are. "Too bad. You make a mess, you clean it up. It's the hardest part of any job. The loose ends."

I washed my hands in the bathroom sink, avoiding my face in the mirror. I didn't want to see the physical mess I'd become, true, but I had another reason for avoiding my own eyes. I didn't want to make eye contact with the person Seth had left a note to. I would have been too uncomfortable.

I dried my hands, picked up the cordless phone by my bed, and returned to the bathroom with it. I punched in my mother's phone number.

"What a surprise, Sydney. I was going to call you about Thanksgiving."

I didn't mean to sound rude, I told her, but that conversation would have to wait. I needed to ask her a quick question about her sister Eunice.

"Doesn't Aunt Eunice have asthma?" I asked.

She hesitated. "What a strange question, dear."

"I know, Mother, but just answer me, okay? I don't have much time." I looked at my alarm clock. It was almost six. I wondered what time Tom would get here.

"Yes, Eunice has asthma. Had it all her life."

"Are you familiar with her inhaler?"

"Well, yes. They've changed over the years, but, yes, I know how it works."

"Tell me, then. Is it all one piece. Could someone siphon the medicine out and put something else in if he wanted to?"

"Well, I've never really thought about it, but I guess it's two pieces. A little plastic container with the medicine in it sticks up into a top piece that is the sprayer."

It sounded like the flea repellent I used to squirt on the haunches of my Lhasa, Butterfly, before she died. "And she has a prescription she gets filled for the medicine container, right?"

"Yes . . . but, Sydney, you must tell me if you're not feeling well."

"I'm fine, Mother. I'm just trying to understand how the inhalers work, is all. For a client."

"Oh, well, then why don't you go buy yourself one at the drugstore? You can buy over-the-counter strength inhalers. You don't have to have a prescription to get hold of a dispenser."

I'd never thought of that. I made a note to find a drugstore in Bredon the next day. I asked Mom to call me the following night. We'd discuss Thanksgiving in as much detail as she wanted.

11

"When I was your age," Tom said to George junior, "we didn't have Chinese take-out. At least not in the small town I came from." He plopped a glob of white rice in front of each of us, then handed us egg rolls. He bit into his, chewed a couple of seconds, then said to no one in particular, "Why do they call it 'egg' roll? I don't taste egg, do you?"

Tom had arrived at six thirty. He'd brought with him several helpings of Beef and Broccoli plus several more of Chicken Cashew. His taste in food is basic, the tried-and-true. His taste in everything else is about the same. Tom doesn't risk where he doesn't have to.

We were all four at the kitchen table, which, even with its leaf in, was pushing its capacity. Tom had pulled in a chair from the dining room and was awkwardly angled at the table's corner. He normally doesn't mix talking and eating, so this talk about the food was something unusual for him. I was just relieved he hadn't brought the USTA schedule book, and I told him so.

"Really?" He sounded mildly offended. "It's in the car. I couldn't carry it with all the food." He chewed a piece of beef with rice on it that had been poised on his fork. He laughed, a strained and small woe-is-me kind of laugh. Then he leaned back in his chair and held his unforked hand up in a gesture resembling that of a fishmonger hawking flounder. "What do you have against planning, Sydney? If we don't go ahead and enter some of these tournaments soon, we won't be giving the organizers time to seed us properly."

I laughed more boldly than he had. "What makes you think we'll be seeded?"

Both kids said, "I think y'all will be."

I looked at all three of them in disbelief. "Based on what? One little old city-tournament championship?" I shook my head. "I don't think so."

"I do," they all said.

Tom continued: "We won't know unless we fill out a couple of these entry forms, will we?"

I stared at him. Why wasn't he eating silently as he usually does?

"I tell you what, Sydney." He became animated, as if he'd hit on a major discovery. "I'll make a deal with you. Let's enter three. I'll pay the entry fees."

I started to protest.

"Hold it, now," he said. "Hear me out. We choose three to enter, with the goal of getting seeded in one. Whoever seeds us the highest is where we'll go. How's that? One tournament in early spring. That's all I ask."

"And if no one seeds us?" I asked.

He thought a second. "If no one seeds us, we don't enter any if you don't want to." He pushed a piece of auburn hair off his forehead, then looked into my eyes. "I don't see why you wouldn't want to play with me though. Even if we don't get seeded."

"I do want to play with you, Tom. I just want it to be more casual. You plan these tournaments. You schedule our practices. You even bought me those barbells," I said while pointing at the silver ten-pound pair currently acting as paperweights on magazines in the basket above the refrigerator.

"You don't use them," he said as if that was the subject.

"You don't know that," I said.

I caught Joan in full animation shaking her head at Tom.

"Cut that out," I said, and we all laughed.

Tom obviously knew the entire schedule without having to get the book out of his car. He chose to talk to the kids rather than me. He named six or seven southern cities, from Richmond all the way down to Tampa.

"What'll it be, George? The mountains might still have some snow in February. The Southern Indoor's in Asheville in February. Want to try it?"

I watched in amazement. George junior loves to ski, so Tom had enlisted him with Asheville during ski season. He hooked Joan with Atlanta and its major mall shopping in early March. As I listened to him building this little battalion of enthusiasts, I realized why he'd suggested Savannah during St. Patrick's Day to me. I love the old city and its funky, quirky ways. He was spreading the pork around the way all good politicians do and getting what he wanted in the bargain. I had to admire his skill. Tom could probably even sell advertising if he wanted to.

While the kids and I were still eating, Tom moved his plate to the counter, fetched entry forms from his car, and started filling them out. When he needed my signature along with his, he looked up at me and smiled so innocently and so enthusiastically that I wished I could have taken his picture. Tom Thurgood really loves tennis.

"Okay, okay," I said, dragging my voice a bit so he would know he'd scored a major victory. "Just promise me you won't turn it into a military operation."

"Military operation?" He laughed heartily now that he had my signature everywhere he needed it. He winked at the kids. "What's your mother talking about?"

George junior rolled his eyes and said, "We had to live through the city tournament with her, remember?"

If I didn't spell out my limits at this moment, I sensed this winter would be hell. "I won't practice in the early morning before work now with winter coming on," I began. "So don't ask me. I won't be badgered to eat those seeds and dried fruit you keep insisting I eat either. I won't jog with you through Freedom Park every afternoon, and I won't lift those silly barbells." I pointed at the top of my refrigerator.

He didn't respond to me. Instead he said to the kids, "Gee, kids, you'd think your mom didn't know anything about sports. You two keep in shape, don't you?"

They nodded.

"Your mom encourages your keeping in shape, doesn't she?"

"Oh, yes." They nodded again.

I didn't think he was so terribly endearing at this point if what he was doing was encouraging my own kids to watch over my habits.

"Look, Tom," I said, "I don't think you know how forceful you are in your suggestions. Your idea of a healthy routine is not mine, okay?"

"You don't follow it anyway," he said nonchalantly. "So why worry about it?" He smiled.

"Because I don't like how it feels. At worst, it's like enrolling in the police academy. At best, it's like being a member of my mother's bridge club. I've never aspired to the rigor or the routine of either." I didn't smile, but the three of them did.

The phone rang.

The person in charge of answering the phone at our house is Joan, so she did. I was throwing the last of the many white Chinese take-out cartons into the garbage can under the sink. Tom and George junior were cleaning off the table.

"Just a minute," I heard her say. As I was closing the cabinet door under the sink, she handed me the cordless phone.

I mouthed to her, "Who is it?"

She didn't know.

Strange how, in the midst of all the good-natured banter at my dinner table that night, I'd forgotten the Wade County coroner was going to call. When he told me who he was and why he was calling, I was taken aback, although I shouldn't have been. There was also something familiar about his voice, something that was distracting me from concentrating on what he was saying.

"Formality," he said. "All the evidence points to suicide, and this note I've got here sort of clinched it for me. You know this boy Seth Bolick was a whole lot like his daddy, and his daddy killed himself the exact same way. Same nicotine concentrate anyway. His daddy ran it through the greenhouse pipes, and Seth here put it in a little squirt bottle he was supposed to have medicine in."

"Nebulizer," I said.

"That's right. His nebulizer."

"Was the note addressed to me?" I had taken the phone into my dark living room, where I could be alone.

"He didn't put it in an envelope," the coroner said. "It's just a short little thing he laid down on top of a pile of paperwork on his desk. Most suicides, they use envelopes with their notes. Seth just put your name on the top of the note."

I sat on my long leather sofa. It was cold through the thin jersey pants I was wearing. I hunched over, pressing my elbows into my knees.

"Can you read it to me?" I asked. My throat was dry.

"Yes, that's why I'm calling. We have to do that when there's a note. I can give it to you after I file my report if you want."

"I just want you to read it," I said quickly.

The rustle of papers hit my ears and traveled down my spine.

"Here we go. It says: 'Sydney, I can't go on. I've

thought about everything you said yesterday, but I'm just not up to it. I wish I was, but I'm not. Hope you'll understand. Sorry, Seth.' "

The words were running around in my head. What had I said to him? "Everything?" I mumbled to myself. What did I say?

"You there, miss?"

"Yes, yes. Can you repeat that slowly for me and let me go get something to write on so I can copy it down?"

He agreed to wait while I ran to the kitchen and grabbed a piece of loose-leaf notebook paper out of our school-supply bin and a hot-pink highlighter. Tom watched me, then followed me back into the living room, where he turned on a table lamp so I could see.

"Go ahead, please," I said when I was back on the sofa with my paper and writing utensil, such as it was, poised to take it down.

When he had finished and I had assured him I had it all, he said, "You can come by here tomorrow morning and get it if you want. I should have my report filed by then."

"Yes, I'd like to have it. Where are you?"

"Right before the last light on Main Street in Bredon," he said. "Can't miss it. Keeter Ford."

Now I knew where I'd heard that voice before.

"Hey, Sheriff Keeter. I was in your place this morning about Sally Ball's car. The wreck out on 29?"

"I thought I'd seen your name before," he said.

"So you're the coroner too?"

"That'd be me" came his familiar refrain.

My eyes stung all of a sudden. I started to thank

Sheriff Keeter but coughed on something caught in my throat.

"I want to tell ya' something, Miss Teague," he said slowly.

"All right," I said. I could barely see; hot tears had filled my eyes.

"Some people just can't be stopped. So you rest easy now, knowing that you did what you could."

"Yes, sir," I said and felt like a child. About ten seconds later I heard the click on his end. I punched the power button on the phone's receiver.

Tom took the phone from me and walked back to the kitchen with it. When he returned, he sat beside me and put his long arm around my back while I cried.

Neither of us spoke for a long while. When our silence was broken, it was Tom who did it.

"Sydney, he must have told you he was going to do it." He said it softly, not in any way accusing. Still, he was waiting for me to give some explanation.

I didn't have an explanation. The note made no sense to me at all. If either of us had acted depressed, it was me, since Seth had got me talking and thinking about my father more than I had in years. If either of us cheered the other, it was Seth encouraging me to try to fix the past. "Father will sit up in his grave," Seth had said to me on Sunday. "He'll shout 'Hallelujah' when the first box of Snake rolls off the assembly line." I could hear him saying that. I could hear him then saying, "Take an action for your dad, Sydney. I guarantee you he'll take note." And I'd told him that was what I was doing by helping him.

"No, he didn't, Tom." I shook my head to clear it,

then put both hands on my face at each side of my nose and evenly pulled them across my cheeks and up into my hairline, like a squeegee on a window. "Not unless I've lost my mind."

George junior called from the kitchen, "Mom, there's a tape still in your video camera. Is it used? Something on it?"

"Damn," I said.

"Is that good?" Tom was being solicitous in his own way.

"They didn't get it," I said. "They thought they had them all, but I must have left the last one I shot inside the camera." Then I yelled to George junior to take it out of the camera and bring it to me.

"I can't tape over it?" he asked as he stood before me. "The Berries have a video premiering on MTV tonight. I wanted to tape it."

I took it from him. "Sorry, Georgie." He shrugged and turned to leave the room. Within a minute I heard his upstairs bedroom door close and his radio come on.

Joan was upstairs too. She yelled to ask me if I was off the phone. Could she go in my bedroom and make a call?

"Don't stay on all night," I yelled back in what was a ritualistic reply.

Tom pressed his large hand into my back at the base of my neck. He gathered my tight muscles together, then let them go. Kneading them like a kitten after its mother's milk. The movement loosened a thousand threads in me. My shoulders drooped; my breathing slowed.

"Thanks. That helps."

Then he rubbed my shoulders. Afterwards he leaned over and kissed me on the cheek. "You'll be okay," he said. "What's on the tape?"

I breathed deeply, then exhaled slowly. "Seth is," I said. "He was all I shot all day. Seth in his lab. Seth in the tobacco field. Seth in his office."

Tom stood up and stretched his six-and-a-half-foot frame. "What were you going to use it all for?"

I bounced the tape lightly off my thigh. "Everything. Anything and everything. Partial tape for a PBS documentary when the time was right. Historical perspective if they'd need it. Probably a year down the road." I thought about Sunday in as much detail as I could. I looked up at Tom, who was still towering over me. "Seth talking a lot about his father. Just because he wanted to. I would have split it up and used it for TV spots in the first market year. There was Seth doing a three-minute explanation of Snake's chemistry. We were going to send that one to doctors when they asked for more information."

"Wasn't all that shooting a bit premature?" he asked.

"How so?"

"Well, you said it'd be a year before the product was offered to consumers. Why'd you spend Sunday out there in the first place?"

"Because I needed a direct appeal from him to give to potential investors. Everything else I shot because I had to get the investor piece. When you're setting up anyway, my philosophy's always been to anticipate and get all you can for future use."

"Did you get the investor tape?"

I chuckled, remembering Seth's reluctance to sit at his desk, look into the camera, and talk to potential investors. "Sort of," I said. "Not really," I added.

"What's funny?"

"The one thing I absolutely had to get—the direct inquiry spot for investors—he absolutely refused to give me. Good Lord, but Seth could be stubborn."

He touched the hair on top of my head. "Would it make you feel any better to take a look at the video?"

"Yes." I gripped the tape tightly. "I need to watch it. I want to see what I missed Sunday. What must have been right there in my face the whole time."

I stared at the black rectangle in my hands and clinched my jaw. I was afraid.

12

Sunday had been beautiful. One of those perfect late autumn days where Nature dresses herself up for one last dance. The sky's blue was so deep it was almost a jewel tone. A soft breeze nudged the fiery red and gold sugar maples that clustered behind Seth's house. They swayed in response as if to a waltz. I remembered the mourning dove pair sitting on a power line, watching with me the departure of a formation of wild geese. It had rained the night before, giving the farm's annual rye its first spurt of growth. That sweet smell came tumbling back to me.

The camera had caught the intensity of the sky and the leaves. Occasionally the sun played havoc with my lens though. Sunspots and sunbursts would emerge and fade with more frequency than desired. Hart would have lectured me on how to avoid these image intrusions, what he, as art director, calls "nature trash."

Tom Thurgood and I were sitting on the sofa in the

basement den of my home. We'd been watching this lone remaining tape for about an hour. I kept hitting the Stop, Pause, and Rewind buttons on the remote every time Seth said anything.

"Sydney, you're starting and stopping the tape so much I can't get a feel for what's happening." Tom was sitting beside me. His long legs were extended across the coffee table so far that his calves were dangling in air.

"This isn't a movie, Tom," I said. "I'm not trying to entertain you." I pushed Stop again.

"You know that's not what I mean," he said. He scooted his rear end back a bit and sat up straighter. "If we're looking for the mood he was in, you've got to let him stay on the screen long enough for us to see it."

I was frustrated. I was looking for something I felt certain would not be found. "I'm not looking for mood. I remember his mood. It was good . . . at worst. I'm looking for specific words out of his mouth, out of my mouth."

I needed a break. I needed, in fact, a cigarette. I reached for Tom's Coke. "Want a refill?"

He looked sleepy. "Okay," he said as he covered a yawn with the back of his hand.

I ran upstairs to the kitchen, where I poured the last of a two-liter bottle into his glass. Then I found my pocketbook on the floor in my living room and, inside my pocketbook, my cigarettes. I quickly lit one and sat in the wing chair beside the fireplace.

What had I said to him? Was it all my talk about living in the present? Is that what made him do it? Could that memorized AA spiel of mine have gotten to him? Could it have broken the link to his father? His wife had kicked him out. His own mother had backed her up. His son—his father's namesake—was not living with him as a result. And his brother thought he was crazy and, on top of that, didn't approve of the work that was his life. Did all this hit him hard after I left Sunday night?

In the dark I studied the little burning ember at the end of my Vantage. Would Snake have glowed like this in the dark? Would it have sorted out the bombarding messages in my jumbled brain? Would I ever know?

I heard Tom call my name at the bottom of the stairs.

"Coming," I said and threw the butt into my fireplace.

When I punched Play again, we saw Seth in his lab donning a white lab coat.

"Wait a minute, Maestro," he said into the camera. "There ought to be a pair of glasses around here somewhere. I don't look much like a scientist, do I, Syd?"

I could hear myself laughing behind the screen. Then I said, "Go ahead, Seth, pick up a test tube or something. You don't need any glasses."

He stood behind a waist-high metal table and did indeed hold a test tube in both hands. The scene looked silly to me on tape, almost like the little tube was a religious icon of some sort. I should have posed him sitting, I thought.

"Okay now, Seth, you want to say something to the health care community."

He settled into seriousness quickly. His eyes pierced

through me even across the screen. The pride was so evident; so was the joy.

"We all know," he began, "that nicotine's great addictive advantage has been its similarity to acetylcholine and its actions within the human neuronal system."

"Does everybody really know that, Seth?" I heard me say.

"These guys do," he said.

Tom said, "Hit Pause for a second."

I did.

"You were going to edit these asides, weren't you?"

"Of course," I said and laughed. "Might have even dubbed in something else entirely. On all three of the tapes I shot I might have gotten thirty minutes that could be used the way it was shot."

I hit Play again, then Fast Forward. "This section's all scientific jargon," I said as I did. "No way I said anything meaningful during this part."

Tom yawned again.

I touched his knee. "Thanks for doing this with me. I know you're tired."

He smiled, then let his hand fall to the base of my spine. I felt a warm, tingling sensation when he did. "When's the funeral?" he asked.

"Thursday," I said. "Church in Bredon, then burial at Bright Snake. All the Bolicks are buried there." I wondered if Seth would be buried beside his father.

"I'm off Thursday," he said. "Is Hart going too? I'd be more than glad to drive the two of you, or just you if he's not going."

I didn't know what Hart wanted to do, but I was

grateful Tom had volunteered to drive. I couldn't see well when I was crying.

I hit Stop when the setting on the screen changed. In the blur of racing videotape, the cool grays of metal slid to warmer tones, yellows and browns. We were in Seth's makeshift home. In the corner of his living room where he'd set up the Bolick Enterprises office. I hit Play.

"I don't know about this, Sydney," Seth said as he came into the camera's view at his desk.

I could hear the rustling of papers on the television screen, then I saw the back of my head in front of the camera.

"Is that you?" Tom asked.

I hit Pause. "I used a tripod in his office. Eventually I used it when we were in his lab too." I laughed. "Still, my head's not supposed to show up on tape."

I hit Play again and watched as I handed Seth a stack of oversized papers. I remembered now it had been Hart's ten different storyboards for the investor appeals. When Seth had originally expressed his misgivings about appearing in it himself, I'd written ten different scripts and visual approaches. My plan had been to anticipate every objection Seth might have and create a spot to remedy whatever each of them was. So the stack I gave him was large.

"Look through these a sec," I said to Seth. "They're all different ways to do this spot."

I watched him put the stack on his desk and leaf through them. He asked if all the ideas had him front and center.

"Some more than others" was my evasive reply.

He looked just to the side of the lens and grinned. I realized he must have been looking directly at me, as I'd stood just to the right, where his eyes were fixed.

"Pretty cartoons, Sydney, but I still think you ought to get Craig Fielding at Interstate Securities to talk to the investors. He speaks their language. I don't."

"You don't get it, Seth. You are Bolick Enterprises. More importantly, you're the mind behind the invention we're telling them will make more money than they know what to do with." I watched him sitting there shaking his head as I gave him my best pitch for doing it my way.

I kept going. "Have you ever played the horses, Seth?" His eyes were still staring at the spot where I stood beside the camera. That was somehow eerie to me now—watching him watch me.

He nodded. "Certainly," he said. "Who hasn't?"

I remembered thinking I hadn't but deciding not to tell him that. "Ever think about buying a piece of a horse? One you heard had great potential?" my voice said.

His face was all grin. "Why?" he said. "You got me a horse, Sydney?" Then he laughed out loud. He was pleased with himself.

"Don't play games with me now. I've been toting this camera all day long, and I'm not in the mood for jokes."

Tom said, "That sounds just like you."

"Well, it should," I said. "It is me."

"That's not what—" Tom began.

"Sh—" I cut him off. "We missed something." I hit Rewind for two or three seconds, then Play again. We heard me say what I'd just said about jokes again, then I said more.

"Seth, if you were considering buying into a horse, you wouldn't want a horse analyst to talk to you. You'd want to look at the horse himself, wouldn't you? Check out his teeth. Look at his body, his legs in particular. Isn't that what you'd want to do, Seth?"

"I'm telling you I don't speak their language," he said. "And I'll tell you another thing."

"What's that?" my invisible voice said.

"It wasn't so subtle." I remembered this part of the conversation and chuckled in anticipation. Tom gazed at me from half-closed eyes.

"What wasn't?"

"Your roundabout way of calling me a horse's ass."

Even Tom laughed.

Dammit, it was all just as I'd remembered it. We were having a good time. Nobody was dropping hints of suicide.

Tom said, "I wish I'd known him. Funny guy. I think I would have liked him."

"He would have liked you too. Seth liked people who take pride in their work."

The tape had continued to run. From under Tom's statement about Seth and my reply, the phrase "everything you said" surfaced from somewhere on the screen. I hit Tom's thigh so hard he twitched in spasm.

I punched Stop.

"Hold it. I heard it, Tom. Didn't you? He said 'everything you said.'"

"Hit Rewind," Tom said. "Let's see exactly what he said."

The tape whirred through awkwardly flailing arms and the jerking of Seth's head in the fast backward motion. My hand shook when I punched Stop, then Play.

It began again with the sound of Seth's laughter and even my own after his comment about the horse's ass.

My voice said, "If that's your definition of stubborn, I'll vote for that. You need to go on this closed circuit network, Seth. These people need to at least see you."

Then he said, "They can see me in the lab. They can see me talking chemistry. They don't need to see me talking about things I know nothing about. If you don't want Fielding, then call the accountants. That's what they're good at." He stood up from his desk, impatient, it seemed, to get off camera.

"Hold it, Seth," my voice said. "Sit back down. Don't get all huffy on me."

He sat in his chair again. His expression told me then and now that he had made his final comment on this subject. Maybe I hadn't heard him say those critical words after all. Maybe I'd just wanted to hear them so badly in some other context than his suicide note.

I saw the back of my hand wave briefly close to the lens. The sound of someone quickly pushing a heavy piece of furniture across a stone floor threw me for a moment. Threw Tom too. He looked at me, eyebrows up.

"Oh," I said to Tom when I realized what it was. I hit Pause. "That's me clearing my throat. Nervous habit. His attitude on this was frustrating me. I knew I was right about making him go on the investor network."

"Of course," Tom said.

I hit Play. The camera perfectly framed Seth at his desk. He had leaned back slightly, waiting, I supposed, for me to say what I was going to say on the subject he had deemed closed. He drummed his fingernails impatiently on the desk. On the screen it sounded like distant wind chimes.

"Will you do me one small favor?" I asked the face on the screen.

"Depends" was his noncommittal reply.

"Those storyboards there next to your right hand."

He looked at the stack, then back at the edge of the camera. "Yeah," he said.

"You've bought them already," I said, then waited—obviously for that to sink in. "I spent an hour on each script. Hart spent two hours on each storyboard. Neither one of us bill out cheap, Seth. Just promise me you'll study those and sleep on it."

He was nodding, but his expression told me now he had no intention of following my professional advice. "Okay, okay, okay," he said quickly. "I'll think about everything you've said." He looked down at the stack of storyboards, then patted them with his right hand. "I'll even take a look at these."

Both Tom and I sat up straight as I hit Stop one last time.

"That's it," I said, smiling so broadly my jaw caught. "The note was about the investors' spots, not a suicide."

Tom was reading the note again. "But what does he mean by 'I can't go on'? I still don't understand that part."

" 'Go on the network,' " I said and turned to face Tom. "That's the phrase we kept using. I'd say, 'I want you to go on the network,' and he'd say, 'I don't want to go on.' Don't you see? He'd slept on it like he promised me he would. Then, I think to make sure the subject was over for good, he said 'can't' instead of 'won't' so I'd leave him alone about it."

Tom nodded, but his expression wasn't what I expected. His jaw had dropped, his eyebrows were furrowed. His gaze was at the floor, rather than at me.

I pulled at his hand to get his attention. He looked up at me, but when he did, all I saw on his face was worry.

"Tom, be happy for me. Don't you know how much this has been bothering me? My God, I thought Seth had killed himself and that I could've stopped him. Don't you know how horrible that knowledge made me feel?"

He nodded, but his expression didn't change. "I'm glad you feel better," he said evenly.

"Well, I do."

Inside my head, a sudden surge of light spread itself quickly. It washed out the joy I was feeling as surely as the sunburst on my camera lens had washed out the blue of the sky. When the light faded, a gray film replaced it, static and dull and dark.

I looked up at Tom.

"Someone did kill him, though, didn't they?" he said.

13

I was angry. Everybody had been so eager to label Seth's death a suicide. Everybody had wanted to wrap it up neatly and just be done with it. Not just Sheriff Keeter, but Seth's own wife and mother. And his brother. I was so mad at Ian for lumping Seth in with his father that Tom had to talk me out of calling him that very minute.

"It's understandable," Tom said.

"It is not," I said. "There's nothing understandable about their attitude. I knew Seth better than that. Why didn't they?"

"You forget, Sydney, you thought he had killed himself too until just now."

"Only because I was told it was fact." I looked Tom in the eyes. I wanted him to believe me. "It certainly wasn't my first thought."

Tom had stopped yawning, but he still appeared tired. I should have been, given the kind of day I'd had.

I wasn't though. In fact, I felt like getting in the Trooper, driving to Wade County and Bright Snake Farm, and telling every one of the remaining Bolicks to go to hell.

"Suicide's common in the children of suicides," Tom said. "That's why their attitude is understandable." He swallowed some of his Coke, wiped the beading sweat off the glass, then put it back down on the bookcases next to the sofa. "Did you know that?" He was wanting me to be in his conversation.

I was wanting to have it another way. "Did I know what?" I asked.

"That a high percentage of children of suicides choose suicide as a way out?"

"Out of what?" I said defensively. "Seth didn't want out. He was bringing his father back in."

"You're not making sense, Sydney. I don't know about Bolick. I'm talking statistics only. I find it interesting, don't you?"

I was sitting on the edge of the sofa, turned to face him as we talked. Ever since I'd realized the truth about Seth's death, I'd been unable to relax. I felt personally wounded by the realization. As if it had been done to me. As if somehow my own life had been dismissed by people who should have known better.

"Do I find it interesting that people kill themselves because their parents do?" I tried to think intellectually, to distance myself enough to gain some perspective. "No, not really, Tom. I think I find that statistic depressing, if it's true. I'd like to think it'd be the opposite, wouldn't you?" Tom and I were not really talking to each other.

"The theory goes," Tom said, "we subconsciously follow the unspoken rules of behavior set down by our own parents all our lives. If your parent chooses suicide as a solution to life's problems, you are more likely to as well." He stroked my hand. "Not pleasant thoughts, I know."

"But if you've lived with the hurt caused by that kind of solution," I said to him, "maybe you will do everything in your power to see that it doesn't happen again. I think that's how Seth was. He even went further. He spent his whole life proving to his father that he didn't have to do it, that there could have been other solutions."

Tom cocked his head to the side, looked into my eyes, then away, in search, I felt, of the distance he was more comfortable with. When his eyes came back to mine, they told me he'd grasped the commitment I felt to Seth, that he understood and, more, he'd been where I was himself. For all his protocol, procedure, and intellectual distancing, Tom Thurgood has as much trouble with the human side of events as I do. But talking about it is something he finds much harder to do.

"I understand" was what he chose to say. It was enough for me.

"Suicide," I said, "is one horrible legacy to bear, Tom."

He patted my hand. "Probably only one that's worse."

I waited for him to finish his own ordering of things, because I, frankly, could not imagine a worse cross to bear.

But he didn't. He squeezed my hand as if the

answer was obvious and his action the punctuation mark on an unnecessary and mutually understood statement.

I finally asked him.

He let go of my hand as if my needing to ask had broken some bond he thought we'd established. "Murder, of course," he said as he hoisted his long body off my sofa. "Try living with that as a legacy."

The tape had been rewinding as we talked. The whirring stopped abruptly. I stood to eject it.

Tom was stretching, which he does with silly looking combinations of exaggerated overheads, forehands, and backhands. With tape in hand, I patiently waited at a distance, since his arms are quite long and tend to require more space than one would expect to merely crank a body up.

When he slowed down, he pointed at the tape in my hand and said, "You'll probably need that."

"The tape? What for?"

"What'd you say the sheriff's name is up there?"

"Keeter."

"This Sheriff Keeter won't take your word for it, Sydney. You'll need to give him some proof your guy didn't do himself in." Tom was starting to sound like the cop that he is.

"That's a fine state of affairs," I said, "to have to prove somebody did not kill himself."

"Look at it from the sheriff's perspective."

"I didn't know sheriffs had perspectives. Don't they just take the facts as they come to them, then file them away appropriately?"

Tom pretended I didn't say that. He continued, "Look at his alternatives. For sure, Seth didn't die of natural causes. And you don't accidentally put a deadly concentration of nicotine in your asthma medicine bottle. When the sheriff is wearing his coroner's hat, his job is simply to classify the means of death."

"So?"

"So the fact remains, Seth's father killed himself. He did it with the same solution found in Seth's bottle. In this case two plus two equals four. The note simply made the addition easy."

That rusty old familiar piece of barbed wire brushed up against some part of me. I felt its prick in my chest, but I knew the pain would gradually spread.

"You need to brace yourself, Sydney."

"For what?" Why did I need to ask? I'm sure I knew.

"Even with your explanation of that," he said, pointing at the note on the coffee table, "the sheriff still may let his ruling stand. He may still decide Seth's death was suicide."

My reaction surprised me. "I won't allow it," I said. I didn't say it frantically. I was as calm and as determined as I am in doing something rote, like a media buy.

"If you think about the coroner's one remaining alternative, you might understand his point of view better." Tom had finally stopped warming himself up.

"And what's that?"

He held up his hand, then spread out his fingers. He took his other hand and held the thumb of the first hand between forefinger and thumb of the second, like he was going to recite a ditty about pigs. "He has only four ways to classify the death. If it wasn't natural, he moves to accident. If it wasn't accidental, he moves to suicide." His eyes lit up the way a logician's does when he thinks he has you in his corner. "What's left for the poor coroner, who also happens to be the sheriff? Only murder." He stopped briefly to make sure I'd followed him this far. Unfortunately I had. "And if there's any way for him to still see it as a likely suicide, believe me, he'll choose it over a murder investigation any day of the week." He kept staring at me. Waiting, I supposed, for whatever was showing in my eyes to shift to a new understanding.

"Even though I'm a homicide detective, I don't go looking for murder. So, if I don't, put yourself in a small-town sheriff's shoes. If he has any other alternative, he'll take it." He paused again. "Does this make sense to you?"

What did make sense, what I understood clearly, is that I didn't relate to the pigeonholing needs of bureaucrats, and whether Tom wanted to see it that way or not was none of my business. What was my business was my loyalty to Seth and ultimately to myself. I don't think Tom would have seen it the way he did if he'd been the one with barbed wire in his gut.

"You didn't use your pinky," I said to him.

He finally let his fingers fall. With his fingers spread, he'd begun to take on a fascist aura. "Did I make sense?" he asked again.

"What do I do with that, Tom? You're not suggesting I just forget it, are you?"

He took a deep breath. "No. I just want you to be prepared."

I flicked the lights out in the family room. We started up the steps to the kitchen.

"How is knowing Sheriff Keeter's administrative needs going to help me?"

"What was Bolick wearing when he inhaled this poison?"

I wasn't expecting the question. Nor was I prepared for the bright fluorescence of the kitchen lights as we emerged from the dark stairwell. I winced.

"He was wearing a suit," I said, then closed my eyes to the memory of him in agony on that stretcher.

"Good." Tom is so matter-of-fact in the way he goes about his business that it's hard for me to tell what a word like "good" really means. It's as if he removes all context.

"When you are driving to Bredon tomorrow, I want you to think about things like the suit. All the physical and psychological reasons you can gather in your head pointing to something other than suicide. Not many people put on suits to kill themselves, do they?"

Thank God, Tom was on my side after all. I watched him gather his barn jacket off the back of a kitchen chair. He stifled a yawn again as he did.

"Give the tape to the sheriff," he said, "and see if he knows exactly where the note was found and by whom."

"I think I know that already," I said. "It was on his desk. That last section of the tape we were watching. That's where we were. In his office. It's in his house."

"Who found the note?"

"I think his son, Johnny, did. And Johnny's mother. They found it when they came back from the hospital."

"But where on the desk?"

A desk is a desk is a desk, I thought. What did he mean?

"Was it on top of those cartoons you gave him?"

"Storyboards, Tom. They were storyboards."

He ignored me. He was telling me what to do, and the longer I've known Tom Thurgood, the more I've come to realize how much he likes to do that. Not just me. But everybody. I am rarely grateful for that. That night, though, I was.

"And another thing," he continued. "If I were you, I'd call Sheriff Keeter good and early. Tell him briefly you'd like to meet him at the courthouse before he files Seth's cause of death. Tell him you're bringing evidence it's not a suicide. Don't get into a conversation on the phone, 'cause he'll try to belittle what you've got. Just tell him it's something he has to see."

"I didn't know Bredon had a courthouse," I said.

"It's the county seat. Yeah, it has one."

I dabbed at a small glob of pasty white rice on the kitchen table while Tom put his jacket on. I couldn't get it off my finger, so I went over to the sink and ran tap water over it. When I turned back around, Tom was removing a piece of paper from the side pocket of his jacket. He looked at it closely, then up at me.

"What's that?" I was drying my hands with a piece of paper towel someone had already used for that purpose.

"The green Cherokee you asked me to check on. I did. It belongs to the Liggon Tobacco Group. Ever heard of them?"

14

All the men in my family are lawyers or judges, always have been. I never wanted it. I would rather make my money in something with at least a chance of everybody winning. In advertising—most of the time— assuming the client has something of value, everybody involved does win. I feel good, the client feels good, the consumer feels good, and my few employees have health insurance. For some, though, I suppose, the assumption of value is too big a stretch.

That morning I was trying to think like a lawyer, and I found the attempt very unpleasant. Not that I was priming for a court battle. Nothing so upending as that. But I was going to need a legal perspective in talking with Keeter.

Tom had called me at seven A.M. to pep me up, even offering to call the sheriff himself.

"Why don't you do that," I said. "Just let me have my shot at him first."

As we talked, the wire crept up the back of my neck, into the nerves that shoot pain to the rest of my body. I no more had a choice in following through with my suspicions than Seth had in creating Snake.

"I owe it to Seth," I said, then added, "Some other people too." I was grateful he didn't ask who those other people were, because I couldn't have told him two men who were dead. Two men who died before they should have, one on a greenhouse floor and the other on a courtroom floor. Two men who did what was right even though it cost them their friends. Even though it cost them the wrath of their own kin. No, I couldn't have told him that.

"I'll call him later in the morning," Tom said. "Chin up. You'll do fine. You'll see."

The following morning had been almost winterlike. No frost at my house, but I bet the low-lying areas outside the city got some. It was the kind of unexpected cold that takes you back to the first cold schoolday mornings of your youth.

On those mornings Dad would rub his hands together and say, "Children, it's as cold as a witch's tit," to which my mother would always reply, "Don't talk that way in front of the children." My dad would then say, "Ah, but there are witches in this world and children must learn how to recognize them." For years after my youth had officially ended, for years after my father had died, I'd awaken on the first cold mornings of the year with the most grotesque image in my head: an old, naked, mean-looking woman with breasts made of metal, sitting on a broom. It was a guaranteed fear-buster. I still missed my dad.

Tom had somehow wrangled Keeter's home number, so at seven thirty I called him. A groggy sounding woman, who told me her name was Bert even though I didn't ask, said she'd get him. He was just then coming out of the shower.

As I waited, I tried to swallow. What actually occurred was a genuine gulp. I was amazed at myself and was trying to remember if I'd ever gulped that way before when he said, "Keeter here."

I told him who I was, but I noticed a lack of the friendliness and concern he'd shown me the night before. He was quiet and passive, waiting, I supposed, for me to say what my business was.

Simple and direct is always best, I decided. "Can you please hold your filing for Seth until I get there?" I asked.

"Why's that?" He didn't sound happy. Was he irritated with me for asking, angry I'd called him at home, or cold from having just gotten out of the shower? At that moment my head filled with an image of a naked Keeter on the witch's broom. I shut my eyes tight in order to concentrate.

"I have some information," I said. Good lawyers don't spill all their beans at the outset.

"What kind of information, Miss Teague? I hope it's not just a feeling."

"No, it's evidence. It's physical, and I plan to put it in my car right this minute and head in your direction." I was pleased to be able to say something without saying something, definitely a lawyerly statement.

Mostly I was pleased because it worked. He agreed to wait.

"But hold up a bit yourself, Miss Teague. I can't get to the courthouse until nine. Gotta go by Keeter Ford first. We're not Charlotte up here, ya know." He mumbled something to Bert, then said to me, "Is this thing you're bringing us real big, too big to get inside the courthouse without causing a stir?"

"Why, no, it fits in my pocketbook." I guess I asked for that with my nonstatement statement.

"Then you bring it on and we'll have us a look-see."

Joan and George junior were up by then. While I fixed us all French toast, them hot chocolate and me coffee, they scurried under their beds for storage boxes, where sweaters had been since March.

Once we'd all three gathered at the kitchen table, it was obvious to me we each smelled of mothballs. And poor George junior even had a lilac underscent to him. Those sachet packets I'd put in the box to diffuse the mothball smell hadn't worked after all. I decided not to say anything.

What I said instead was "Children, it's as cold as a witch's tit out there this morning."

They giggled. I did too. I wish they'd known my dad.

I knew it would probably warm up after lunch, so I'd dressed for stripping. I had on a white, long-sleeve weskit blouse over a simple straight black skirt. I put a camel cardigan on top of that and camel hair coat on top of that. As the thermometer added to itself, I could take away from myself. The tape went inside my pocketbook and, at the last minute, a pair of yard-work tennis shoes into the backseat. I was tired of the mud in Wade County.

The drive from Charlotte to Bredon in the morning rush hour was a confidence builder. All the commuters were going in the other direction. The mere reversal of my traffic pattern made me feel I'd held to some conviction. Like Ben Hur turning his chariot around and moving through the ranks of infidels. I hoped I was ready for Sheriff Keeter.

At precisely nine I opened the Trooper's door in front of the old courthouse. I was surprised I hadn't noticed it before when I'd been through Bredon. It was a lovely old building, mostly granite, with massive, round antebellum pillars. More impressive than the building, though, were the hundred-year-old oaks flanking its entrance. Their size and the fact that their leaves hadn't started falling until now were probably why I'd never noticed the building.

There was even more oak inside, in the paneling that covered every bit of every wall in the rotundalike central room. The oak was repeated on the railing of the wide stairs that led to the second floor, then continued around the balcony up there. The floor I stood on was marble, though, a fine intricately laid Italian marble. I couldn't believe a town the size of Bredon had such a beautiful building.

My expression must have made my thoughts evident. Behind my back, Keeter said, "Pretty impressive, huh?"

"Very," I agreed. "Good morning, Sheriff Keeter." I

extended my hand, but he didn't take it. I really don't think he saw it, because of the angle of his girth and the gray trench coat that hung all around it.

We stood together looking at the fine old paneling.

"Wade County used to be the seat of progress in all of North Carolina. Do you know why?" He began walking, a slow and lumbering walk.

"No, I don't," I said quickly, even though I knew the question was rhetorical. I was following him across the big room.

"The earliest gold in all America was found just down the road from here." His eyes seemed nuggets themselves, they burned so brightly.

"I thought that was Cabarrus County," I said.

The sound he made in response was dismissive, slightly guttural. "That's their story. They got the word out. Our people didn't bother. Wade County never has known how to brag."

He spoke with such passion I would have thought we were discussing a close relative or friend, someone jilted by a lover or, at the least, drummed out of a job unfairly.

He stopped at a heavy, eight-panel door, turned to me, and said, "Then, after the War Between the States, we all got into tobacco. It was just like the gold. Could have been gold for the money it brought in." He sounded like a man who'd been there. His eyes surveyed the opulent walls and ceilings as if seeing them for the first time. "Tobacco built this here building, Miss Teague."

We went into a room like all other bureaucratic, administrative rooms of its type, except this one had stood still a couple of decades earlier. I didn't see a computer anywhere. Row after row of old putty-colored file cabinets lined the room on three sides. A tiny gray-haired woman sat at a black metal desk trimmed in walnut-simulated vinyl, probably a sixties purchase.

"Bert, this is Miss Teague from over in Charlotte. Bert here's the missus."

The woman smiled, said good morning, and went on with her typing. Her machine looked to me like an IBM Selectric of the seventies and early eighties. At least it was the size and shape of one, a drop smaller and a bit more rectangular than a VW Beetle. The typewriter was the most up-to-date item in the room, including Bert, whose polyester blouse wasn't one of the blends you see today, but a true polyester relic, the kind that never wrinkled and always kept its shape.

He removed his trench coat with some difficulty and hung it on an old-fashioned hall tree in the corner near the door. I didn't know if this conversation would take fifteen minutes or an hour, so I put my camel hair coat there as well.

Sheriff Keeter picked up a couple of pieces of paper off the counter in front of his wife's desk. He pushed open a swing door that I'd thought was part of the counter itself, then turned sideways to get himself through it. I followed him to another metal desk, although this one was larger than his wife's and had a blond oak captain's chair in front, where he asked me to sit.

"So, what is it you have for me, Miss Teague?" he asked once he was settled and held the paperwork on Seth in his hands.

I knew by now he'd have no VCR or even a television in this office. The tape, if he needed to see it, would have to be viewed elsewhere. I removed it from my pocketbook anyway and put it on his desk.

"Seth Bolick didn't kill himself," I said. "The note he wrote to me was about something else entirely." I don't believe I could have been any more clear or any more direct, but when I looked into his Keeter's eyes, there was confusion.

His bulbous fingers crept across the desk to the tape. He looked down at it and tapped it with his fingers, all the while not saying a thing.

In sales I've learned to make a statement, then shut up so the prospect is forced to commit to the conversation. I was the one who wanted something here, so I sat and waited. I listened to the unusual quiet of the office: the tinny clicking of Bert's typewriter, the slow moan and clang of old pipes. The aroma of oil heat wafted from a register in the corner.

"Is this what you brought me?" he asked with his fingers still drumming the tape.

"Yes, it's a tape of Seth talking the night before he died."

"Talking to who?"

"Me." I wanted to blurt the whole thing out but forced myself to hold up and let Keeter ask the questions. He pushed himself back in his large burgundy Naugahyde chair. It was an old-fashioned type with four small spiderlike legs coming together into a central hollow tube with a rusty bolt or two holding it together. The contraption creaked under his weight.

"The exact phrases he uses in the note you have. Those same phrases he uses on this tape."

"What's the tape about? Who taped it?"

"Well, I taped it. I was at his house all day Sunday taping him for use in some advertising. Seth hired my agency to promote a product he was going to introduce. I wanted to tape him talking to investors. He didn't want to. That's what the note's about." Slow down, Sydney, dammit. Slow down.

He pulled the tape toward him, sliding it across the table. He picked it up and turned it around, squinting his eyes as he did. I'd never seen anybody stare so hard at something as intangible and innocuous as a videotape. You would have thought a bomb was inside it. "You want me to look at it or you just want to tell me what he said?"

"Do you have a VCR here and a TV?"

"Got both those things at home," he said, then looked around his own office. "Don't have 'em here though. Never had call. District attorney's office might, but that door's locked."

"Why would the DA's door be locked?" I had never heard of a public servant getting away with locking out the public before.

"We share him. Cabarrus and Union and Wade take turns having a district attorney." He looked at his watch, then back up at me. He smiled jovially. "Let's see. Today's Thursday, so he's over in Union County. He'll be back Monday if he doesn't get involved in something over there." He scratched his forearm with the tape. "He keeps his door locked."

I have to admit I'd never heard of counties sharing the services of a DA before. Of course, I'd never lived someplace where the sheriff and the coroner and the Ford dealer and the town wrecker were all the same person either.

I said, "Maybe I'd better go ahead and tell you about what's on the tape."

He reared back in his chair again. This time I heard metal biting metal. Abruptly the whole seat dropped a couple of inches. "Damn this chair," he said. He straightened himself again, although lower than he was before. His reduced presence made me feel better. "Go ahead, Miss Teague. Tell me what Bolick said on that tape."

"Where's his note?" I asked Keeter. "You should be looking at it when I tell you."

He glanced over at the papers on his desk, removed the paper clip that held them together, then picked up a small piece of paper on top. It wasn't much bigger than a Post-it note. "Okay, got it here. Go ahead."

I took a deep breath, told myself this would be all Keeter would need if I told it clearly enough. "Seth said to me, 'I don't want to go on.' He said this to me in reference to a closed network show I wanted him to do. I asked him to think about what I was saying. We agreed to talk about it some more Monday morning. So, when he says there, 'I thought about everything you said,' he's talking about the fact that I asked him to do just that." I let my breath out and stared hopefully at Keeter.

He looked at the tape. He looked at me. "Why was he sorry? He says he's sorry."

"Because I wanted him to do it so badly, and he knew it. It's also why he changed 'I won't go on' to 'I can't go on.' He wanted me to leave him alone about it."

Keeter was squinting his eyes at me.

" 'Can't' is a stronger word, don't you think?"

He nodded his head, but I think it was more from a genial habit than understanding.

"You say you and Bolick were going to get together Monday and talk about it some more?"

"Yes. At nine Monday morning. Only he didn't show up."

"Where was this meeting?"

"Charlotte. At his new office."

I sat back in the uncomfortable captain's chair and watched Keeter think. He would gaze at me for a couple of seconds, then at the tape again, and finally at his wife's back up at the front of the room. He repeated this rotation three times before speaking again. When he did, I was shocked at what he had to say.

"Miss Teague, you're a fine woman, coming here like you did. But I don't know how to say this. You see, I don't want to get you more upset than you gotta be already. It's a whole bunch of trouble you're going to so you can ease yourself of guilt over this."

I shot up out of my chair. "Guilt? That's ridiculous. I've brought you facts."

He had stood up as well, although slower than me. He reached both arms across the desk in an attempt to hold my shoulders and ease me back into the chair. I winced at the first touch of his hands and turned my shoulders away. I backed up. I didn't want contact with him.

"Calm down, Miss Teague." His voice was hushed. I could have sworn the whisper was so we wouldn't disturb his wife, because I saw him glance in her direction as he spoke. The whisper continued: "Sit back down here so we can talk sensibly."

I continued standing. I refused to whisper. "That's what I'm doing, Sheriff Keeter. I am sensible. You haven't said one sensible thing."

Again he looked at Bert's back, then looked down and shook his head. "Maybe so, maybe so." He motioned me to sit again with his hands pushing down against the air, since I'd removed my body from his reach.

I sat, but all the warning I'd been giving myself about how to talk with someone in Keeter's position disappeared from my head. In fact, I shook my head to clear it completely. I no longer needed a sales coach. I needed boxing gloves, because I was entering the ring.

I asked him why he was so convinced Seth had died by his own hand. I was going to get aggressive if I had to.

He was reluctant at first and almost mumbled when he said it, but I distinctly heard him say, "Seth was Jonathan's son." Tom had warned me about this kind of attitude.

So I said, "Ian is Jonathan Bolick's son too."

"Not like Seth," he said. He began to loosen up and talk about the father and the sons. "Small towns are funny, Miss Teague. They make up their own myths and legends to help understand their own. Bredon thinks the Bolick boys were north and south pole, black and white, hot and cold. Any way you want to make up your opposites, that's how this town would peg those two boys."

"And good and evil? Is that one of the antonyms? Look," I said, "Ian worked the tobacco farm even before his father died. He loved it already. Nothing changed for him with his father's death." I was willing to have a long philosophical conversation if that's what he wanted as long as he was willing to open an investigation into Seth's death.

"Maybe so." He chuckled softly. "Or maybe he was finally free to love his land with the love Jen taught him. Legend around here has it Ian made his commitment the day his daddy died. His commitment to the land." His tiny eyes twinkled when he looked at me. "You know, though, how these old legends are. Just rumor passed down. Who knows the truth?"

I do, I wanted to scream. I know the truth. I said, "But what you said about Seth is true. When his father died, he became obsessed with his father's obsession. He became possessed by it." I stared hard at Keeter. "Just not the way you think."

He scratched his thick neck the way I'd seen him do when I met him. Little spots resembling prickly heat had erupted there since yesterday. It must have been his aftershave. He opened his mouth as if he was about to speak. I knew I couldn't let him. I had to get it all out.

"Maybe Seth had a mission, Sheriff," I said forcefully and loud enough for Bert and anyone else who came into this room to hear. "His mission was proving his father's work had value. Value, do you understand? To carry that work all the way through to a great discovery, a great invention, so people would say, 'Yes, that began with Jonathan Bolick.' He was his father's defender in this world"—I hammered my fists against

Keeter's desk to emphasize the words—"not in the world hereafter."

I held my forefinger no more than an eighth of an inch from my thumb. "And this, Sheriff Keeter, is how close Seth Bolick was to showing the world his dad was not a crazy, dejected old fool. Do you really think someone on the verge of being able to right such a wrong would cop out through suicide?" I shook my head and spread my hand on his desk. "No way, Sheriff. No way."

We were silent for a full twenty seconds. I had disoriented myself, was trying to get my bearings. He tapped his fingers. "Anything else you want to tell me?" he said.

"He had on a suit," I said. "He was dressed for our meeting."

Keeter was taking notes now. I felt victorious, although I didn't know if I actually was.

"Also, can you find out exactly where that note was on his desk? I bet you it was sitting on top of the paperwork I'd given him on the taping he didn't want to do. If it was sitting with the storyboards I gave him, that's just more proof the note was about business."

"Okay," he said and continued to write.

"And why would he go to the trouble of emptying and then refilling his own inhaler with nicotine? There are simpler ways to die, don't you think, Sheriff?"

"Don't ask me to read the mind of a crazy man." He stared at me. He really believed what he'd just said.

"He wasn't crazy." I held his gaze until he looked away.

He put his pen down, pushed the thin papers on

Seth away from him with some difficulty. As if they were all of a sudden heavy.

"Do you know what you're asking me to do?" His eyes no longer twinkled. They were, in fact, dull. Keeter looked a little ill.

"Yes," I said as steadily as I could. "I'm asking you to open an investigation into Seth's death."

"A murder investigation," he said. "I don't expect you to know how hard that's going to be, if I do it."

I knew Tom would be calling him. Charlotte-Mecklenburg could help and often does when its outlying counties need manpower and technology otherwise unavailable. All Keeter had to do was ask. "Charlotte homicide and the SBI will help if you feel you need them," I said and was sorry I had. Of course he knew this, so it wasn't my business to bring it up.

He leaned forward. "If I decide to open it up—and mind you, it's my decision alone—if I decide to, it'll be the biggest mess this county's ever seen."

"Because the Bolicks are prominent?" I asked, not able to imagine what kind of "mess" he was talking about.

He laughed. This time, though, it had none of the playful merriment of a few minutes ago. This time it was sardonic and laden with irony.

His tone was hushed again, but it had a loud breathiness to it. "Wade County's only got twenty thousand people in it. Half of them commute to Charlotte and just sleep here. We keep Main Street all gussied up for them. Wade County don't mean no more to those people than a quaint Holiday Inn. Know their kind? Just passing through?" He gave a dismissive swipe with his hand through the air. He hesitated, chewed on his lower lip. "The rest of us were born and raised here. Wade County's like our own mama. You know what I mean by that? The county, the land: it raised us. Made us who we are. We love this county. We protect this land. So that's a good ten thousand people feel pretty strong about this place."

He looked deep into my eyes. I felt he was trying to communicate with a part of me deeper than what I could tap today. The experience was unnerving.

"I think that's wonderful, that people care so much about their home." I didn't know why he was telling me this.

Sweat had collected on his cheek. He brushed it away with his knuckle. I was beginning to feel hot myself. He kept staring at me. He wanted me to understand something that I wasn't getting.

"So, what are you telling me, Sheriff?" I asked with more than a modicum of nervous impatience. "What does it mean?"

"It means, Miss Teague, that ten thousand people are glad Seth Bolick's dead. Only question is, which one did the honors."

15

I called Tom Thurgood from my car phone while I was still sitting in front of the courthouse and told him about my conversation with the sheriff. I told him I honestly didn't know if I'd convinced him or not.

"I hope you're calling him soon," I added. "From what I've seen, he hasn't the manpower or the inclination to find Seth's killer. He might not think it's worth it."

"I'm afraid you're right," Tom said. "Everything I'm finding out corroborates what you're saying."

"What have you found out?" As I asked this question, I saw Keeter leave the courthouse and get into his official sheriff's car, a new Taurus.

"For one, I called the state attorney general's office on that Liggon Tobacco Group. They're a start-up a couple of years old, but word in Raleigh is that they've got two or three brands getting ready to hit the market within the year. Big bucks behind them. Liggon's in

Forsyth County, not Wade, but these people have a whole lot to lose if Seth's synthetic nicotine were to take off."

"All tobacco companies would lose, Tom." I watched Keeter pull out of the parking lot. He didn't drive toward his dealership. He went east instead. In the direction of the Bolick farm.

"Yes, they would," Tom agreed. "But most of Wade County's involved with tobacco one way or another."

"That's what Keeter was talking about when he told me half the county was glad Seth was dead."

"He said what?" A surge of static flooded my ear. "Did he really say that, Sydney?"

"Yes, Tom. Ten thousand people, he said, were happy now."

"There's even an organization called the Wade County Tobacco Growers Association lobbying Congress." Tom sounded like he was reading the name.

I was only halfway listening to Tom at this point. He was just confirming what Keeter had already told me, namely that more than a few people could have wanted Seth dead. I was more interested in where the sheriff was going. I switched the phone to the speaker mode, put the handset back in its cradle, and pulled away from the curb.

"Yeah," I said so he'd know I was still listening.

"You sound different. What'd you do?"

"Changed to speaker. I'm driving now."

"Oh," he said. "Going to the hospital?"

"No, I'll go there next. I'm just curious. The sheriff headed out toward Seth's farm. I thought I'd follow him there—if that's where he ends up. See what he does with my request."

Tom was silent. In fact, I thought I'd lost him.

Then he said, "I don't know if I'd do that, Sydney. Leave it alone. I'm coming over to Wade now."

Keeter had a head start on me by a few minutes and probably was barreling down the road, as all rural law enforcement types seem to do. I was driving at a snail's pace, since I was talking to Tom. At this rate, Keeter could come and go before I even got to the farm.

"Well, I'm glad of that, Tom. They're going to need you up here. And none too soon." I pushed in my car lighter.

"Sydney, listen to me now. You go on to the hospital. You don't want to get tangled up with either Keeter or Ian Bolick."

"Tangled?" I lit my cigarette. "I'm not getting tangled. I just want to see if the sheriff's doing what he said he'd do. That's all."

"And what's that?"

"He said he'd look into opening an investigation. I want to see where he's looking."

"That growers' association I was just now telling you about?"

"Yeah?" I saw another formation of birds. They were spread at least a hundred across at their widest point and moving faster than the geese I'd seen out here Sunday. Twenty or thirty of the birds had fallen out of wing and were flapping desperately to realign themselves. These birds were too small to be geese. I was wondering what species they were when Tom spoke again.

"Bolick and Keeter are both on the board. Bolick's the treasurer. Keeter's the secretary."

"Of that association? I'm not surprised, Tom. What does surprise me is where Sheriff Keeter finds the time. By my count, if he's growing tobacco, that's his fifth occupation. Hard to believe." We were starting to lose our connection under the tall oaks arching across Highway 29.

"Not really," Tom said over the static. "You grew up in Charlotte, so you don't know. Where I grew up, lots of people dabbled in three or four things. Nothing in itself was big enough to support a family. My father called it 'stringing a living together.'"

"That's not really how I meant it." We were losing each other. "You haven't met Keeter yet. You'd think a guy that busy would be thin."

Static took over our airwaves completely. I punched the power button and pressed a little harder on the gas pedal. I just needed to see for myself what Keeter was doing. Was he beginning his murder investigation or was he planning a defense strategy for all the growers?

I would have sworn the rye had grown since the day before. As I knew so well, it had rained out here. I could almost hear the red clay giving way to the power of the grass's roots as they spread out and down. Seth had explained the rye's role to me that way. About its roots reaching deep into the packed clay, breaking it up, making it friable and easy to plant come spring. He had told it from the rye's point of view, taking me on an animated journey into a sea of mud and solid, almost impenetrable rust-red walls. Seth loved this land too, I thought. Nobody could tell me he didn't.

Ahead of me the gravel road curved slightly. Beyond the curve, gray dust gave the illusion of smoldering fire. No matter how much rain falls, when someone drives fast on a road like this one, the gravel kicks up. I didn't register the smoke as an oncoming car, though, because I'd never run into anyone out here before. But the green Cherokee came out of the curve so quickly and at such a high speed that it veered to my side of the road. Thank God my instincts took over. I found myself and the Trooper oddly angled in a drainage ditch between the road and the rye. It took shifting into four-wheel drive to get back onto the road. I was both angry and shaky. So much mud had been heaped onto the Trooper's tires that each rotation slapped a glob onto my axle.

I didn't think the guys in the Cherokee had targeted me. At least I hoped they hadn't. But they were driving so fast I knew something was going on. They were either racing a clock to get somewhere or running away from somebody they feared or from someplace where they shouldn't have been. I knew already the latter was true: They had no legal business at Bright Leaf Farm.

Seth's lab sat in what would have been the road itself had this been a public road. As it was, the gravel road merely bulged on both sides into half-moon swing-outs, sort of like an aneurysm in an artery wall. The lab was on one of these bulges and on the other side of the farm road, where the road expanded again, sat Seth's

tiny shotgun house. I had to swing onto the house side
of the road because of all the cars at the lab. They were
sticking out into the road proper because there wasn't
enough room up next to the concrete building. I recognized Betty's car and Sheriff Keeter's too. But it took
me a moment to recognize the third car: Ian's Chevrolet
truck.

Why was Ian at the lab? What business did he have
with Betty? Perhaps he was telling her to close up shop
and go on home.

Poor Betty. As upset as she was yesterday, I imagined how she might be reacting to this particular set of
visitors. And, if the Liggon men had been to see her as
well, she'd probably be ready to leave the work, in spite
of what she'd told me about continuing it.

I drove slowly around the property. Jen and Sara
Bolick were home; at least their cars were. A couple of
late model Japanese trucks were in front of Ian's house. I
assumed they belonged to his sons.

I was trying to kill some time so those cars would
leave. I wanted to talk to Betty alone. I couldn't wait to
share with her the good news. She'd been even more
shocked than I at the news Seth had taken his own life.
Surely she'd be as relieved as I that he hadn't. And I
wanted to find out what Keeter had had to say about our
conversation. If he'd decided what he was going to do.

I turned off onto the next road parallel to Jen
Bolick's, thinking I'd turn around after this one and go
back by the lab. Down at the end, all flanking a big circular turnaround, were shotgun houses just like Seth's.
There must have been ten of them plus two large dor-
mitorylike structures in their backyards. I didn't see

anybody but wouldn't expect to at ten something in the morning. These buildings were obviously where the farmworkers lived.

To the right of this small village I saw two large production greenhouses and one smaller, more the size of those you see in hobbyists' backyards. My first thought was of Jonathan Bolick. Surely he had died twenty years ago in one of those greenhouses and a sixteen-year-old Seth had come home from school and found him. I shuddered. A sadness welled up from the very pit of my stomach and caught me by surprise. Quite unexpected. Seth's eager face filled my head.

A man and a woman came out of one of the larger of the greenhouses. I stopped the Trooper and pushed the window button for the passenger front seat. I leaned across to get a better view of the two people. They were both wearing some kind of rain gear, the kind trout fishermen wear—only more. They had on hats, boots, pants, and jackets, all shiny and water-repellent. Then the woman took off her hat, and I saw it was Sara Bolick. I honked a friendly toot and got out to speak with her. I figured I needed to kill a few more minutes.

Sara seemed much more relaxed than she'd been yesterday. Talkative even. She was cleaning out the greenhouses, she said, for her orchids and other tropicals.

"I thought you started the tobacco plants in there," I said.

"We do, Sydney," she said, then introduced me to Lorenzo Guava, who she said was her greenhouse manager. "Tobacco's not started until the early spring, so Lorenzo and I get to play with my plants the rest of the year."

"I wish you had room for my geraniums in there. They looked frozen as I left my house in Charlotte this morning."

"We've got room," Sara said. "Bring them on out."

I asked her how Jen was this morning, and she said, "Still crying off and on." We agreed that was normal.

"What could be worse," I said, "than a mother losing a child?" Sara nodded. "And Johnny? Is he feeling any better?"

Sara didn't answer right away. She unbuttoned the top two or three snaps on her rain jacket. Then she shook her head. "Not really. He doesn't talk much, but when he does, it's only about his dad." Some of the strength slipped from her voice, and then she seemed to remember that Lorenzo was still standing beside her. She asked him to go start the fumigation in one of the greenhouses.

"What do you fumigate with?" I asked out of curiosity.

She seemed distracted, probably still thinking about Johnny. "Tobacco concentrate for insects," she said. "Maneb for fungus and mold."

I almost gasped. The concentrate that had killed Seth had probably come from one of these greenhouses.

"You know," she began, totally unaware of the shock that must have been showing on my face, "I told Johnny on Sunday that his dad would be real busy on Monday. His Charlotte office would be opening. I knew he had business with you. I told Johnny all that. I told him not to bother his dad. I didn't think he'd go by there on his way to school." She looked out into the green fields. "But Johnny's as stubborn as his father was. He went by anyway. Now he's going to have to live with what he saw." Her concentration drifted, then she seemed to rouse herself out of it. "Why are you here today?"

I didn't expect the question. I mumbled something about it being such a beautiful day, then became disgusted with myself for hemming and hawing for no good reason. I finally said I was here to see Betty. I hoped I didn't have to say why. "You know, I don't think I got her last name," I said hoping to preempt the possibility of why entirely.

She smiled. "I never have either. All year she's just come and gone, never has talked to the rest of us. Just Seth." She stopped smiling. "I don't know why she's still here. I think she's strange. Jen does too. Sort of secretive."

I chuckled at her suspicions. "Snake was a big secret, you know. I'm sure Seth primed her to be secretive."

She contorted her features, dropped her chin as if she were about to say "Duh," and emitted a sharp, sarcastic one-syllable laugh. "Not with us," she said. "We were his family, remember?"

Not much of one, I was tempted to say, but I held my tongue and looked at my watch. Almost eleven. I wanted to visit with Sally before lunch. I excused myself and returned to the Trooper.

Ian's car had gone. All that remained was Betty's and the one car that could keep me from stopping. Sheriff Keeter was still there, dammit. I slowed to less than five miles an hour and actually considered going in anyway. For what though? To simply prove I was meddlesome? I wanted to ask her what he had said, and I certainly couldn't do that with him still there.

Then I remembered Tom was on his way here. I could find out from him what Keeter had decided to do. I pushed in the clutch, shifted to second, and drove out of Bright Snake Farm.

At the turnoff to the hospital, I remembered the inhaler. I really didn't know how easy it would be to remove asthma medicine and replace it with nicotine. I flipped off the Trooper's turn signal, passed the hospital's entrance, and kept driving into the heart of little Bredon.

Hutchins Drugstore was on Main, like everything else. Its quaint, old-style, hand-lettered sign said "Since 1879." I wondered if this was Sara's family. I'd seen a Hutchins Florist too. Odds were, I decided, the Hutchinses were as established here as the Bolick clan.

The parking on that part of Main Street was at forty-five degree angles to the curb. I pulled in and deposited a dime into the meter. The ten cents gave me an hour if I wanted it. I couldn't remember the last time I'd gotten an hour of anything for a dime. Even the electricity to a twenty-watt bulb probably cost more than a dime.

I fell in love with Hutchins Drugstore. As I entered, I was greeted by barrels of old-fashioned, homemade candy—the long stick kind. A barrel of grape, a barrel of lemon, and a barrel of cherry. Shelf after shelf of kitchen gadgets took the whole wall behind the barrels. Across from them a genuine soda jerk served customers at a counter that could have been painted by Norman Rockwell. I felt I had stepped back in time. If I hadn't been planning on going to the hospital from here, I would have sat on a stool, swiveled awhile, and ordered a heavy-syrup cherry Coke.

The deeper I went into the store, the more it resembled a modern drugstore. In the far back the druggist was filling a prescription at a station two or three feet off the floor level. A small, thin man with thick bifocals was counting pills, then scraping them into a plastic bottle. The rows of goods were laid out like every other drugstore I could have entered. They had the same headings too: Eyes and Nose, Feminine Hygiene, Digestive, Teeth, and so forth. I found several different types of asthma inhalers in the respiratory therapy section on the Eyes and Nose aisle.

I asked the druggist which of them was designed most like their prescription counterparts. He thought about it a minute, then pointed at the brand on the end of the row. I picked up several for experimentation. Then I asked him if he had anything for a sharp stomach pain.

"Is it for you?" he asked.

I nodded.

"Indigestion?"

"I don't know. It doesn't seem to happen after I eat, if that means anything." I touched the area high in my diaphragm where the barbed wire was knitting itself into random rows.

Out of the corner of my eye I saw two men enter the front of the store. This closely I saw that one was blond and the other brunette. All else I'd noticed before: the short haircuts, strong jaws and weight-lifter necks, their white oxford-cloth shirts, navy suits, and dark solid ties. The druggist watched them too. I would bet a dusty green Cherokee was parked outside near the Trooper.

"Probably gas," the druggist said.

They spotted me but pretended they didn't. They stood together by the magazines and paperbacks between me and the front of the store.

"What causes gas?" I said, not liking the sound of it.

The druggist chuckled. "Some people are just prone to it. What causes anything?"

I pressed the area again where my stomach hurt. He watched me, then said, "Up that high, it might be heartburn. You drink a lot of coffee?"

"My share," I said, but I was watching the two men.

He sold me a bottle of chalky, pastel-colored disks that he instructed me to chew when the pain struck.

I was paying him when he said, "I saw you watching our boys there." He opened the cash register, then nodded toward the two Liggon men.

"Do you know them?"

"Been coming around close to a year now. Occasionally at first. A lot recently." He closed the register, gave me my change and a bag with my purchases, which he stapled out of prescriptive habit.

"Do you know who they are?" I whispered the question even as I was certain they couldn't hear.

"The missus and I think they're Mormon boys. They send 'em out in pairs like that, you know. They're so neat we couldn't figure out how they'd be anybody else."

I chuckled. Mormons? I couldn't wait to share this with Tom. "Have they ever tried to preach to you?"

He smiled. "No, ma'am, those boys know their manners."

"What about bicycles? Aren't Mormon missionaries supposed to ride bicycles?"

"Those boys don't have bicycles? They walking or you seen them riding something else?"

I put the bag into my pocketbook. "A green Cherokee," I said. "A far cry from bicycles."

He pushed his heavy glasses up the bridge of his nose. "A car?" he said. He shook his head. "Wait till I tell the missus. The Mormon boys in a fancy car. Before you know it, the Amish will get out of their wagons."

16

Intensive Care was quiet except for the rhythm of a pump. I couldn't tell if it was pumping blood or breath or the hospital's sewage. Two nurses were hunched over paperwork. I was pleased to see that one was a man.

I arrived at the glass window where Sally had been on display inside and stopped. An octogenarian, and a male at that, was in Sally's bed. The pump I'd heard was attached by a flexible tube to the mask over his face.

The sound I let out of my mouth wasn't a scream, but it wasn't exactly "Oh" either. I turned to find the male nurse at my side, his hand on my shoulder.

"Sally Ball," I said, gasping. "Where did you take her?"

The nurse shushed me, as rightly he should have. He explained Sally had been moved out of ICU and onto a "regular floor." I chose not to argue semantics with him although I knew Wade Community had only one floor, and instead asked for directions to her room.

It had to be a good sign, this move of Sally's. It must mean she'd be alert. And maybe not her old self, but at least on the mend.

As I walked toward her room, I felt myself smiling. I didn't intend to. The life the smile had was its own. I put my hand to my cheeks and there it was. It was like finding a new facial wrinkle in the bathroom mirror. You wonder where it came from. I passed a woman with a cleaning cart. She smiled broadly when she looked at me, said "Good morning" even. It must be contagious, I thought, then remembered I used to know such things. It seemed a long time since I'd felt this kind of genuine happiness, the kind that dances all over you.

My smile turned to an all-out grin when I saw Sally. She was sitting up in the bed, sipping a ginger ale through one of those wonderful, bendable hospital straws. Although she still looked weak, her eyes had a spark to them, not the dull, drugged glaze of yesterday. Her bruises were turning from angry purple to dirty yellow. In some places on her face they had almost disappeared.

Mrs. Ball stood in a corner of the room arranging well-wishers' cards. Word of Sally's wreck had gotten out. She smiled when she saw me. Then Sally looked up and smiled at me as well.

"I'm sorry," I teased. "I thought I had Sally Ball's room here. She's in terrible shape from a wreck. You are certainly not she."

"Come here, you," Sally said and pulled me close for a hug.

As I finished hugging her, I noticed she winced in

some pain. Still, I was genuinely shocked at how well she seemed to be doing.

"Here, Sydney, take this chair." Mrs. Ball pushed to me an orange plastic chair that looked like an unattached cousin to the ones in the emergency room.

I sat and took a good, hard look at Sally. I grinned again. She was actually looking back at me.

"When did you move into this room?"

Sally seemed slightly confused by the question. "This room?" she said.

Her mother answered: "Dr. Fritz authorized it early this morning when he made his rounds." She looked at her watch, then walked over to the head of Sally's bed and stroked her shoulder. "We've been here a couple of hours at least, haven't we, honey?"

Sally nodded.

I asked her how she felt.

"My head hurts," she said, not surprisingly. "Dr. Fritz says I'll be fine. He says I'm his best patient."

I'd forgotten about the good doctor.

"He says Sally is making amazing progress," her mother said.

"She certainly looks better," I agreed. "Does this good news speed up the timetable for getting you home?"

"Next week," Sally said. "Dr. Fritz says he'd keep me forever if he thought he could get away with it."

Oh God, I thought. Here we go again. The signs were unmistakable. Sally's monstrous weakness is men. She is infatuated with every man she meets and in love every other week. Literally. She has never been married, came close only that one time in Las Vegas, and is out of love as quickly as she goes in. There is no discernible pattern to the men she falls for. Hart and I have seen her with accountants, wrestlers, artists, lawyers, one school bus driver, and several admitted bums. Every client is fair game. Fritz was the first physician I'd seen her do this with though. Only, however, because I go out of my way to avoid medical clients. To paraphrase Hart, they usually make me sick.

Normally I jump in and criticize every man she goes gaga over like this. It's the role we established for me years ago. That day, however, something stopped me. Maybe it was her weakness. Maybe it was my relief that she was okay. Whatever it was, it kept me from asking her if he'd figured out her name yet. Or was she still Ms. Bull?

"He told me you'd be here about a week, so I guess that hasn't changed," I said.

"You've met Douglas?" Sally said.

"Douglas?" I repeated.

"Dr. Fritz. Douglas Fritz." She said it as if it wasn't unusual for a patient to be calling the doctor she only just met by his first name.

"I didn't know he had a first name," I said blandly. Watch it, Sydney. Don't spoil Sally's fun.

Sally and her mother both laughed. I didn't understand the humor. They had the same laugh, a teenage, girlish laugh.

While they were sputtering to a stop, Dr. Douglas Fritz entered the room as if it were his own. I saw the old familiar look in Sally's eyes, bloodshot though they were, and I had to turn away. How many times had I seen it?

"Well, well, well . . ." He glanced at all three of us

as if to say that life could resume now that he was here. My resentment of him was mingled with gratitude. He had, after all, saved Sally's life or at least acted promptly enough and with enough skill to insure that she'd be okay.

I stood to reintroduce myself to him. I said my name, but before I could add a reminder that we'd met Monday, he interrupted me.

"I was hoping to meet you," he said.

Uh-oh. He had no recollection of me whatsoever.

He turned to Sally, then back to me. "Sally told me she worked for the best advertising agency in Charlotte. I wanted to meet her boss."

He took my hands and held them in his. His smile really looked genuine. If I were meeting him for the first time, I would have thought him charming.

"Sit back down, Ms. Teague. It is Ms. Teague, isn't it? Allen Teague?"

I nodded, but Sally piped right in. "Sydney's the Allen and the Teague." She looked pleased with herself for knowing this. Considering that her brain had been drilled into recently, she had a right to be.

It was getting hot in the room. I took my coat off and folded it in my lap as I sat down again.

"Did Sally tell you?" he asked.

"Tell me what?" I looked from him to Sally. All of a sudden I thought he was going to tell me they would be married.

"About the hospital. That we need an agency."

I perked up.

"We'll be merging with Carolinas Medical Center," he said. "I head up the committee to promote it."

"When's the actual merger?" I asked.

"Technically, financially, we already are merged. The public date I'm shooting for is January 1. With the New Year, I thought it would be easier for people to remember."

His ego came through in the tone he was using. Also in his choice of pronouns. Where was the rest of his committee when this big decision was being made?

"If you're 'shooting' for January 1," I said, "then you'd better load your gun fast. You're too late already for most opportunities."

He looked personally offended. Then his expression turned to a certain haughtiness that was definitely directed at me. "It's just advertising, Ms. Teague. Why so much lead time?"

I thought, That's right, Bozo. Belittle what I do for a living and you'll gain my undying loyalty.

I said, "Magazine print goes to bed at least a month before pub date, and TV's usually full by now for the first week in January. You could do an *Observer* campaign, but that won't get you quite the same image. Besides, someone has to create your look and your message. That takes time."

"How much time?"

"What do you need?"

"Isn't that your job to tell me?"

This exchange was getting us nowhere. I removed my camel cardigan and piled it on top of the coat on my lap. No wonder people got sick while they were in the hospital. This heat could bake up a healthy batch of germs.

"You need a typeface for your new name and a logo." I made sure he was listening to me by making eye contact with him—no matter how distasteful. "Unless, of course, there's a legal reason not to."

"What kind of legal reason?"

"Well, sometimes when you merge, you become an extension of something else, usually the bigger party in the merger. You, in effect, lose your identity. In that case there's nothing to promote. And if there is, the work for it would probably come out of Carolinas Medical's agency. Have you discussed this with anybody in Charlotte?"

He snickered, a rare facial contortion on an adult. Obviously it was directed at me. I just wasn't sure which one of my remarks had garnered such disdain. So I asked him.

"What's that about?" is the way I put it. I contorted my face into a weak mimic of his snicker so he'd be certain to know what I was talking about.

He sat on Sally's bed. No, he sat on Sally's foot, which was on the bed. She pulled it away and smiled sweetly as if she'd been blessed. He didn't seem to notice.

"The public view is this," he began in lecture mode. "In becoming Carolinas Medical North, Wade Community Hospital has finally become what it says it was all along."

"Whoa," I said. "How long's the hospital been here?"

"Fifty years, give or take a few."

"So you're going to say, 'For fifty years we lied to you. Now we'll tell you the truth.' Is that what you want to say?"

Sally said, "You don't understand, Sydney. Douglas, explain your idea to Sydney like you did to me this morning."

Fritz nodded and cleared his throat. He could have

been an opera singer readying himself for the stage. "What we call health care has really been sick care."

That's because you were paid to find sickness, Bozo, I thought.

"As we become part of the network, our emphasis will change to health."

That's because insurance is sick of all the trumped-up charges, I said to myself.

"Wellness centers, cardiac prevention programs, self-diagnostic tools, diabetic screenings . . . Wade never had any of that in the past. We were just the place where the sick people came."

As if there was something wrong with that.

He smiled self-servingly at Mrs. Ball, then Sally, and finally at me. "So my idea is 'From Sick Care to Health Care—Carolinas Medical North.' "

God help me. Did I dare touch this? Hell, with the loss of Snake, Allen Teague needed some quick business any way I could bring it in. Over here in Wade County, Dr. Douglas Fritz was probably the only prospect I'd run into.

I smiled back at him and hoped my expression was appropriately admiring. Of all the people I deal with, health care professionals are the most frustrating. Once Wade became absorbed into the big Carolinas Medical network of hospitals, I'd be willing to bet all critical procedures would shift to Charlotte and little Wade would be left with a few primary care physicians and some exercise physiologists. Fritz, being a brain surgeon, would leave this place to a pulse-taking corps of generalists.

"Dr. Fritz, are you yourself moving down to Charlotte?"

"How did you know that?" he asked, genuinely astonished. He turned to Sally. "Did you tell her?"

Sally crossed her chest and shook her head. "Cross my heart, I didn't."

"Just a guess," I said. Maybe even he didn't understand what he'd bought into.

"But I'm not leaving until after the first of the year. Not until this new name is out in the community and working for us."

I took a deep breath. "The first thing you need is a logo and logotype." I caught his eyes and held them. "And you need them fast. Like yesterday," I added.

"How fast can you get them to me?" He grinned pompously over his shoulder at Sally. My guess was he had people turning flips for him all the time.

If he only knew, I thought. Yesterday would be fine with what I planned to sell him. "Maybe by tomorrow. I can show you something then anyway."

He was impressed. Anybody would have been. Even Sally's mouth had dropped open.

I promised to bring him something in the morning. If I couldn't find him, I'd leave it with Sally and he could look at it when he had time. I reached inside my pocketbook and handed him an Allen Teague card so he'd have the phone number.

When Fritz had left, I picked up the phone on the table beside Sally's bed. "Does this dial out?" I asked Sally.

She said it did.

"Long distance? Can I call long distance?"

"I guess so. What are you doing, Sydney?" Sally scratched lightly at a loose piece of tape at the base of her skull. I looked closely at one of her pale bruises and saw a bit of caked powder. Sally had on makeup.

"Tell you in a minute," I said as I dialed. I glanced at my watch to be sure Hart hadn't gone to lunch yet. His schedule was usually clockwork. Eleven forty-five. I was safe.

Leslie answered. I told her I needed to speak with Hart if he was still there. He was, she said, and was starting to transfer me. "Oh, do you want your messages?" she asked.

"Are there many?" I asked, not wanting them if there were.

"Just two. Mr. Ian Bolick confirming your four o'clock appointment here at the office and a Betty Zebrinski."

"Who is Betty Zebrinski? Did she say who she's with?"

She hesitated. "She sounded like y'all knew each other, Ms. Teague. When I told her you were in Wade County this morning, she said that's where she was."

The only Betty I knew in Wade County was Seth's lab assistant. I'd never heard her last name before, but it must have been that Betty. I wondered if she'd called before or after the visitors to her workplace.

"What time did she call, Leslie?"

"Bright and early. Nine o'clock at the latest. Then she called again fifteen minutes after that. She finally asked for your voice mail. Do you want to listen to it?"

"No, I'm going where she is when I leave the hospital. Give me her number though." I pulled the pen off my checkbook and *The Charlotte Observer* off Sally's lap, where she had it carefully folded to the daily crossword puzzle. I wrote Betty's number in the margin while Leslie transferred me to Hart.

"Make a copy of the Snake logo right after lunch," I said when he said hello.

"Why?" came his matter-of-fact reply.

"We've got a new client who needs a quick logo and logotype. The caduceus we used for Snake can work for them if you take out the cigarette. Let that stylized Snake wrap itself around something else."

"Like what?"

"God, Hart, I don't know. You're going to have to think of something. These people are a hospital, though, so the cigarette has to go. Put something healthy in its place. Like broccoli."

"Quite a content switch," he said and chuckled. "From synthetic nicotine to health care, all through the same image." He paused. "How about a carrot? Broccoli's too fat."

"Whatever works, Hart. Pick up a pen so you can write down the name. You're going to have to do this today."

There was total silence on his end. I expected it. Typical of Hart when he thinks I'm being unreasonable about a deadline. I ignored it.

"Got it?" I asked after I'd given the name to him.

"Got it. Will I see you today?"

"Oh, yes. I'll be there before four for Ian Bolick. Please see that Leslie's worked up our hours. I forgot to ask her about it."

He said he would, then we hung up.

I grinned at Sally. I was quite proud of my idea for

the defunct Snake logo. Recycling had always made me feel useful. Why not with images?

Sally wasn't grinning back. "You can't give the Snake logo to the hospital," she said.

"Of course I can. It's not being used, and you heard me, we're changing it enough where it won't be the same thing."

"Why isn't it being used? I thought Seth liked it a lot."

Oh my God. Sally didn't know about Seth. How could she? She was on an operating table when he died, unconscious when he used the deadly inhaler. If she'd seen him two days ago when she picked up the tapes and camera, he must have seemed fine. In fact, I am sure he was fine at that point. His demise happened quickly. From what I understood of nicotine as concentrated as it was in Seth's blood, one shot of the spray would have begun to paralyze his respiratory muscles. And he probably reached for it again, thinking it was the only thing that could help him in his distress. He couldn't have known that the more he sprayed, the closer he came to complete respiratory failure.

"Sydney, has Seth changed his mind?"

I had to tell her, but I didn't want to. If a brain is already scrambled, adding emotional hurt to it is bound to slow down recovery.

"Sally, I don't want to tell you this. You don't need to hear it right now."

"Then don't tell her, dear," her mother said. "Can't whatever it is wait?"

Mrs. Ball couldn't have known what the subject

was. She knew only that her daughter was sick and that everything we did should be to get her well. I agreed, but I couldn't see a way out of this conversation. Maybe I could soften it somehow.

"Sydney," Sally said with a strength in her voice I hadn't heard since last week. "Sydney, what's going on with Seth? Did we lose him?"

Of course she meant his business, but she took the euphemism right out of my mouth. I had no choice now but to be direct with her.

"He died," I said.

I watched her closely. She looked deep into my eyes to see if they matched the words I'd just hit her with. Her features drew taut, and I thought I saw physical pain jab at her temple. She held her hand there and her other hand over her mouth as she choked out a sob. Her mother rushed to the other side of the bed. As Sally pulled her hand from her mouth, I took it with both of mine and squeezed tight. Mrs. Ball gently stroked the back of her daughter's bald, taped head while she glared at me in obvious disgust. I mouthed to her that I was sorry, but her expression didn't change. Sally finally looked at me again.

"What happened to him?" The weakness had returned to her voice.

I decided to fudge the truth. His death was hard enough on someone in her shape. "He had a reaction to his asthma inhaler," I said, rationalizing that as long as I didn't use the word "medicine," I was telling some form of the truth. "He died here Monday morning after you'd been brought in." I quickly glanced at her mother, hoping to see some forgiveness. I didn't. I looked back at

Sally. "I was here," I continued. "They did everything they could to save him."

She flinched again. "I don't understand it," Sally said. "He was fine. He was even joking with me. His lab assistant said the two of us were enough to cheer up the devil." She gazed into my eyes. "Those were her exact words, Sydney. 'Cheer up the devil.' So you know he felt good. We were teasing each other like we always did."

"You went to his lab?" I was confused. When did Sally ever meet Betty?

"No, his house."

"What was Betty doing in his house? Are you talking about Monday morning, Sally?" I thought her memory was playing games with her.

"Of course it was Monday morning. Right before I had my wreck. Is that her name? I don't know why she was there, but she'd been crying."

"Betty had? She'd been crying? What about?"

Sally's eyes were blank. "I don't know. I thought maybe they were having an affair." She smiled. "You know me, Sydney. I like to imagine that when I can. But I do remember wondering myself why she was so upset."

"She didn't say anything else? Just that you and Seth could cheer up the devil?"

"No." Sally shook her head very slowly.

A slew of scenarios jumbled on top of each other. My mind couldn't stop racing long enough to grasp what any of them meant. Betty was clearly upset when I'd seen her yesterday. Did I only imagine that her emotions were for Seth? Could she have been distraught over something else? Did she know something the rest of us didn't?

"Was Johnny there yet?" I asked.

"Who's Johnny?" Sally looked confused again.

"Seth's son," I said.

"Oh . . . I think I knew he had a son." She put her hand to her forehead again. "I can't remember everything, Sydney. But, no, I don't remember seeing his son."

Had Betty left by the time Johnny came by on his way to school? Where did she go? Was she in the lab when Seth was murdered? Had she slipped him the tainted nebulizer before she left?

"Do you remember anything about the wreck, Sally? Do you remember why you drove off the road?" I held my breath.

Her still-bloodshot eyes grew smaller. She shook her head. "I remember leaving the farm. A car was following me real close. No, maybe it was a truck. It was bigger than my car. I remember thinking how stupid the driver was not to pass me if he was that impatient. There weren't any yellow lines. No traffic was coming from the other direction." She shook her head again. "But I don't remember the wreck. The driver behind me must have seen it, though, because I don't think he ever passed me."

"Do you remember the color of this truck or car or whatever it was behind you?"

A smile spread slowly over Sally's battered face. "It was green. I remember now thinking how pretty that green was against all the colorful leaves."

"Honey, you're doing well," her mother said. "I think your memory's going to come all the way back. Don't you think so, Sydney?"

I patted Sally's knee. "Yes, I do. You're going to be fine."

Finally, I thought, I have the answer to one question at least. The green Cherokee had indeed run Sally off the road. The two men inside had been willing to do that to Sally for my videotapes of Seth. But why? What could be so valuable to the Liggon Group? And what did Betty have to do with all this? I still couldn't believe my instincts about her were so far off base. She didn't seem to be capable of hurting anyone. Dammit, I was going to find out.

"I need to make one more call," I said to Mrs. Ball. "This one's local."

I picked up the phone and the newspaper with Betty's number on it. I assumed she'd been calling me from the lab. My anxiety was such that I wanted to get in the car, drive straight to the farm, and just confront her. I tapped my toe impatiently as the phone rang six times. I was beginning to think she wasn't there and I was deciding what to do next, when the ringing stopped abruptly.

"Thurgood," the voice said.

17

"So Keeter has asked you for help," I said. "That's great. He must have listened to me after all."

Tom said he was awaiting a callback from his superiors. He told me to hang up so he could get his call.

I asked to speak to Betty instead. I wasn't going to be told what to do. "She called me," I added. "I need to tell her something quickly."

"Can't do that, Sydney." His speech was clipped, the way it gets when he thinks I'm delving into his business.

I raised my voice. "She called me, Tom. What are you doing in the lab anyway?"

He was silent.

"Did you at least tell her Seth didn't kill himself?"

"I haven't told her anything." He hesitated. "I'll talk to you later," he said abruptly. "I'm going to hang up now."

And he did.

I just stood there for a minute. I held the receiver away from my ear and looked at it.

"Tom Thurgood?" Sally asked.

I nodded, still holding the receiver in my hand.

"I thought you were making a local call."

"I was. To Seth's farm. He's out there." I placed the receiver back on the cradle.

"Why is he over here?" She paused, and when I didn't answer immediately, she added, "Is he coming to see me?"

"I knew he was coming," I said aloud, but communicating only with myself. I put on my cardigan but couldn't decide whether it was still cold enough for my coat now. I decided to carry it over my arm. I looked at Sally and suddenly remembered she'd spoken. "He's working, I think. At least he sounded like he was." I smiled at her. "Besides, as far as he knows, you're still unconscious. Everybody's going to be surprised when I tell them how well you're doing." I squeezed her hand quickly and brushed her cheek with my lips.

I walked the long, meandering hospital halls at a record pace. As I did, I passed the friendly cleaning woman again, but she didn't smile at me this time. Something told me I was the difference, not her.

When I arrived at Seth's lab, Sheriff Keeter's car was still there, as was Betty's. Ian's truck wasn't there. It had been replaced by Tom's navy Toyota, his "company car," as he called it. The sun was high in the noon sky and had warmed the earth as I had thought it would on this classic autumn afternoon. I left my coat in the Trooper.

The first thing I noticed was the smell. Even though

someone had left the door opened to air it out, the combination of chemicals was almost overpowering. Then I saw why. Test tubes lay broken and scattered all over the place. Large jars of stored chemicals had shattered too, and the liquid had pooled in streams and puddles all over the vinyl flooring.

I stepped into it, since there seemed to be no way around. I followed the sound of the voices to the lounge area in the back of the building where I'd gone with both Seth and Betty. Tom and Keeter had their backs to me as I entered that room. If the atmosphere of the place had not been so ominous and the smell so sickening, I probably would have laughed. Tom's six-foot-six body next to Keeter's of the same diameter would have made a good cartoon. I did start to smile until I saw the body at their feet and the pool of blood that was unmistakable even in the midst of all the chemicals.

"Good God, what happened?" I said, my voice shaking.

Both men turned when I spoke. As they did, the shadows shifted and a ray of sun streaked through a window and softly lighted the entire body, including the face, of Betty Zebrinski. Amazingly, her glasses were still on her face. Her neck, however, held a puncture wound, a wound so deep as to have drained her body of its blood. Her starched white lab coat had turned crimson red.

Tom placed himself between the body and me, his hands on my shoulders. I knew he was trying to shield my view, but what I'd already seen I'd remember forever.

"Who did that?" I barely got the sentence out.

Keeter was now standing beside Tom. They were so close to me I felt claustrophobic.

Tom spoke first. "We're trying to figure that out, Sydney. You shouldn't have come."

"Shouldn't have come? How was I supposed to know this is what I'd find? The woman called me, Tom. I was trying to find out what she wanted." He has a nasty habit sometimes of making me feel I've done something wrong—even when I haven't.

Keeter said, "The Zebrinski woman called you? What would she want with you? You think she knew this was going to happen to her?"

"I doubt that, Sheriff," I said sarcastically. "I certainly wouldn't call an ad agency if I feared for my life, would you?" I was coming down from anger at Tom and had no business being so sarcastic. "I'm sorry, Sheriff Keeter, I didn't mean to jump on you." I glared quickly at Tom, then lowered my eyes.

"S'all right, Miss Teague. I guess you're nervous. What do you think she wanted with you though?"

I didn't know how to answer that. I'd been trying to figure it out myself. Here was Seth's only real employee during the critical research of this past year. Her loyalty to him and his work had seemed evident to me when I'd spoken with her. But something had obviously been bothering her. Why had she been crying Monday morning when Sally had come by for the camera and tapes? And here was the biggest question of all: Had whoever killed Seth also killed her?

I shook my head. "I don't know," I said.

Keeter scratched what had become a raging rash on

his neck. He took out a large bandanalike cloth tissue and dabbed at watery eyes. I looked at Tom. His eyes were watery too. I felt my own eyes sting.

"Have you got all the windows open?" I asked. "Who knows what's in the air in here."

The three of us spread out to open the windows. If this had been Tom's turf, he'd have kicked me out without a word. Since Wade County was Keeter's jurisdiction, I don't think Tom knew quite what to do. I stayed in the general area of the lounge, with Tom and Keeter both heading toward the front part of the building. When I had been here before, I'd noticed the large jars of chemicals, about the size of commercial water dispensers. There had been so many that the volume of chemicals had impressed me. Now every bit of it was on either the floor, the counter surfaces, or the walls. I would probably need to throw away these shoes.

Betty's desk had been so neat when I'd been here before, the kind of neatness that's so pristine you don't even register that what you're seeing is, in fact, a desk. Now it was in total disarray. All the paperwork had been ripped into many pieces and scattered around so that you couldn't tell which pieces had fit each other originally. Her journal was missing all its pages, and I wondered if they were the shreds that were lying around.

I opened the refrigerator. A few small vials of chemicals were placed inside the door. I assumed whoever destroyed this place forgot to look there, but I doubted this small remaining bit of Seth's work would make any difference to Betty's killer. The rest of the refrigerator held only a sandwich in a plastic bag and several six-packs of those generic, store-brand sodas I'd seen Betty drinking yesterday.

On the floor beside the refrigerator, wedged there next to a cabinet, was what looked to me like Betty's pocketbook. It was a large, black pocketbook with several outside compartments. Because of where she'd placed it, it wasn't as drenched in chemicals as other things I'd seen in the lab. Still, I grabbed the roll of paper towels I found on top of the small refrigerator, pulled off a few pieces at the perforations, and swiped the pocketbook several times before I sat in the chair with it. As I held it, I noticed it was made of a poor quality leather, too stiff and made even more so after being doused with the spill. I sighed, then asked myself what in the hell the quality of Betty's leather had to do with anything at this point, and, thank God, the better part of me said, nothing, absolutely nothing.

The insides were much like mine. Lots of shredded, unusable tissue that couldn't blow a newborn's nose. Four or five pens and a leadless pencil. Two glasses cases, one with prescription sunglasses, the other empty. I glanced at the body no more than ten feet from me and saw the other pair, then squeezed my own eyes shut to block out the image. I shifted myself in the chair to face away from her.

She'd carried her money in a cloth pouch instead of a traditional wallet. At least, I couldn't find a wallet. The pouch was a vivid African print in orange and red. I zipped it open and confirmed for myself that it was indeed used by her as a wallet. Receipts that had obviously been hastily stuffed in fell out and onto my lap. I looked at a few of them and saw nothing odd.

One was for this pocketbook. It was from a Belk store in Winston-Salem and it said "handbag." My quality assessment was confirmed when I looked at the twenty-dollar sale price. Her driver's license showed her as Elizabeth Caudle Zebrinski at an address in Winston-Salem. I wondered if she'd commuted over here every day. Winston-Salem is in Forsyth County, and the drive to Wade County would probably have taken her an hour each way.

I was wondering if she was married. Was Caudle her maiden name or merely her middle name? Or if she had children. Tom called out from the front of the building. He wasn't calling to me, but to the other police officers whose cars I could hear beginning to arrive. They would secure the lab, pull their bright yellow tape all around its perimeter so that it looked like a poorly wrapped present.

Betty's charge cards were the ones I'd expect. A couple of bank cards, a Belk, and a Sears. A pang of guilt hit me, then floated away like honeysuckle on a summer's night. I could hear my mother telling me not to go through other people's belongings. I mumbled aloud to stop my mother's voice inside my head and kept searching for pictures of children. I found none. Her only snapshot was a posed photograph of an elderly couple with fake bookcases behind them. It looked like my mother's church directory photograph. The couple must be her parents, I thought.

I could hear the officers entering the building and coming with Tom in my direction. Of course, they'd be coming back here, I thought. The body's back here. I turned myself around again in the chair so I could see her. I breathed deeply and thought I could smell the iron in Betty's blood. Like liquid rust. It mingled with the other chemicals, and, even now with ventilation in here, it had become a heavy sickroom smell.

I reached into the pouch again. When I touched the card, I thought it was merely another charge card. But it was a smoother, thinner plastic like her driver's license. I pulled it out of the pouch and looked closely. It was an identification card. Betty's face stared out at me, bespectacled and serious, wearing her lab coat. A typical head-and-shoulders pose. The card carried both her typed name in full and her signature. The word "Research" appeared right under her name as if it was a title or the name of a department. A bold tobacco leaf logo was surrounded by a circle with the words "Security Clearance" inside the circle, creating the illusion of a permanent stamp. It looked to me like a company identification card denoting that Betty was free to come and go. At the top of the card was the company name, and it wasn't Bolick Enterprises. The Liggon Tobacco Group name was set in bold Helvetica type and spaced proportionally to fit the entire width along the top of the card.

I was still staring at the card when I noticed the lounge had filled with a half dozen Charlotte uniformed policemen, a couple of whom I'd met through Tom. One of them spoke to me by name, asked me if I was okay. I don't think I answered him. My mind was so full of images and words and scenes at that moment, so full of stuff that didn't connect and didn't make sense, that I couldn't connect either. Over all the disjointed pieces in my head was a film of great sadness and disappointment. I had read her wrong. I thought I'd seen the same commitment I had to Seth and his cause in her. Had my own commitment blinded me, rendered me incapable of seeing her for what she obviously was?

As disappointed as I was in Betty and myself and, if I am to be honest, all human beings at that moment, the sadness I felt for Seth was overwhelming. His joy in discovery, his sense of triumph for his father, had kept him from seeing the reality of his creation. He may as well have unleashed a tornado for the impact his invention would have on people's lives. He had known that, of course, but he'd concentrated instead on the lives Snake might save. Seth knew only too well the economic implications on the tobacco industry. The industry had made his family wealthy, after all. He knew how many people would eventually be wiped out because of what he was doing. When I had said something about people being put out of work because of Snake, Seth had looked at me like I was stupid.

"You can't think about things like that," he'd said. "You can't stop progress simply because people will have to learn something new. You sound like my brother."

He was right, of course, but I thought even then that some things were so deeply ingrained in people that taking those things away probably felt like you were taking their lives. I'd been thinking of farmers, growers, people of the land. Not tobacco companies themselves and the people who ran them. Betty was a corporate thief, and I was having a hard time with the knowledge of it.

"Sydney, you need to go on now." Tom's thighs were in front of my glazed-over eyes.

I didn't know what to say to him. I simply handed him Betty's Liggon ID.

After thirty seconds of staring at it, he said, "Makes sense. She was working with the guys in the Cherokee."

"They were leaving the farm when I got here."

"The sheriff saw them too," he said.

"Did they kill Betty?" I asked.

"I don't know." He looked at the card again. "Corporate spies aren't normally into murder."

"They did run Sally off the road." I held his green eyes. "She remembers them behind her." My hands had begun to shake. I dropped one of Betty's receipts onto the floor, picked it up, and had some difficulty putting it back into the pouch. "I bet there's green paint on the back of her Honda."

"That sounds like something their type would do. Not this. I have an APB out though. They won't get far."

"I saw them in town in a drugstore. After this had already happened, I think. They probably don't know to run."

Tom said nothing.

"Where's Ian?" I'd almost forgotten his car had been here too.

"I'd like to know that myself. Keeter found him in here. The girl was dead when Keeter arrived." He pushed a piece of hair out of his eyes. He took the pouch from my lap, put it back in the pocketbook, and put the pocketbook under his arm. He stooped and cradled my elbow with his hand. "Come on," he said. "Let's get you out of here."

He walked me to the Trooper, opened the driver's side, and told me to sit. He remained outside.

"What was used to make that puncture wound?" I'd been afraid to ask it until now.

"Looks like a piece of glass. A large piece from one of the chemical containers."

"So someone first destroyed the place, then cut her throat with the shards?" I cringed at that level of violence.

"That looks like the order of things." He nodded. "There was a piece beside her body. It had skin on it." He glanced at the building, at the officer busy unrolling his crime scene tape, then back at me. "I bagged it before you got here. We'll get fingerprints off of it, if there are any to be had."

"Do you think Ian did this?" I hoped to God he hadn't, for the family's sake more than for his own. "He had motive, Tom. Betty refused to halt the research."

He hesitated. "Sheriff Keeter doesn't like to think so."

"Sheriff Keeter might even have the same motive, you know." I studied him carefully. "You didn't answer me. I asked what you think."

He had been leaning over to talk with me. He stood back and stretched. I didn't see a tennis stroke this time.

"I just got here," he finally said. "Keeter wants us involved, but I don't know enough. I've got to rely on his knowledge of the people involved."

I understood. I nodded. "Makes it hard, though, doesn't it? Keeter and Ian having so much in common?"

"Sydney, you know more about what's going on here than I do."

He was right. I did. Why, then, did I feel I understood nothing?

"Tell me about Ian Bolick," Tom said. "Is he like his brother?"

I raised both eyebrows, hoping the action would create enough room in my brain for a new thought to form. I didn't trust anything I thought I already knew. "I met him only twice, talked to him only once—after Seth had died. Yesterday, I think."

"And?"

"And what?"

He squatted and held on to the window frame to keep from falling backwards. "Was he grieving for his brother? Was he angry? Was he relieved? What's your take on him?"

"I think he's all those things." I rubbed my nose. Only a slight stinging remained from the chemical smell in the lab. "He's not at all like Seth," I said slowly. "After twenty years he's still angry at their father for the work he was doing. That anger is what came through to me, nothing else. He wanted no part of Snake now that Seth was dead."

"Was he even sad about his brother?"

"I don't know. I assumed he was. And expectation tends to fulfill itself. All I cared about when I talked to him was the product. I wasn't thinking about anything else." I fiddled with my car keys, lined up my ignition key and my house key on the big brass circle. "Tom, I'm sorry. I just don't know."

He stood up. "He left the scene. I could pull him in for that alone, but I sort of wanted to talk with the fellow first. I'm in a bad spot here. This really isn't my case, you know. Keeter seems to think a lot of him."

"He would think a lot of him, though, wouldn't he?

You're the one who told me about their being in that growers' group together."

Tom's pained expression told me his mind was beginning to clog up as much as mine was. I felt sorry for him. He wasn't used to relying on someone else's instincts.

"I'll call you tonight," he said. "I still plan to drive you over here to the funeral tomorrow. Maybe we'll know some more by then."

I started the Trooper and put it in neutral. "For what it's worth," I said, "Ian Bolick's supposed to be at my office at four o'clock today."

Tom said, "I doubt if he'll show now. Who knows where he's gone."

"Oh, I think he will," I said. "I owe him a bunch of money, and he's coming to pick it up."

Tom and I both checked our watches. We had three hours until Ian was supposed to be at Allen Teague.

"He called to confirm this morning," I added.

He nodded back toward the lab. "But that was before this happened."

"Where else is he going to go?"

He chewed on the side of his lower lip, let his one unruly piece of hair stay in his eyes, then tapped his hand on the windowsill of the Trooper. "I'll get things started here," he said, "then come back to town. Four o'clock?"

I nodded.

18

I was having an old familiar reaction to death.

It started the day we buried my grandmother, this odd empathy I have with the dead. I was eleven, a year younger than George junior is now. Granny lived in the bedroom next to mine the last two months of her life. In that short time, we established a daily ritual of after-school snacks and long talks about her childhood and mine. I remember in vivid detail the harsh Pennsylvania farmland in winter, how she'd ride her loyal pony five miles to school, how she watched helplessly as three of her six brothers and sisters died of TB.

Other than her stories, what I remember most from those days were the snacks themselves. Mother would make them and have them ready when I got home from school. Pitchers of pink lemonade with sprigs of mint, homemade chocolate chip cookies, frosted lemon squares, sometimes triple-decker sandwiches with two kinds of cheeses and meats. Usually Granny would eat with me.

Always she'd drink the lemonade, even toward the end. These were very important days to me, although I've never understood quite why.

Granny died while I was in school. She turned over in bed and the tumor in her diaphragm cut off the flow of blood to her heart. It was a peaceful death, like a heart giving out while the person's asleep. At least that's the way Mother and Dad told it.

That night I wouldn't eat dinner. The very thought of food repelled me. I thought my family barbaric for sitting down together as if life just goes on. Instead I sat in Granny's room, on her bed, and wept. I fell asleep there.

The funeral was the following day, I think, although it could have been the day after that. I just remember the first family meal after Granny had been put in the ground. Food was all over the house from the moment she died. Neighbors and friends had inundated us with trays of every imaginable raw vegetable and meat. Frozen casseroles overflowed the freezer. I disdained it all. I didn't understand how anybody could ever eat again. After all, Granny couldn't. In my young mind it was disrespectful to even consider it.

Then it happened, and I was shocked that it did. When I smelled Mother's roast in the oven that night, a dizzying hunger overwhelmed me. I was appalled I would want the meal so badly. Ashamed that I would choose to live when Granny no longer had that choice. I ate that meal in its entirety. Sobbing and gulping the whole time. The only feeling greater than my shame was my hunger. Whenever anybody dies, I have that personal tug-of-war inside me.

I had it inside me today as I passed the Bredon Family Restaurant on my way back to Charlotte. Something was being hickory-smoked. The aroma pulled the Trooper, my guilt, and me into the parking lot. My watch said one thirty. Breakfast had been early this morning. I had to eat something.

The restaurant was bustling but not the way a Charlotte restaurant bustles. Wherever I eat in Charlotte, the atmosphere is charged like that of a sales presentation, people wanting something from each other. Charlotteans bring agendas to lunch that have little to do with the food. I confess I oftentimes do lunch the same way.

I slipped into a front corner booth and studied the laminated menu I found wedged between the sugar dispenser and the bottle of vinegar. The special today was smoked pork chops. I ordered it along with turnip greens, cabbage, and a sweet potato. The smiling young woman put a basket of homemade biscuits, a plate full of butter squares, and a jar of fruit preserves on my table.

As I sipped my coffee, I noticed everyone else was drinking ice tea. There must have been sixty or seventy people sitting inside that restaurant in a space about the size of a typical family great room. Shiny, vinyl-upholstered booths lined three of the walls. Some of the booths were patched with large pieces of gray tape. Three or four men sat in each booth carrying on intense conversations about the weather, tobacco prices, and personal stories of friends and families. Occasionally I would hear a joke followed by robust laughter all around. I overheard two men discussing hog production in detail and the problems they were having with state inspectors. The whole time they talked, they were eating the smoked pork chops. I was jealous of lives so neatly compartmentalized.

Square and rectangular tables took over the center of the room. Men and women together occupied those tables. I thought it strange no women sat in any of the booths. Except me, of course. But I didn't feel I counted here. I was an observer of a way of life I wasn't part of.

The women all wore dresses, the kind I remember Granny wearing. Cotton, floral prints, waists with belts. Most of the men had on overalls, not the designer corduroys I've seen in the stores lately, but heavy blue denim. Their shirts were either knit or flannel.

Their faces were weathered, both the men and the women. In the younger ones the effect of the sun and wind was a certain healthy looking glow, a ruddy, rich look. The older ones seemed etched by it, though, as if the sun had driven deep staples into their cheeks and foreheads and the wind had sealed them there.

Almost all of them were smoking, so I did too. I couldn't think of a single restaurant in Charlotte where the practice was still tolerated. The busy but attentive waitress brought me a glass ashtray. The coffee, the cigarette, the clang of plates and the buzz of people enjoying each other was a comforting combination. I settled back in the booth and relaxed for the first time in two days.

When my meal arrived, I tried hard not to think of Betty. This was a wonderful country meal. I was determined to enjoy it and I did. The pork chops were laced with fat that bulged when it cooked and moistened the meat to mouthwatering perfection. Totally unlike the cardboard that passes for pork these days. I smothered the potato in four or five patties of butter, then set it off with several shakes of both salt and pepper. Its sweetness lightened the heaviness of the pork and piqued some taste buds I hadn't used in years. Since the cabbage and greens were both cooked in fatback, they would have tasted the same had I not dribbled vinegar onto the turnips. The vinegar was just enough tart to cut through the fat of all else. I punctuated each bite with biscuit smothered in what I finally decided was plum preserves. After thirty minutes of nonstop eating, I was devoid of shame and burdened instead by the volume I'd consumed. A nap would have been nice.

As I was drinking a final cup of coffee and smoking a particularly wonderful cigarette, I noticed a party get up from one of the center tables to leave. Two young men in their twenties, an attractive woman of about the same age, and an older woman, probably five to ten years older than me.

One of the younger overalled men from a booth yelled, "Hey, Bolick. Get all your rye in?"

Both young men turned in response and smiled.

"We're finishing up this week," one of the two said.

The young man with him laughed and added, " 'Bout time, don't ya think? Looking forward to a nice quiet winter."

"We hear ya," said the man in the booth. "Everybody needs a rest."

So these were Ian's sons. Given Ian's age, the woman was surely his wife. I think her name was Bev. She was attractive in a very plain way, looked, in fact, a lot like the daughter I'd met at the farm. The younger woman was quite pretty, though, with vivid red hair and the complexion to match. She put her arm through the arm of one of the young Bolick men. She must have been his wife.

The cashier laughed with them. Several "amens" were exchanged all around. The cashier took cash from one of them and leaned almost imperceptibly forward. I could barely hear her say, "Sorry about your uncle." The young man didn't look her in the eye. Instead he hung his head, stared at the floor, in fact, and muttered his thanks. He was clearly more embarrassed than sad. Was this the effect Seth had on his family? If his death was an embarrassment to them, his life could only have been more so. Was he so much of a burden to bear?

I glanced around the restaurant and, for the first time, understood that he was. These people were the true inhabitants of Wade County. The land was their common bond, their entire lives. Working it, loving it, yielding to it, harvesting it. And the land was synonymous with tobacco here. From their point of view, Seth Bolick had been out to destroy it all. This family I saw here, his family, had been his primary victims. How far would they have gone to stop him?

I felt sick. I didn't know if it was from stuffing myself or from the realization that had been so long in coming that Seth's mission cut two ways. My stomach hurt though. That old piece of wire had something, if not everything, to do with it.

There's a stretch of the interstate as you approach Charlotte from the north where the city is set off like a jewel. The road dips at that point and the city is above you at a distance. It reminds me of the animated Magic Kingdom of the old Disney TV series where Tinker Bell hovers above the castles as the show starts, then sprinkles gold dust just before the first commercial break. As I drove through that stretch on my way back to town, I was struck again by the resemblance. Charlotte was shaped like the Magic Kingdom. It came to a point in the NationsBank towering spire just as the Kingdom did in its castle. I didn't see gold dust, but the mid-afternoon sun reflected off the building's glass, sparkling like a topaz caught by the light.

It was three thirty as I exited the ramp off the loop around uptown and drove the four short blocks from West Boulevard to East. I wanted to talk with Ian alone. I needed to understand what had happened between him and Seth, when it had started, what part he had had in Seth's death and Betty's. Was he involved with the Liggon Group, and if he was, had Seth known that before he died? The naive exuberance I'd carried with me like a flag now sat on my chest like two tons of fool's gold. My simple attempt to take an action for Dad had become terribly complicated.

I saw my chance to talk with Ian as I was turning left into the Allen Teague driveway. His truck was illegally parked along East Boulevard a couple of buildings down from mine. I left the Trooper in my building's lot and hoofed it toward the street. The sun was so strong now that I left both my coat and my cardigan inside the car. Whether from the increasing heat or my increasing anxiety, I had begun to sweat. My pantyhose and shoes had trapped the sweat along with the chemicals I'd stepped in at the lab. My sweat had diluted the chemicals to a point of irritation, as if sweat was a catalyst for something new and dire. My calves had begun to itch and my toes were stinging. Adding these woes to the pain in my stomach, I was not in very good shape.

He literally jumped off his seat when I knocked on the passenger window. "God, Sydney, what are you doing?" he said.

I smiled and motioned for him to roll the window down. "Park in the back of my office," I said. "You'll get a ticket out here."

Ian nodded, a blank look in his eyes. "The least of my legal worries," he said ironically.

I stood back and let him pull away from the curb, then followed him to the back of my office.

"Can I talk with you a minute before we go in?" I said. "My employees are in there. I wanted to talk with you alone."

He got out of the truck, removed a worn leather jacket, and draped it over the driver's side windowsill. He wore a heavy wheat-colored canvas shirt. His right lower arm from the cuff to the elbow was splattered in blood. He saw it when I did and quickly rolled up both sleeves.

"Okay," he said carefully, leaning against the truck door and folding his arms. I placed myself next to him, back against door, my shoulder rubbing against his upper arm. We both stared at Allen Teague's back door.

Before I could gather my thoughts, he said, "I didn't kill that woman."

Okay, I told myself. I'll start wherever he wants to

start. I bit my lip to keep from saying anything. He needed to talk.

"She was dying when I got there. Blood was flowing out of her neck." He looked at his own hand, then folded his arms again. "I tried to stop it, but the gash was too deep . . . too jagged. I think it was too late then anyway." He closed his eyes, opened them again. "There was blood everywhere."

"Was she conscious?" I asked, hoping she'd told him who'd done this to her.

"Briefly." He resumed staring at my back door.

I wanted to scream, to pull it out of him. Something about his presence stopped me though. He and Seth may not have gotten along, but they were of the same gene pool. Seth couldn't be pushed; he might have been the most stubborn man I've ever known. I felt that stubbornness as I stood here now. If Ian was going to tell me anything I wanted, he was going to do it on his terms. I looked at my watch. Three fifty. We didn't have long before Tom would show up.

"I thought she was dead when I walked in. Her eyes were half closed. I tried to stuff the bottom of her lab coat into the hole in her neck. She was gurgling, choking on her own blood." He shook his head. "Then her eyes moved. She looked directly at me while I was fooling with her coat. I was so close to her face . . . six inches, no more. She whispered two words to me."

My heart was racing. The words had to be "Liggon Group."

Ian leaned forward so he could look me directly in the eyes. "She whispered, 'Love Seth.' " He paused and resumed his position parallel to mine. "That's it." He shook his head back and forth again. "I've been thinking about it for five hours now, and I still don't know what she meant." His voice thinned out, got weaker. "Was she telling me she loved Seth, or was she telling me that I should?"

A tear had joined the perspiration on my face. "Maybe both," I said.

He nodded and a partially stifled sob escaped his mouth. "I did love him. I do love him. He's my brother." Ian coughed, pulled a big cloth handkerchief from his corduroy pants, pressed it on his nose a couple of times, then put it back into his pocket. "I was a teenager when Seth was born. The early sixties. I was about the happiest kid in the whole world. My father owned the biggest farm in the county, damned near the biggest tobacco farm in the state. I loved working it. I knew someday it'd be mine and my baby brother's. Hell, we had enough land for ten brothers to farm. I couldn't wait to teach him. Then our father went crazy, Sydney. He really did. I don't see how you can possibly know how bad it was."

"Seth told me he had depression."

"The first time he was hospitalized, I dropped out of State to take over the work. I never left again."

"Must have been hard on you," I said, and I really meant it.

"The work wasn't. I loved it, always have. I love it now. The hard part was Father. He felt personally guilty for every person who'd ever died of cancer. You know how much money he gave to the Lung Association?"

"How much?"

He laughed sarcastically. "About a hundred thousand a year. Sometimes more, sometimes a little less. He hated himself for having grown tobacco. He was like a born-again." He cleared his throat. "No matter how much money he gave, the depression kept coming back. It was cyclical, although at the time, there didn't seem to ever be a break in it.

"I worried about Seth because he was with Father all the time. I was married by the time it got really bad. I had three kids of my own when Father built the lab and contracted with those idiots to develop the safe cigarette." He laughed sardonically. "I like to say he contracted to save the world, 'cause that's what you would have thought to hear him talk about it. Seth was old enough to buy into it." His shoulders dropped. "I guess he did."

"What did your neighbors think of your father? How did Wade County people take all that?" I had to know. Ever since lunch, it mattered to me.

"You mean the safe cigarette stuff?"

"Uh-huh."

"At first people were happy he'd stopped harping about the killer that tobacco was. His old friends were glad he had something that gave him back his meaning. Most people still thought he was crazy though. I was just grateful he stopped showing up in the fields every day to tell me how many people I was killing. Can you imagine what a daily lecture like that can do to your morale? Especially coming from your own father?"

"So people didn't hate him?"

"Nobody hated Father. I think they felt sorry for him."

I needed to say it. My time was running out. "But not so with Seth?"

He nodded. "Not so with Seth. He wasn't fixing tobacco. He was getting rid of it entirely."

19

"Ian, did you understand why Seth had to?"

"No. I'll never understand it. I loved him. Why didn't he care about me? Why didn't he care about Mother? She's held the land together for us always. Father would have thrown it away. She wouldn't let him. And, for Christ's sake, what about the land? Those six thousand acres have taken care of every Bolick who's lived in this country."

I could feel his anger building again. Just as I'd felt it when we were in the field. But it was born of frustration, not hatred.

"You told me why a few minutes ago, Ian."

He stood away from the truck and turned to face me.

"You said Seth was with your father all the time. You experienced your father at an earlier time in his life. It's why you love to work the land. I bet he did too when you were young." Ian nodded. "When Seth came along, your father had changed. He spilled his soul, and

Seth was there to drink it up." I paused; it was so hard to find the right words. "Ian, for what it's worth, I don't think Seth loved you less; I just think he loved your father more."

"But Father's been dead twenty years . . ."

"Not to Seth," I said.

A sob escaped him again. "Why did he do it, Sydney? I'd get rid of the farm to have him back. I blame Father for this too."

I said, "Sheriff Keeter didn't tell you about my visit with him this morning?"

"What are you talking about?"

"I hope I convinced him Seth didn't kill himself. I thought he was going to talk with you about it. Maybe he would have if Betty hadn't been murdered."

"If Seth didn't kill himself, then what happened to him? Could he have inhaled that much nicotine accidentally?"

"No. I don't think so." I felt a chill and realized the temperature had been dropping while we talked. The sun was moving toward the west.

"Then . . ."

"Ian, did you run into the guys in the green Cherokee?" I rubbed my upper arms and wished I'd kept my sweater on.

"Yeah," he said, his tone one of disgust. "They were leaving the lab when I got there this morning. Running out of it is more like it. I told Keeter. Damn Liggon spies. They had to have killed that woman." He faced me again. "Christ, do you think they killed Seth too?"

From where we stood in the parking lot, I could see East Boulevard. I watched Tom's navy Toyota ease past the drive. None of the rest of us could get away with parking curbside as he was preparing to do.

"Sheriff Keeter thinks lots of people had cause to kill Seth. Do you agree with that, Ian?"

He didn't answer me. Instead he said, "That woman was spying for them. Did you know that, Sydney?"

"Yes," I said. "How did you know?"

He scratched his wrist, then his arm up to where his bloodied sleeve was rolled back. "Those goons destroyed her notes. It was the last of the patent work."

"But the patent's already been filed, Ian. My brother's the lawyer on it."

"That was just the initial patent, the one for the compound. Some of the delivery devices were still under development."

I wondered how Ian knew anything about the patent work. Betty had said he knew nothing about the business. "You mean the smokeless blend and the hard candy? They're not patented yet?" I felt like a fool if this was true.

"The blend's filed, but not the others. Seth didn't see the rush. Three or four devices would have been filed by next week though."

So that's why Betty had been working so feverishly. Snake was the smokeless blend, was already in FDA trials and was getting ready for market through us, but all the other means by which synthetic nicotine could be delivered were neither laid out nor protected by law.

"Tell me, Ian," I said, "why did Seth share this work with you, knowing how you felt about it?"

He stared at me, then said bluntly, "He didn't. He knew better."

"Then how do you know what's been filed and what hasn't."

He clinched his jaw. A vein popped out on his forehead. I'd tripped his anger again. How? What was Ian hiding?

"Let's go handle our business," he said, then walked in front of me into Allen Teague.

All of a sudden I was glad Tom was here to question him.

Tom and Hart were sitting in Sally's reception area. Leslie had walked to the post office for stamps.

"I told her none of us ever walk anywhere, Sydney, but she insisted." Hart didn't need to share our corporate weakness. Especially in front of Tom.

"She's young," I said. "She'll learn," I added as I smiled at Tom.

I reintroduced Hart to Ian. I wasn't sure if they had officially met out in the rainy field or not. I introduced Tom as just Tom Thurgood. No Detective Thurgood, no title today. He could talk with Ian when our meeting was over. To make certain he understood the order of things, I said, "Tom, I hope you'll excuse the three of us. We have a few minutes' worth of business to take care of."

Tom nodded and picked up an *Ad Age* magazine sitting on the table beside him. The thought of him actually reading it almost made me laugh. I made a mental note to buy a broader variety of magazines for the room. Perhaps a *Newsweek*, a *Field & Stream*, or, for Tom, *Tennis* magazine.

Leslie had neatly stacked the Bolick Enterprises paperwork on Sally's desk. I picked it up and led Hart and Ian up the steep stairs to our second-floor art department. Hart's lair, I'm fond of calling it.

Hart had cleared the conference table except for all the Bolick corporate art and the Snake logo work. As the three of us were taking our seats, I looked over at Hart's board to see what work was in progress. Immediately I wanted to cover it. There curled the animated snake of the Snake logo, only it curled, not around the stylized cigarette of its original conception, but around a variety of other objects. He must have had six or seven ideas under study. I saw a carrot, as I knew I would. And a celery stalk, but it looked top-heavy from where I sat. He'd tried it around a thermometer, but although it was graphically balanced and made sense historically, Hart didn't know that doctors would no longer care for the sick in the brave new health care world. A thermometer might imply such a possibility, encourage it even, so it would have to go. From the angle I had, the snake looked like a winding path. It spawned a quick flash of creativity. I scribbled "Path to Health" on my copy of the Bolick time sheets.

Ian wasn't very interested in the art we gave him. He had no plans, after all, to go ahead with the product. He was interested in the money Seth had paid us, most of which, I gathered, was family money. We kept just under ten thousand of the hundred thousand dollars Seth had advanced us. I should have kept more, but I decided I'd spent some time because I simply wanted to. Not because I needed to.

After Ian whistled, he said, "Lord, that's a lot of money. What did you do for that? I really don't understand."

Hart seemed to shrivel in his seat. Although he's fond of discussing finances with me, he is rarely around when a client brings up money.

"Actually it's a fairly small amount of money for the time I gave Seth," I said, hoping to be clear for him. "We each charge by the hour." I further explained everything we did carried different rates. "From seventy-five an hour to one twenty-five depending on what it is." I even went over Hart's rates. "Ian, I got so involved in Snake I didn't even charge for some of my time. I was so swept up I literally got lost in it."

He was nodding as if he understood, but I could tell he didn't. When he spoke I understood why. "Where I come from," he began, "time doesn't count for much. Only people on time are the field-workers. They come cheap."

He looked down at the balance sheet again, checked a figure off with a ballpoint pen he'd pulled out of his shirt pocket, and then looked up at me again. "Two weeks of you is the same as a decent backhoe, you know that?"

The way he said it, I must have paled in comparison. For what he could now do with the work I'd done, I'm sure that I did.

"We put our money in equipment," he said. "You Charlotte people go around charging each other for your time." He laughed. "A big game, that's what it is."

"I'm sorry," I said. I didn't know what else to say.

Each of us had restacked our sheets, I had given Ian the check, and we were in the process of standing up. It was then that I remembered the hours that Leslie had put in at Bolick Enterprises.

"She put in nine or ten hours altogether," I explained. "I was concerned she'd fall between the cracks since you didn't even know she existed." Suddenly I remembered the mysterious Mr. Little, who'd said he'd send her a check. "Who is Mr. Little, Ian?"

"Who?"

"Leslie said there was a Mr. Little at Seth's new office early Monday morning and again yesterday morning. She said he had a key, seemed to come and go like he had a reason to be there. He was even the one to let her go. So I guess he had the authority to do that too."

Ian didn't say anything, just shook his head. "I'll make sure the girl gets her check," he said. Suddenly he looked very tired. As if all that had happened in the past couple of days was descending on him at once.

I patted him on the back. "It'll all work out, Ian. The important thing is, and I believe this with all my heart, your relationship with Seth. Dead or alive, you still have a brother." I wasn't going to tell him how hard it is to set right a relationship once someone dies. How he might spend the rest of his life trying to do well what he failed to do in life.

With Ian on the landing, I stuck my head back into Hart's room. He was sitting at his art board. He hadn't said one word since the subject of money came up. "Oh, Hart," I said, loudly enough for him to look up from the hospital work. When I had his eyes, I said, "Path to Health. How's that sound?"

He tilted his head several times, then pursed his lips and nodded.

"Try it, okay? And put a human body inside that snake. It has the right proportions."

He tilted again. "Which sex?"

"Does it have to have a sex?" I asked.

His lips drew thin. "Most human bodies do."

"Well," I said, "make one up that doesn't. Play God." Honestly, Hart is always letting details keep him from exploring an idea's potential.

I led the way down the stairs. Leslie was back at Sally's desk. Before we even reached the room, I heard her putting away sheets of stamps in Sally's bottom drawer. Tom waited eagerly. I could tell by the way his rear end was now perched on the edge of the seat. Ian followed me into the room. Leslie closed the desk drawer and looked up at us.

She stammered, but she eventually got it out. "Hello, Mr. Little," she said to Ian.

20

Trying to remember the details of what happened next is difficult for me. I think sometimes fear is such a mental rush that the brain is flooded. What would normally attach itself to memory banks gets thoroughly washed out in an onslaught of adrenaline.

I do remember turning to Ian though. What Leslie said was such a shock I think I was expecting an explanation.

But Ian was staring at Tom. Tom had stood up, pulled out his identification, and was walking toward us. Maybe Ian would have reacted differently if Leslie had not recognized him. There would have been no reason for what he did otherwise.

My mouth was open to say something when Ian turned me abruptly. It was like being a partner in a violent dance. He pulled me tight against him and was pushing a small, hard object into my back just above my waist. My head didn't register what was happening until

I saw Tom's expression. I had never seen fear in his face before.

"Not a step further, do you hear?" Ian jabbed me twice with the object.

Tom stopped moving forward.

"Don't you come near me or she's dead. I've got a knife in her back and I'll use it."

Tom held his hands away from his body. He was still holding his ID. "I just want to talk with you," he said. "I'm not a threat."

Leslie began to cry.

I began to shake. No matter how hard I concentrated, I couldn't will myself to stop. I thought I had just bonded with this man. I couldn't reconcile the person who had just cried in front of me with the man who was now threatening to kill me. The transition was too quick.

"Back up against that wall. Keep your hands out like that." Ian's voice was shaking just as much as my body was. I could feel the unsteadiness of his hands as the knife jerked from point to point on my back.

As Tom backed up to the wall near the front door, Ian and I inched backwards toward the door leading to the parking lot. An image of myself dead in a ditch off Highway 29 flashed through my head. I blinked hard to get rid of it.

"Nobody wants to hurt you, Bolick. And you don't want to hurt Sydney. She hasn't done anything to hurt you." I heard the fear in Tom's voice. I wondered if Ian could hear it.

"She won't be hurt if you leave me alone."

"I am leaving you alone. Let go of her and walk out that door. We can talk later."

"I don't want to talk to the cops at all. What I had to say I told Keeter."

My office is an old house with lots of old-house features such as loose boards. The sound we all heard was unmistakable: the strident moan of an old oak plank underfoot. Poor Hart was on the stairs. Ian and I were standing beside them.

"Come down here," Ian commanded. He waited. No other sound. A full thirty seconds went by. "Now . . . or your boss loses her kidney."

The creaking of the boards began again. Hart slowly emerged at the base of the stairs. No more than a foot from where we stood. He was more pale than I've ever seen him. I would swear to seeing the large vein on his forehead throb.

"Over there," Ian said, indicating where Tom stood with a nod of his head.

Hart stumbled getting over there. Nothing was in his way. I really think his knees buckled on him. Whatever the reason, Hart was on the floor. Tom instinctively reached out to help him.

"Stop that," Ian screamed. "Don't touch him." He looked down at Hart and yelled, "Stay there. On your stomach. Spread out. Arms straight out."

Hart spread himself as if on a crucifix. He didn't even turn his head to the side, instead buried his nose directly into the kilim.

Leslie's crying had turned to a whimper. I don't believe Ian ever heard her.

At some point during the situation, I made a conscious decision not to think. Not that I hadn't tried to use my brain. It just wasn't working for me. All I could summon were visions of myself dead. When those visions were successfully blocked, one word kept attacking me. Why? Why was he doing this? Could a man love his brother and kill him still? Had Ian killed Seth, then Betty too to keep the patents from being filed? In spite of the love he professed for his brother, I didn't think anybody had as much reason to kill either one of them as Ian. But the thought of him doing it blew my mind. What he was doing to me blew my mind as well. So I blanked. I couldn't handle it. I cleared my brain completely.

I never said anything to try to save myself. And I didn't try any heroic moves either. I was totally incapable. Tom told me later I looked like a deer caught in headlights.

"She and I are leaving now," Ian said with increasing resolve in his voice. "If any of you move before we're out of the parking lot, you'll be responsible for her death."

The room was silent.

"I want to hear you say it. Say you understand that. You, cop, say you understand those consequences."

Tom nodded.

Ian screamed, "Say it!"

"I understand, Bolick."

"You on the floor. Say it."

Hart's muffled voice managed "I understand." He must have eaten some fibers in the process.

Leslie whispered it but not to Ian's satisfaction.

"Can't hear you," he said. So she said it again, this time meeting his invisible standard.

We backed out the door. Behind me, he dragged me. My feet lost their step, tangled on his shoes. He lifted me until I could find the floor again. His weight was on my back.

Until this moment skydiving had been the most terrifying moment of my life. Not sailing out in the air. That part was exhilarating. The frightening moment was the second I left the plane. The instructor pushed me out backwards. The weight of the gear on my back tilted my body out the door and away from the plane. Ian felt like that gear now as the door began to close after us. What I saw were the horrified faces of my friends. The skydiving instructor had told me it would have been scarier for me had I been looking at the open sky when he pushed. I disagreed. There is nothing more frightening, I told him, than watching what you are leaving, where you know you are safe, and having no power to stay.

It was almost five o'clock. East Boulevard was carrying a full load of cars and trucks. From behind my building, the sound was a deep, steady hum like a harmonica on the low notes. I remember being cold. The sun had fallen behind the trees and would be gone within the hour. Everything was gray, on its way to black.

Ian pushed me into the truck through the driver's door. "Don't move," he said once he was behind the wheel.

I finally said something. "This is stupid" was my one and only contribution. I wonder now what I could have said that might have made a difference. Something wise. Something to defuse him or at least divert him. He'd told me enough about who he was that I should have been able to find those magic words. But I didn't. It occurred to me more than once, however, that Ian wasn't who he said he was. So which Ian would I talk to anyway?

He stripped his gears going into reverse too quickly, then again shifting to first. His leg was shaking too badly to hold the clutch all the way down. Cupped between his right hand and the steering wheel was a large Swiss army knife. It was folded, and I realized from the memory of its shape against my back that it had been folded the whole time.

As we were almost to the end of the driveway, about twenty yards from the street, I noticed how very heavy the traffic was right then. At this time of day I'd sat at this spot for twenty minutes just waiting to be let into the traffic. What was Ian going to do if nobody let us in? How was he going to make his escape when nothing was moving less than forty miles an hour and no lanes were open?

I was thinking he'd probably just bulldoze the truck on into the traffic. Bang up any fool who didn't stop for him. That's what I would have done. I thought about putting on my seat belt, as if that safety precaution was all I might need.

I actually had my hand on the belt when Tom backed his Toyota across our exit. It was too late for Ian to stop. I don't believe he would have even if he'd been able to. His choices were limited now. Besides, he'd made the decision to run. We hit the passenger side of the Toyota going about twenty miles an hour. Thank God Tom had gotten out, because the impact turned the Toyota and sent the driver's side into the oncoming traffic.

As Ian struggled to turn the truck and move it around the wrecked Toyota, Tom opened my door. He pulled my arm with so much strength I tumbled into the dwarf hollies that run along that side of the building. A hundred pointed leaves all bit me at once. I may as well have landed on a hornet's nest.

The pain kept me from standing up, from seeing what happened next. I heard it though. The truck's rattling acceleration, the screech of brakes, Tom yelling above the horns and sounds of metal hitting metal.

Suddenly four or five police cars were in the road and up on my sidewalk. I could see as far as the sidewalk. The hostage-trained tactical unit was there too, its van doors sliding open and five black-clad and heavily padded men and women spilling into the yard. I found out later Hart had called 911 when Ian first took hold of me. The mistake he made was deciding to eavesdrop while waiting for them to show up.

I heard Tom yelling orders. I was relieved to hear his voice. His first order was for someone to call an ambulance, then he quickly yelled to call for another one. I stayed in those bushes as long as I could. A part of the reason was the difficulty I knew I'd have in standing up. The spread of the hollies was such that my hands couldn't find ground. If I were going to hoist myself to a stand, I'd have to press against more prickly leaf endings to do it. I couldn't make myself endure more pain. I knew instinctively, though, that the greater pain was seeing what had happened on the street. I stayed right where I was. Even when Hart stood before me and offered to help.

"No, no," I said. "I'll get up in a minute."

"Doesn't it hurt?" he asked.

"Not anymore," I said.

He left and returned with Tom, who asked me if I'd broken anything.

"A stem or a limb?" I asked.

"Not a good time to crack jokes, Sydney," he said.

I couldn't help it. I was still scared. Every bit of that tension was still with me. It all had to do, I knew, with what I'd see if I stood up.

"I'm sending you in an ambulance," he said.

"No. I won't go."

"Decision's made," he said. "The department's not going to be liable for you too."

"But nothing's wrong with me."

"It's standard procedure. I have to. I'll follow you in your car, okay?" He turned away, left me there in those bushes.

Why did I think that by not looking at the street and by not asking Tom what had happened, I could make it go away? I was like a crawling infant who covers her eyes and, in doing so, makes herself go away.

I let the attendants step into the sprawling hollies and lift me. To their credit, they were gentle and knew to angle me straight up so that no new dagger could impale me. They rolled me on a gurney across the lawn, across the bump of the sidewalk, and into the street. I leaned my head to the side and saw a second ambulance adjacent to several cars that seemed to have come together in an ill-timed do-si-do. A man sat in that ambulance, the door open. Blood was covering his face. A female attendant was bandaging his head.

I looked around for Ian, was afraid I'd see him lying in the street. Other than the bleeding man and three or four wrecked cars, I saw nothing else. The Chevy truck was gone and so was Ian.

Tom climbed up into the ambulance just as the two attendants were hooking me up to a glucose drip.

"I'm fine," I said. "Why are you doing that?"

"Possible shock," one said.

"Precaution," said the other.

"Because it's their job," Tom said. "Let them do it."

I looked down at my left arm as I lay there. Twenty or thirty small red spots covered it. The rest of my body must have had hundreds of these little mounds of blood. Every surface vein in my body must have been pricked by the holly bushes. I felt stupid that it hurt so badly.

"Where's Ian?" I asked Tom.

He leaned over me, kissed me on the lips, and whispered, "I'm sorry I hurt you, Sydney. We'll find Ian. Don't worry. We'll find him."

21

Why had Tom's presence been such a threat to Ian? He said he'd already talked with Keeter. Why not repeat what he had to say to Tom? Why'd he concoct such a charade at Seth's office? This Mr. Little persona. What was it all about? He was on the board, after all. He could have said he was there for all sorts of legitimate reasons. Why'd he feel the need to lie? Ian had told me, as we stood in his tobacco fields, he'd be willing to do whatever it took to keep Snake from becoming a product. Could he have meant even murder?

Hart and Leslie followed my ambulance to Carolinas Medical. It's less than five minutes from my office, so Hart didn't have to do any heroics to accomplish that. In spite of saying he'd follow me in the Trooper, Tom wasn't there when the men wheeled me into the emergency entrance. The attendants handed my paperwork to an intake nurse, who looked at me, then at the paperwork and left me in a corner of the wide hallway while she went in search of more-needy patients.

"I'll give them thirty minutes," I said as I lay there. "If they don't feel the need to see me by then, I'm leaving. I could care less about the police department's liability."

Hart rolled his eyes. Leslie, the young and inexperienced girl that she was, said, "Oh, Ms. Teague, you don't mean that, do you?"

I was flat on my back. The IV had been removed. I rested my hands on my stomach, watched my thumbs twiddle, and thought about how I could figure out what was driving Ian Bolick so hard. If I could go through the files at the Bolick Enterprises office, maybe I'd find some answers. Something had to be worth looking at there for Ian to have done what he did.

Ian's timing had been strange though. At the very time he'd been posing as Mr. Little in Seth's office, Seth had been inhaling the fumes that would kill him. That alone didn't mean Ian was innocent of Seth's murder. He could have tampered with that nebulizer long before Seth used it. Seth didn't use the inhaler daily. What had he told me? He'd said his asthma wasn't bad. That he medicated only when he exercised or on cold mornings. I was certain that's what he'd told me. I thought back to Monday morning. It had been cold, probably the first morning this fall that signs of winter were in the air. Whoever tampered with his inhaler could have done it a long time before Monday morning. But if that person knew Seth well, they would know, as I did, that he would use it that morning. So . . . my circuitous thinking led me to one overriding conclusion: Ian would have known Seth would use that inhaler Monday morning. Therefore, there would have been no reason for him to masquerade as someone else when coming to the Bolick Enterprises office. If Ian had tampered with Seth's medicine, he would have known his brother was dying or dead. For that reason, more than any other, I decided Ian was innocent. At least of Seth's murder.

Leslie still had the Bolick Enterprises NationsBank keys. She agreed to go with me to check for missing files. Hart had driven her to the hospital, though, so I needed him to go with us as well.

"I think you're crazy," Hart said. "Everybody associated with that company has died, in case you haven't noticed."

"Not in the middle of uptown Charlotte, they haven't."

He thought about what I said, narrowing his eyebrows and looking genuinely mad at me for confusing him. "Nobody said the link was geographic, Sydney."

Leslie said, "Mr. Johnson, I don't think it's dangerous in the NationsBank building on a Wednesday evening. They have real good security."

"If you're so worried about us, Hart, why don't you go with us?" I stared at him without so much as a blink.

He began shaking his head, but it didn't look like a negative shake. It looked instead like more of the exasperation I'd seen building in him. He began to stare back at me as I had at him.

We were in a stare-off when Tom arrived. When I look back on it, neither Hart nor I was being such a great role model for poor Leslie.

"Why haven't you been seen?" Tom said before anything else. "Where are the ambulance attendants?" Tom handed me my pocketbook. "I thought you might need this. It's certainly heavy enough."

By now Leslie, Hart, and I were all three sitting on the edge of my stretcher. I suppose to Tom we looked as if we were socializing. I told him nobody had come by to look at me. "The attendants don't stay, Tom. They have work to do. They gave some paperwork to a nurse, then were gone."

"Where's that nurse, then?"

I pointed in the general direction of the intake desk, and Tom headed that way. Hart slid off the gurney.

"I guess I'll go on home," he said.

"You can't, Hart." I looked at Leslie, then back at him. "You're our transportation. I saw you two get out of your Jetta."

"Doesn't Tom have your car?" Hart seemed anxious. He forgot to close his mouth.

I nodded. "I'm in no shape to drive him or anybody else. He can call someone to meet him at my house. You're my ride, Hart." I raised my eyebrows and gave him a questioning smile, not sure which way he would go on me.

Hart challenged me. "You told me you felt fine."

"Relative term, Hart. Please. We'll only be in the building five minutes."

"It takes five minutes just to ride the elevator, Sydney," he said with great satisfaction, as if correcting me was his victory.

He could have his moral victory as long as he would drive. "You're right, Hart," I said in defeat. "Fifteen minutes, then. Five going up, five in the office, and five coming back down."

His nod looked more like a pout to me. "Okay," he said. "Just promise me that's all it'll be."

"I promise. So does Leslie," I added. I looked at the eager girl. Leslie didn't have a clue why we were going to her old office.

Tom reappeared with a female nurse who asked Hart if he was Sydney Teague. Although this wasn't the first time someone had made that assumption, Hart's cheeks blushed anyway. Everyone turned their heads toward me as I raised my hand. She asked me if I could walk. I admit that question flushed my cheeks just a bit.

"I'm fine really," I said as I slid off the gurney. I nodded at Tom. "This was his idea. The city of Charlotte doesn't want to be liable."

"Just check her out," Tom said, sounding like a man about to embark on a long road trip with his trusty old car.

I told Tom he could leave since I had Leslie and Hart with me. "Get one of your men to follow you to my house. You've got a lot to do, I'm sure," I added and knew it had to be true.

"What about Joanie and George? What should I tell them?"

I knew what he meant. Would they be worried if they knew where I was? Would they wonder why I wasn't driving my car?

"Tell them you wrecked your car. After all, that's the truth. And tell them I'm running a little late. Hart will drive me through somewhere so I'll bring our dinner home." Hart made a small martyrlike sound; out of the corner of my eye I saw him fold his arms. Five more minutes for a drive-thru wasn't going to kill him. Sheesh, I thought, just wait until he needs the slightest thing from me.

Tom agreed he had a lot to do. He left saying he'd give the kids my message. He'd call me tonight.

My pocketbook was still on the gurney. I reached for it before following the nurse. Tom had been right. The damn thing had gained five pounds since the last time I carried it. I opened it hurriedly as I walked toward the treatment rooms. No wonder. The druggist's bag with the inhalers and stomach medicine was still inside.

"Don't all those scratches hurt?" the nurse asked as she dabbed my scores of holly wounds with some form of alcohol.

We were in a tiny treatment room, not much larger than the room at Wade where Dr. Fritz had taken me to talk about Sally. I was lying on a table with all my clothes removed.

"Sort of," I answered her as I lay there. "Whatever you're putting on me is helping though."

She smiled.

"Can I ask you a question about something? Can I show you something I have in my pocketbook and you tell me what you think?"

"What is it?" she asked, then stood back from me. "Sit up now. I need to get your back. You've got hundreds of these scratches."

"Some medicines," I said. I followed her instructions and swung my legs over the side of the table.

"I'll answer what I can," she said as she continued working. "Let me finish you up first. Hmm, what happened to you?"

"There were several bushes, all planted in a row. I ended up in them."

"What kind of bushes were they?" She continued to dab.

"Dwarf holly. Burfordii, I think."

"Good to know. I'll never plant them at my house after seeing what they've done to you."

"Hopefully no one will ever throw you into any bush," I said a bit sarcastically.

She chuckled. "This happened at work?"

"Uh-huh."

"What do you do for a living?"

"Advertising."

We laughed together. I never did tell her that my alternative to holly bushes was possibly a knife wound or two.

When she had finished sterilizing me, she handed me back my clothes, which I wadded loosely in my lap while I pulled the Hutchins Drugstore bag out of my pocketbook. I ripped open the staples and poured the contents beside me onto the gurney.

The nurse leaned over the two inhalers and the container of disks. "What have we here? You have stomach problems and asthma too?"

"No. The stomach medicine's mine, but I want to ask you about the asthma medicine. About the container part that holds the medicine itself. How hard is it to take the medicine out that's in there and put new medicine in?"

She didn't react as if my question was crazy or even out of the ordinary. She'd probably seen and heard much stranger requests here in the emergency room. She picked up one of the containers and examined it all around, finally focusing on the top where it connects to the sprayer when attached. She pointed at that small area.

"This is soft plastic here," she said. "The tube from the sprayer perforates this plastic to access the medicine. You can squeeze the medicine out once the plastic is pierced." She began putting the nebulizers back into the bag.

"What about replacing it with another medicine?" I asked as nonchalantly as I could feign.

"Well, that would be harder." She stopped and studied the soft plastic again. "But not impossible. A hypodermic or something like a hypodermic could introduce another substance."

"Thanks," I said.

"I can't recommend experimenting like that though. If you're planning on mixing medications, you could get yourself in lots of trouble."

I put the disk bottle back into the bag with the inhalers. "Oh, it's not for me. It's not for anybody really. I'm just wondering."

She raised her eyebrows. I'm sure it sounded lame. "Experimenting with the antacids too?"

"The little disks?" I put the bag into my pocketbook. "No, they're for me."

She asked me to describe the stomach pains. I told her it was sharp, but I didn't tell her the pain was like barbed wire. She was suspicious enough of me already.

"Sounds like an ulcer," she said. "You under much stress?"

"No," I lied.

22

Uptown Charlotte at night used to be as deserted as an abandoned movie set. Like a lot of cities, it lost its anchor department stores to the malls in the seventies, and although big banking took off in the eighties and revitalized uptown, bankers go home at five. Even the restaurants that had begun to creep into the center city were open only at lunch. Uptown was so dull that when Charlotte hosted the NCAA Final Four in 1994, it had to erect a temporary nightclub district so our visitors would have somewhere to go at night. In the past couple of years the trend has finally begun to reverse itself. Whoever decided to put Ericsson Stadium uptown when we won the NFL franchise put excitement back into the city too. Now the old abandoned Ivey's department store is even being converted to condos. Uptown still can't compete with the malls at night, but at least I see people other than security guards and the homeless there.

But that night it was security guards, the Nations-Bank Corporate Center guards. Of course they'd be there. I don't know why I wasn't expecting them. Luckily Leslie had identification still, and the three of us were let inside. If Ian had known what he was doing, he would have let them know she was no longer an employee. He also would have asked for her keys.

In spite of Hart's stopwatch approach to this foray, I paused at Ben Long's triptych frescoes in the lobby. I always do. The paintings haunt me with their religious style and color on images of robotlike workers and menacing overlords. The work is Dante's *Inferno* for corporate America, visions of hell for modern man. Why would a bank commission such a depressing portrait of capitalism?

"Move," said Hart.

We took the elevator to the fortieth floor, where Leslie used her key to get us inside. I noticed the Bolick Enterprises sign I'd ordered two weeks ago. It had arrived and the sign company had put it on the door exactly as Hart had specified in our order. My breath caught when I saw it. Hart's did too.

"Anything else we need to cancel, Sydney?" he asked.

I couldn't tell by his tone if he was seriously asking me or if it was merely more of his sarcasm. "Maybe we need to meet about that," I said in case he was serious.

The reception room was as I remembered it, including the armless chair Leslie had such a hard time controlling. Leslie flicked all the switches on a wall panel, throwing both office hallways into bright fluorescent light.

"Which way did Ian—Mr. Little—go when he was here Monday and yesterday?" I asked Leslie.

She pointed to the right, so I went down the hall. Other than a bathroom, all I saw was a conference room with a traditional long, rectangular table, a wide-screen TV inside a state-of-the-art media center, and a copier behind a tastefully carved mahogany screen.

"What's down the other hall?" I asked her.

"Mr. Bolick's office. It's where he interviewed me for the job."

"Did Ian go to Seth's office while you were here?"

She sat in a chair by the door and dangled her keys. "Yes, he brought paperwork out of there. And he took it into that room." She pointed toward the conference room.

I walked into Ian's office. The furniture was sparse: desk, file cabinet, credenza, desk chair, and an odd chair that looked as if it belonged to his personal bridge set. A portable computer lay atop the credenza, with a combination printer and fax beside it. I pushed the desk chair out of the way, stooped down, and started looking inside the credenza. The corporate checkbook and financial records were there but not much else that Ian would be interested in. I didn't really think he'd be interested in the books either. Money, in and of itself, was not what motivated either of the Bolick brothers.

The file cabinet was a different story. An entire drawer held patent information, including the Snake patent itself. Ian wouldn't gain anything by copying this stuff, I thought, because the patent was a matter of public record. The next drawer held FDA paperwork though. During the next year this drawer would have overflowed with paper, given the volumes that agency tends to produce. I supposed there were lots of people who'd have made good use of these files if they had access to them. A third drawer Seth had set up for marketing and investors. All my correspondence and proposed plans were in this drawer. Seeing it made me sad, wistful. Like finding copies of old love letters when the love hadn't ended the way it should have. I squatted at the bottom to go through it but found only two files, both of which he'd labeled Miscellaneous. His office lease was in there, as were owner's manuals for the equipment he'd purchased just last week.

What would Ian have been after? Was it all the paperwork or something more specific? I remembered the tobacco growers' association and what Tom had found out. Ian was an officer of that group and so was Keeter. Everything in these drawers no doubt affected the future of growers everywhere. If that's why Ian was in this office, then Keeter would know about it.

I returned to the reception room, where I'd left my pocketbook.

"Can I help?" Leslie asked. She was still sitting in the chair by the door.

"Thanks, but I don't see anything obviously out of place or missing. Do you?" I was sifting through my pocketbook in search of my checkbook and deposit slips, where I'd written Keeter's phone number.

Hart had stationed himself behind the desk in the receptionist's chair. He made a show of looking at his watch. The smirk etched on his face was part of the performance as well.

"I'm almost through here, Hart. I'm still at less than five minutes, aren't I?"

"You don't appear hurt to me, Sydney."

So that's what was bothering him. "I told you that was relative. Do you want me to lift my skirt so you can see where those bushes attacked me?"

He didn't answer.

"Would it make you feel better if I were to limp?"

He shook his head, then crossed his arms. When he did, his chair shot backwards across the floor. He was trying to pull himself up to the desk as I left the room to look for Leslie again.

She was going through the file cabinet just as I had.

"Find anything out of place?"

She closed the drawer and turned to me. "I don't really know. Mr. Bolick showed me what was in each drawer, but I don't remember what was where. It does seem to all be here though."

I nodded as I picked up the phone to dial Keeter's number. He probably wouldn't tell me anything, but I still had to ask. If my hunch was right, Keeter knew exactly why Ian was sneaking around here.

Bert answered as she had this morning. When I asked for the sheriff, she hesitated, obviously reluctant. "He's tired and upset, Ms. Teague. I'm getting ready to feed him. Can't whatever this is wait until tomorrow?"

"I promise I'll take only a minute of his time."

She was silent.

"Bert, is he upset about Ian? About what Ian did over in Charlotte?"

"How did you know about that?"

"I'm the one he held at knifepoint. Have the police found him yet?"

"Good Lord, girl. I didn't know. Last we heard, they haven't found him, no. The sheriff's in the basement listening to his scanner. Your man issued an all-points on Ian."

She said that last sentence as if Tom should be tarred and feathered for putting out the APB. We were both silent for a few seconds.

"Can I speak to the sheriff now, please?"

I listened as she called her husband. Her voice grew more faint, and I realized she'd had to leave the room to get him. I used the time to think about what to say. I had no idea how Keeter was going to react to me.

When he picked up the phone, he did sound tired. And, I supposed, depressed as well. He'd probably been friends with Ian all his life. I couldn't help it though. I saw no reason in beating around the bush because of that friendship.

"Why was Ian copying Bolick papers, Sheriff?"

He didn't answer me, but then I didn't give him a whole bunch of time either. I took his hesitation for guilt. Of course he'd be in on it. I should have known that instinctively.

"Why did the two of you do this to Seth?"

He spoke then. "That's not fair" was all he said.

"What's not fair?"

"We didn't have anything against Seth. Ian loved his fool brother. It was what he was doing."

"Who were you funneling your copies to? The Liggon Tobacco Group?"

His laugh was tinged with sarcasm. "They didn't

want our help. They had their own source. You know that now."

How did he know that? If Tom Thurgood told him, Tom would get a piece of my mind. Why couldn't Tom see that Keeter was the enemy?

"Did Tom Thurgood tell you about Betty?"

"Tom Thurgood? Hell, no. We've known about Betty from the moment Liggon planted her. Everybody else was happy to get our reports." He tried laughing again. This time the sarcasm wasn't there.

"Sheriff Keeter, who is 'everyone,' if not Liggon?"

"Everybody who needed them. Everybody we could think of."

"Other tobacco companies?"

"Yeah. All of 'em."

"And other growers' associations? You sent them copies too?"

"Of course. And Friends of Tobacco and the Tobacco Institute. Everybody whose livelihood depends on tobacco."

I couldn't believe what I was hearing. The extent of this spying never entered my mind. I felt certain Seth hadn't thought about it either.

"How long have you and Ian been copying Seth's paperwork?"

"About two years, I guess. Ever since he started sending papers back and forth to the patent office. We all just laughed at him until that started."

"Why did you do it?"

"Ian and I talked about it. We just couldn't see not letting the industry know what was happening out there in that little lab. Wouldn't you appreciate bulletins—

status reports—if the world was coming to an end?" He waited as if he really expected an answer to that baited question. I wasn't about to jump in on that one.

"Not a damn thing wrong with Ian copying from Bolick Enterprises, Miss Teague. Not a damn thing."

Keeter sounded very sure of himself. I think he truly believed neither he nor Ian had done anything wrong. Ian's actions at my office told me he knew though. He was afraid he'd been uncovered. Tom's showing his ID was all it took to turn him into a frightened man. I was still not convinced, though, that he wasn't afraid of being caught in something bigger than conspiracy.

I sighed into the phone's receiver. "Sheriff, you should know better. What you and Ian did was illegal."

"No, it wasn't," he said. "It was Ian's company as well as Seth's. Legally anyway. He could do what he wanted." He was starting to sound defensive.

"No, he couldn't. Not with a corporation. As a board member, he was charged with taking care of it, not raping it."

Keeter snorted into the phone. "Ian is a hero in my book." He paused. "I hope they never find him."

"Seth was my hero," I said, but I don't know why I told him that.

"Well, it looks like we got different philosophies, Miss Teague. Don't it?"

Hart was motioning to me and looking at his watch. Hell of a time for me to be under his thumb. I turned my back to him.

"I got those Liggon boys. Picked 'em up headed

back to Forsyth. Got 'em together in my only cell." He said it with pride.

"You do know they ran my secretary off the road, don't you?"

"Done a damn sight worse than that." He snorted again.

"Are you telling me you think the Liggon men killed Seth and Betty?"

"Who else, Miss Teague? Those boys don't follow no damn rules."

Look who's talking, I thought but didn't say. "Do you have proof they killed them?" I asked.

"I don't know what I have tonight. I'm having myself some dinner, then going to bed. The sun's done gone down."

He hung up.

"We've been here twenty-two minutes," said Hart.

23

I was eating Colonel Horton's Fried Chicken in the kitchen with my children. The two of them were discussing mutual friends. Gossiping, I supposed, although George junior didn't know that's what he was doing. I was grateful to be left out. I needed to sort through things.

Nothing was as it seemed. At least that's how it all sequestered itself inside my head. Three days ago two people were alive who were now dead, Seth a supposed suicide and Betty a brutal murder. I didn't understand why either of them died. I thought back to Monday and how I hadn't even suspected anything when Seth died. In fact, I would have assumed it a cruel accident of fate that happens to more of us than we like to admit. If all of Wade County hadn't been so determined to write him off as a suicide, that's where it would have stayed with me. An accident. As Tom says, you don't go looking for murder. I would have thought Ian murdered him, if he hadn't shown me how much he loved his brother. Or did he merely love his idea of a brother, a brother he never really had? A cynical little voice in the back of my head was saying brotherly love didn't matter in this case, that Ian still could have killed Seth. I didn't want to listen to that voice. I like emotions to stand alone, uncluttered clean, ringing true. Not this smoke screen I was getting from everybody. And what was I to make of Betty? Hers was the most arcane agenda of all. She'd truly seemed devoted to Seth. Can a person be devoted and still murder the object of her devotion? I didn't think so, but my thinking hadn't been the most logical throughout this whole week. But who killed Betty? The men who employed her? If she was on their side, that hypothesis made no sense. But, to make matters even more complicated, if she was on their side, Betty was likely to have killed Seth. But what did she mean when she said "Love Seth" to Ian? Maybe I identified too closely with Seth and couldn't see any more clearly than he could before he died. Was it possible, after all these revelations, that Seth killed himself after all? If he'd found out the people he trusted were all out to get him, he just might have chosen to deal with it the way people have for centuries. To be completely honest, that amount of betrayal would surely have overwhelmed me.

"Earth to Mom," Joan said as George junior waved his hands in front of my face.

I blinked, then clapped my hands around George junior's as if his wiggling fingers were late summer flies.

"You're quick," he said with admiration.

I smiled. "Don't ever forget where you get your eye-hand coordination."

"Dad says we get that from him," he said.

Joan and I locked eyes and laughed.

She said, "Then why did Mom beat him at singles all the time?"

George junior said almost sheepishly, "Dad says she didn't. He calls it 'Mom's Myth.'"

I put a biscuit in my mouth. "Your father's a liar," I said, although the bread distorted my words. I swallowed a good portion of it, sipped some Pepsi.

I picked out the largest, most perfectly formed breast from the bucket in the center of the table and bit into it. Its facade crumbled. Literally. What had appeared to be a sturdy rib cage was the placement of individual little bones that weren't attached to anything. There was no structure to the breast at all. I picked up a thigh and examined it as well. Same thing. The thigh bone, which normally runs all the way through a piece, was missing. Instead, small vestiges of bone bulged at two ends, giving the illusion of a whole bone. These were rebuilt chickens, no different than rebuilt motors for cars. No, even worse. Cars are rebuilt to be as they were before. This chicken was an imposter, all facade and surface succulence. Why would anybody do this to a chicken when all they had to do was drop it in the deep-fat fryer and count some minutes off on a timer? I pushed myself away from the table without eating another bite.

"May I have that piece?" Joan asked me. "I just love Horton's."

"Me too," said George junior. "I thought you liked it too, Mom."

"I do, I guess," I said as I stood up. "But I'm running out of steam tonight."

He grabbed for the thigh I left on my plate. He looked up at me and said, "Mom, what are those spots on your neck?"

"What spots?" I asked, automatically putting both hands on my neck.

Both of them said, "You have spots everywhere."

Ah, the attack of the holly bushes. I would have thought they'd seen my holly wounds before now. So I told them I fell into my office bushes. They laughed long and hard. Their laughing made me tired.

I was reminded again of how small the intersection between my life and my kids' lives really was. I was the only one who could expand that territory and include them in my world. But something in me didn't want to. My world included Seth and Betty's murders, and I wanted to protect them from that. They needed their innocence; I needed their innocence too. I wanted them to love people, not to be suspicious of them. My dad probably rationalized the way I was doing tonight. The daily drama of a courtroom wasn't something to share with your kids. No wonder I knew nothing about his work. For all my children knew, I took a break from writing ad copy, went for a walk on this beautiful autumn day, and tripped during the stroll.

I don't believe I had ever even mentioned Seth's name, which isn't unusual, since I rarely talk about work at home. They did know Sally, though, and were, in fact, close to her. I should have told them she'd been hurt. One question usually leads to another, and before you know it, you're into a conversation you don't want to have. Is this how Dad had been with me? Avoiding the tough issues until one day they could be avoided no longer?

The phone rang. Joan took it out of George junior's hands as he was attempting to answer it. I frowned at her. George junior looked mad. In another year or two she wouldn't be able to get away with bullying him like that.

Her eyes lit up. She slipped quickly into her little girl voice. Even if Joan hadn't spoken her name, I would have know from Joan's voice the caller was my mother. "Granny" treats Joan as if she's still ten years old. For my mother, Joan gladly plays the part.

"Granny wants to know what day to come to Charlotte for Thanksgiving," Joan said, holding the phone away from her mouth.

"Whenever she wants. That's what she's going to do anyway," I said loudly enough for Mother to hear.

Joan talked to Mother for a few more minutes, then gave the phone to George junior. Mother had moved to Asheville in North Carolina's mountains ten years ago. When the children were little, we'd visit her for the holidays. Now she came here. But she always makes such a big deal about not wanting to interrupt our schedules. I'm of the opinion it's all show, because, as I said, she ends up doing exactly what she wants in the end no matter what she says up front.

George junior handed the phone to me. She and I talked about which one of us had the best fresh turkey source for a few minutes, then what she would bake before driving down. She wanted to know numbers, specifically who I was inviting.

"Will that nice policeman you've been dating be there?" she asked.

"We haven't talked about Thanksgiving. I don't know."

"You should have, Sydney. It's a week from tomorrow." She breathed heavily through her nose, which is one of her ways to show displeasure with me. Her repertoire is quite extensive.

"I don't know," I said. It wasn't that I hadn't noticed it on the calendar every time I looked at it. In the scheme of things, however, the date seemed forever distant. "I've been busy," I added.

"You're always busy. You should stay at home with your kids more."

"I'm not landed gentry, Mother. Besides, they're busy too. I'd be at home by myself."

Joan whispered to me, "Don't argue with Granny."

I suppose to her that's what it seemed we were doing. I'd never thought of my conversations with Mother as arguments though. I felt certain Mother didn't either. Our disagreements sprang from generational gaps that didn't exist between Joan and me. The cultural distance between Mother and me is three times the distance between me and Joan. Oddly, though, Mother and Joan understand each other better than Mother and I ever will.

"Your father insisted on family times, you know. They are very important to children. You should make more of them, Sydney."

"I agree, Mother." I wasn't placating her. I did

agree. "I've been thinking a lot about Dad recently. More than I have in a long time."

What she said then had become her mantra over the years, I'd heard it so often: "Your father was a wonderful man." Then she added, "He cared so much about you, honey. He just wanted you to be happy."

"I know, Mother. I know. I've just been thinking about him a lot. Do you remember the Samson Hall case?"

"Of course I remember. That was a terrible time for him. You too, honey."

"I was so mad at Dad for not telling me he was going to defend him until that morning it was all over the newspaper. Do you remember that?"

"Yes, honey." Her voice had grown soft. "Why do you want to bring this up again, Sydney? Your father wasn't trying to hurt you."

"That's not my point, Mother. I know he wasn't. I've known that for years now. He'd never have done anything to hurt one of us. Not if he could help it," I added, knowing all too well some things are beyond our control.

"What I want to know," I continued, "is how long Dad knew he was going to defend Samson Hall. How long before the paper announced it? Do you remember?"

"He always knew."

"What do you mean by 'always'?"

"Why, the day after it happened. He told me it didn't add up. He told me that little girl must have been so traumatized she didn't know who'd hurt her. He just didn't want to upset you with his thoughts."

"Upset me? How could that have upset me?" It was the first I'd ever heard any of this.

"Sydney, it would have. Believe me. Your father didn't know who did it. He only knew Samson Hall didn't. Everybody needed someone to be guilty." She paused, then continued more softly. "Including you, honey. Your father didn't know how to tell you. You were only sixteen. We talked about it. He came close to telling you several times. He said he couldn't bear making you unhappy. But, Sydney, he had to do what he had to do. You never understood that."

I couldn't bear hearing this all again, but I needed to. "Yes, Mother, I did understand. Just not for a long time."

I had started to cry. My children were staring at me in total confusion.

"Mother, tell me something. Okay?"

"Why are you crying, Sydney?"

"Answer something for me," I said through my tears. "Did Dad ever say he forgave me for being so damn self-centered? Did he?"

She was quiet for a few seconds before answering. "He didn't feel there was anything to forgive, Sydney. He blamed himself for not telling you sooner. He always said it would have been different if he had."

I should have suspected as much from my dad. No matter what he did in that difficult situation, he'd been prepared to blame himself for my reaction.

Later I bathed, then discussed Napoleon and Hitler with George junior for about an hour. I still didn't understand why his social studies teacher was assigning the two together.

Tom called just before ten. I'd been deciding what

to wear to Seth's funeral and had chosen a basic navy suit with a red shell and pearls. I'd also found the stone Seth gave me in the pocket of my corduroy jacket. I was sitting on the edge of my bed studying the stone when the phone rang. I picked it up before Joan could.

Tom confirmed what Keeter had told me about the Liggon men. They'd been stopped on Highway 52, headed back, it appeared, to Forsyth County. When questioned about Betty, the men expressed horror themselves. They said the lab had been destroyed by someone before they got there and that Betty lay dying in a pool of blood.

"Do you believe them?" I asked.

"I don't know. We still have questions."

"Don't we all," I said. "Why didn't they help her?"

"They panicked when Ian's truck pulled up. At least that's what they told us."

"Panicked about what? For God's sake, the woman was dying. They might have been able to help her. There's no excuse for leaving her there."

Tom sighed. "There's no law in this country about panicking, Sydney. We've got them on hit-and-run with Sally, leaving the scene. And they've got trespassing charges and a host of other charges related to the spying. Don't worry. They're not going anywhere."

Some consolation, I thought. "What if they did murder Betty and Seth?"

"We'll find out if they did," he said, although the confidence I usually hear in his voice wasn't there.

"Good Lord, Tom. What's going on here? What were those men after?"

"The tapes. Just as you suspected. They were hell-bent on monitoring everything Seth produced. They admitted all of it. They said the whole tobacco industry's been watching for well over a year."

We were both silent.

Tom then said, "You didn't know any of that was going on the whole time you were working with Bolick?"

"No," I said and sighed. I decided not to tell him about looking through Seth's files tonight or about my conversation with Keeter. I could tell him tomorrow. He wouldn't see Keeter until then anyway. Tom trusted him though. My information would most likely change that.

He said he'd pick me up at nine thirty for the eleven o'clock funeral service in Bredon.

"Can we leave a little earlier than that?" I asked. "I need to make a couple of stops."

"Okay, Sydney. You name it. I'm just your chauffeur tomorrow. What time do you want me at your house?"

Bless Tom Thurgood. I don't know what I would have done without him during this whole confusing time. He was the one sure thing I could hold on to, a man who is always exactly as he seems. As for everybody and everything else, especially what I'd experienced in Wade County, it all seemed somehow veiled.

After we said good night, I checked on the children and walked around the house turning out lights. As I did, I rubbed the lapillus absentmindedly. I returned to my bedroom and sat on the edge of my bed.

Seth had told me his father had brought the stone

home from a trip, one of his many trips to the Far East. A lapillus was a stone ejected from an active volcano, he'd explained. Unlike the rock formed of lava flow, which is porous and so full of air it hardly looks like rock at all, this stone came instead from the very center of volcanic activity. There, I suppose, the fire is so intense no air intrudes, no smoke exudes, and the flame itself burns white. I held the glassy stone up to the lamp's bulb on my bedside table. I'd once told Seth the dark gray swirling patterns looked like veins seeking a heart. He'd laughed at the time and called my observation "wishful, at best. An illusion, Sydney. That's what you want to see," he'd said. "The stone's power is in the rub."

I peered more closely at the small stone. The patterns trapped inside were too vague to be veins; he was right about that. Now the patterns looked like swirling smoke. As if the heat had trapped volcanic smoke before it could escape. The lapillus then became its capsule, holding the smoke forever.

I yawned, then slipped under the covers, pulling up my grandmother's old quilt for the first time this season. The phone rang just as I was reaching to turn out the light. I grabbed it quickly so it wouldn't wake the kids. My brother Bill wanted to know why I hadn't called him, hadn't kept him informed.

"Informed about what?" I asked. Had Mother called him assuming I'd asked him and wife there for Thanksgiving? This sort of miscommunication happens all the time in my family. To head it off, I added, "If this is about Thanksgiving, Bill, I haven't called anyone yet. I've been too busy."

"I couldn't care less about Thanksgiving," he said. "Why didn't you tell me Ian Bolick went off the deep end? He's my client, for Christ's sake."

"I didn't know you wanted to be informed," I said, his anger tickling a deep genetic challenge in me. I sat up, away from my soft pillows, and added, "You hung up on me last time we were discussing the Bolick family."

"Don't get personal. This isn't about us. Ian Bolick's in trouble."

"Damn right he is," I said. "And Seth Bolick is still dead."

Bill's anger was gone when he spoke again. "Please, Sydney, tell me what you know about this mess. You won't even understand this, but my obligations, my loyalties are to the patents involved—not any of the players."

I was more than pleased to hear my brother say that. For years, ever since he went the way of corporate law and, I have to admit, the way of marital infidelity, I hadn't thought him very ethical. He was showing me he was—at least, in the realm of corporate law. So I told him everything. From the truly odd circumstances of Seth's supposed suicide to Betty's gruesome end to Ian's masquerade and his near violent reaction to Tom Thurgood. I even told him about going through the Bolick files tonight and getting the confession out of Keeter. The whole story took about thirty minutes.

"Goddamn," Bill said when I had finished. "You're telling me Ian Bolick's been sabotaging his own company? Snake and the rest of it would have made him billions of dollars eventually."

"I don't think money really mattered. Not to either Bolick." I was tired now.

"So the patent for Snake's been broadcast all over the tobacco world and the rest of the device configurations have been destroyed? That's what you're telling me?" Bill sounded disgusted.

"So what?" I said. "The patent for Snake's been filed. It's protected legally, isn't it?"

His laugh was sarcastic. "What makes you think that?"

"Doesn't filing a patent protect it? Isn't it safe then no matter who sees it?"

"Wrong, Sydney. Filing is only the first step, and all it does is obligate the federal government to secrecy until the patent is issued. Nobody else is obligated."

I couldn't respond. As he explained the process to me, I realized Snake wasn't protected at all, that any of these people who'd been recipients of the file copies could do anything they wanted with the formulas. Well, maybe not literally anything, but close enough to call it that.

He continued, "The process from filing to issuance takes a couple of years. Corporate espionage happens. It's how we lose patents all the time." Bill sounded tired now too.

"So even if Seth had lived . . ."

"Snake would still have been in trouble. Yes."

"How could one brother do that to another?"

We were both silent as my question hung between us. Finally Bill said, "From what you've told me, it sounds as if Ian asked that question first."

I needed sleep. I was totally drained. "I've got to get off, Bill. You going to the funeral in the morning?"

He told me he wasn't. "I've got to be in court."

That was a surprise. "I didn't think you went to court, Bill."

"I don't like to, but sometimes we can't avoid it. We'll talk about Thanksgiving later, okay?"

After we hung up, I turned out the light and lay back down on my side. With the stone still in my hand, I cradled it in the bend of my fingers and rubbed it with my thumb. I decided to give the lapillus to Johnny the next day. It had meant so much to Seth. It seemed the right thing to do. Seth had said rubbing the stone helped him focus, helped him see what needed to be done. The smoothness of the glass against my skin did calm me, but it didn't help me see what I needed to do. I fell asleep talking to Dad and asking him instead.

24

The year's first true frost fell on Charlotte overnight. The morning was yet chilly and immaculately still when I walked outside to get in Tom's car. Anything that could reflect was doing so: car tops, roofs, and evergreen trees threw their shimmers onto windows, car bodies, power lines, and each other. Giddy with its power to transform, winter premiered that morning. This wasn't winter as I'd remembered it, and told Tom so. He agreed, said he'd wondered about the sparkle himself.

I wished I hadn't promised to take the logo by the hospital on the way to Seth's funeral. The fact is, I was uncharacteristically depressed, and talking advertising with Dr. Douglas Fritz was the last thing I wanted to do. I didn't have a choice, though, the way I see things. I'd promised the work and Hart had dropped other things to do it for me.

I asked Tom to drive me to the office first. He'd

brought his own car, a rusty gray Honda. Seth's funeral was personal and today was his day off; besides, he'd also lost his Toyota yesterday, although neither one of us mentioned that.

"When we get to the hospital, I might ask you to take it inside. It'll give you a chance to see Sally. She'll like that."

He tipped an imaginary hat to me as he parked the Honda illegally in front of Allen Teague. "Whatever you say, ma'am," he said.

"You need to move, Tom," I told him. He wasn't a cop that day, so he shouldn't have been using the privileges of one.

"I'll take my chances." He grinned, leaned across me, and pushed my door open.

"This is the first time I've ever hoped someone gets a ticket, Tom. You bring out the worst in me." I got out and walked briskly toward the office as he jogged to catch up.

The logos were interesting, if not outstanding. I didn't want to hurt Hart's feelings, but the celery-anchored caduceus looked too much like Road Runner. Among the raw vegetables, the carrot worked better. And orange was a better logo color than light green too. Looked sort of like Mercurochrome. When I took one glance at the human within the snake, the sexless one I'd requested, I was taken aback. Hart had connected the beginnings of the snake where a man's penis would be. He'd wrapped it over twice so not many people would notice, but he'd attached it just the same.

He saw my expression and said, "I couldn't help it. I told you I couldn't do a sexless human figure."

"But, Hart," I began, but he wouldn't let me get a word in.

"It goes against everything I was taught. I am a reality-based artist."

I watched him closely and decided I wasn't going to win this one.

Tom saw it now too and walked away so Hart wouldn't see him laughing. Leslie didn't understand what we were talking about.

"Did you try a woman too?" I asked. I didn't expect an answer, but he gave me one anyway.

Hart gestured with his hand about his chest as he nodded to me. "There were two of them. I couldn't make it work." He blushed. "Besides, they were too high. No balance."

"Like the celery," I said as I nodded in understanding. He had a point, although merely an artistic one. Tom was choking in the corner of my office.

I gathered the six treatments together inside my portfolio, heaved it to the top of my desk to zip it up, and noticed the light flashing on my voice mail.

"Have I had calls already this morning?" I asked Leslie.

"Yesterday's," she said. "Betty Zebrinski."

I let the portfolio drop to the floor. How had I forgotten Betty's voice mail message? Tom and I gathered around my telephone as if a miracle were about to occur. Would she tell us who killed Seth? Would she be able to foretell who would kill her so shortly after leaving this message?

As prepared as we thought we were, I don't think

anyone could have anticipated what Betty said into my voice box. It was so shocking and unexpected I dare not paraphrase it here. The following is what she said:

"Sydney, I want someone to know the truth of what went on here. So I'm leaving you this message because I won't be around to explain it to you. . . . You will find out sooner or later I've been a Judas to Seth Bolick. The most wonderful man I've ever known." Her voice broke. "And the worst part of it is, I told him." An unmistakable sob was the next sound heard on the tape. She fought for control and began again. "And, when I did, I saw his heart break. I told him the morning he killed himself. I didn't want to believe he'd done it, Sydney, but now I know he did. I drove him to it. Why I told him, I don't know." We could hear her ragged breath. Then she repeated "I don't know." She inhaled deeply like someone who was about to swim underwater. "I've hidden my journals in the small greenhouse. It's the least I can do for Seth. Please take them and see that they are protected, that they at least will not go to the enemy. As for everything else in this building, I've already destroyed it. The vultures are coming. I can hear their car a half mile off on that gravel road. . . . The last bit of evidence I need to destroy is me." She laughed, but it wasn't a bitter sound. I know I heard relief in her voice and an eagerness to get the job done. "God forgive me. . . ."

I stared at my telephone for a full minute. My eyes suddenly stung, then my vision blurred from tears. I didn't want to believe what she'd said. I didn't want to believe what it meant. Betty had killed herself because she thought she'd driven Seth to do the same.

I felt Tom's hand at my back. None of us said anything for a good while. The shock had run through all of us, I assume, as lightning does to a group when standing on a hill.

"It's too bad," Tom said finally. I remember thinking this was understatement of huge proportions.

If Seth had mattered any less than he did to me, I would have forgone his funeral entirely. Betty's prologue to her own self-mutilation was more than I could handle this morning. The hardest part of listening to her tape, though, was how it made me feel about myself. I identified with her. I identified with her humiliation and, to a lesser extent, her self-loathing. To have betrayed someone you love—and she clearly loved Seth—is the second most horrible feeling in the world. The worst feeling, and I mean the absolute worst, is for the person to die before you can correct what you've done.

I was almost in a trance by the end of Betty's message. Tom was shaking his head. I know how he thinks. His reaction was pure dismay at the waste of a life, any life. I'd seen that look on his face before. When I saw the confused expressions on Leslie and Hart's face, it slowly dawned on me they didn't know Betty had died yesterday. They both looked at me, not at Tom, for some kind of explanation.

I sat in my desk chair. I put my hand on the message box again, even poised my index finger to punch Repeat. Why play it again though? If Betty were to talk again, would that make her any less dead? If she were to talk again, would she explain herself any better to Hart and Leslie so I wouldn't have to? If she were to talk again, would she allow me to talk back to her, tell her that Seth didn't kill himself so there's no need for her to take her own life? Allow me to be a friend, to commiserate, to help with her burden?

"What did she mean, Ms. Teague?" Leslie's voice was soft, her tone meek enough that I didn't have to answer if I didn't want to.

Tom sat on my desk, his back to me. He said to Leslie, "Betty Zebrinski killed herself yesterday." He placed his hand over mine on the machine. "This message to Sydney was the last thing she did before she died."

Leslie began to cry. Even Hart looked as if he might. I didn't though. I really don't know why except that I'd cried for Betty already. I'd cried when I thought she'd been murdered. My sadness had sunk deeper now. I felt it somewhere below my chest—where my feelings for Seth had settled, where the sadness mingled with anger.

Hart stood before me and said quietly, "So Seth Bolick killed himself after all."

"No, no," I said louder than I needed to.

All three of them were watching me.

"No. Don't you see? I was going to tell her. After I saw Keeter . . ." I looked up at Tom. "Tom knows he didn't. The note was misread . . . misunderstood." Then I finally started to choke back tears I didn't know were in me. "Everything . . . all of it . . . misunderstanding."

Tom towered over me as I whimpered into his crotch. He pressed my head against him as he rubbed his hands in a circular motion on my back and my shoulders. His dark suit was wool with the musty odor of storage. As comforting as his hands felt, I couldn't breathe. I pulled myself away and took a deep breath.

He squatted in front of me so we'd be eye to eye. He pushed my unruly hair behind my ears. He smiled the warmest smile I think I've ever seen. "Hey," he said, "I'm with you on this. Seth didn't kill himself. I know that." He then looked up at Hart and Leslie. "Sydney's right. Seth Bolick was murdered. We're going to find out by whom."

I reached into my pocketbook and found the jar of antacids. I took two, a green one and a pink one.

Tom acted as my courier. I couldn't bring myself to go into the hospital before the funeral. Not just because I was devastated by Betty's words, but because of the way I knew I'd act in there if I were the one to represent our work to the doctor. When I'm off my game for any reason, I sabotage myself with inappropriate comments and behaviors. I'd probably point out the penis to the good doctor. Might even tell him we'd used him as a model. I know because I've behaved that way before. I am recklessly honest when I am down.

He stayed longer with Sally than I expected him to. I tried not to smoke while he was gone, but I failed. I cursed myself for failing the whole time I did. When he returned, he assured me he hadn't even seen Dr. Fritz. He'd left the work with Sally, who'd said the doctor would be by shortly. She'd told Tom he was having lunch in her room. I was able to laugh about that. I couldn't wait for her to be well. Fritz could even come to lunch at Allen Teague as long as he got Sally well again.

Tom smiled while I was laughing. "That's a good sign," he said. He patted my thigh with his free hand as he drove. "You had me worried for a while there." He drove awhile longer in silence, then said, "Leaving that message was selfish of her, you know. Just one more confession. Good for her soul but no thought to how it would affect you."

"I think she was trying to help," I said wearily. "At least we're no longer looking for a murderer. Not hers anyway." I looked at his profile as he drove. "Thanks for defending Seth with Hart and Leslie. I'm not naive though. I know there's still a chance he killed himself."

Tom glanced at me briefly, almost dismissively. "I meant what I said, Sydney."

The residue of that morning's frost sparkled off the red tin roof on Bredon's hardware store. Straw bales, pumpkins, and potted yellow mums were quaintly arranged at the door. Two doors down, the Nations-Bank branch had an antique wagon in its side yard. Colorful gourds overflowed it and dangled over a wheel. The bank itself had a wood shake roof and cornflower blue siding. The sheriff had said they "gussied up" their downtown for the commuters. Funny how I was noticing it for the first time. Now I saw it everywhere. Even down to the barrels of apples outside the produce market and the American flags at several storefronts. How horrible, I thought, to turn the town you've lived in all your life into a stage set. All for the tax revenues of city folk gone country. I unclasped the pearls from around my neck and slipped them into my pocketbook.

"Why'd you do that?" Tom asked.

I pointed at the flag in front of the Bredon Presbyterian Church. "I was beginning to feel thematic," I said.

Tom put the Honda in park, then stared at my red shell and my navy suit. He laughed, shook his head. Then he saluted me.

Thank goodness the church was small. It could seat a hundred at most. Counting Tom and me, no more than thirty people were there. Other than Tom and Johnny Bolick, no men were in attendance. Since Tom was mine and Johnny was Seth's, that meant no men at all had come to pay their respects. Not even Ian's sons. Most of the women were elderly. Jen's churchwomen, I assumed. And there was Jen herself, who, I had to admit when I saw her, was a remarkably strong woman. She'd buried her husband before his time and now a son. Ian had said she'd held the family together. As I watched her with her hands on Johnny's shoulders, I could see it. The Bolick men had abdicated. Jen had stepped in when she needed to. Sara stood on the other side of Johnny, her hands gripping the back of the empty first pew. I understood her anger now when she'd thought Seth's last message was to me. Her anger too at Betty. Betty's adoration of Seth, so obvious in her eyes. Sara still loved Seth, but her anger was so deep she couldn't see it herself. A smattering of women Sara's age were there, and one young girl who could have been a friend of Johnny's. Sheriff Keeter wasn't even there. He'd been right about the county's feelings. They may not have killed Seth, but his passing was surely good riddance.

I felt hypocritical for being in their midst. Suddenly I wanted out of that church, that mockery of mourning. As the music began and everyone was rising to sing, I whispered to Tom, "Let's leave."

Although the mild shock on his face was unmistakable, he was being true to his word today. He was my driver, nothing more. We left out the side door as a decidedly soprano rendition of "Rock of Ages" hit the second stanza.

"I'm sorry, Tom. I just couldn't stand it. I felt like they were celebrating, not mourning. I—"

He put his hand up to stop me. "You don't have to explain anything, Sydney." The Honda was idling at the church lot exit. "Where to now? The farm?"

I nodded.

He looked over at me.

"The greenhouses," I said.

25

This close to noon and with the sky so clear, the frost had retreated from all but the shadows. On the lower leaves of the grove of pines, I could still see it shimmering. An occasional rock caught the Honda's reflection as we drove. On the rye, though, the freeze had turned liquid and washed each blade to newborn green—lush, verdant awakenings—like spring.

Tom noticed it too. "Sure is green," he said, "just when everything else is turning brown."

We hit a long stretch of the road without a curve. The wind kicked up a November gust. It blew a current through the fields, turning them to flowing, swelling oceans of green. I was overcome by the beauty of it. For the first time I understood how people could love the land so deeply that all else in life seemed false.

"It's beautiful out here, isn't it, Tom?"

"Nothing else like it," he said.

The smaller greenhouse was behind the other two. Tom pulled over where I had parked yesterday when I'd seen Sara here.

"Do you want me to go with you?" he asked as he turned off the ignition.

"Hang on a second. Let me check out our distance to the graveyard. We might want to just park here."

There's a slight hill between where we parked and the greenhouses. When I'd been here the day before, I'd noticed the backs of both Bolick houses not far from the entrance to the smaller greenhouse. The family grave-yard was somewhere near as well. I hated doing it to a second pair of good leather shoes, but I hiked through the wet red clay up the grassless bank to a point where I could see the other side of the smaller greenhouse. As I'd hoped, a nice brick path ran from the greenhouse en-trance to the family plot, split into a V there, ran as two paths along each side of the graveyard's black wrought-iron fence and on to the back doors of each house. We should have parked at either Jen's or Ian's. Dammit! My shoes were unnecessarily caked in mud at the heel. No sense in Tom ruining his as well.

I yelled back down the hill to Tom, "Drive back a road. Park at the house. There's a sidewalk from here to there."

"You want me to park and walk over?" he yelled back.

I shook my head. "The grave site's between here and there. I'll meet you at it. The service is probably let-ting out now."

Tom nodded, got back into the Honda. I watched him drive away.

I walked along the side of one of the commercial-size greenhouses to get to the smaller one, then along its side to the entrance. Thank God someone had placed a row of gravel for drainage up close to the structures. I crunched my way wobbly through the gravel, mercifully losing some of my accumulated mud in the process. Replacing it, I feared, with scratches.

The greenhouse was about the size of a large living room, a fraction of the size of the other two. Its door was ajar. I smelled the odd odor even before I entered. What I recognized as chlorophyll was part of it, but it wasn't the clean, refreshing effect I thought defined chlorophyll. Its cleanliness was sullied by an underlying sweetness, a sweetness akin to mildew in a wash load left overnight. What held both scents was air so thick and musty I coughed on my first intake. It was like being trapped in a truckload of Tom's wool pants. At the same time my eyes began to water.

Around the inside walls of the greenhouse hundreds of young tobacco plants sat in individual pots. Some of the plants looked healthy to me, but most were covered with a grayish soot, or a mounding, dusty mold. The air must have been rife with spores. No wonder I was having a hard time breathing.

I easily spotted the journals. They were on a deep rectangular table directly in front of me as I stood just inside the door. The massive, raw-oak table held bins underneath it of potting soil, peat moss, and rooting powder. On its surface were some bottles made of brown glass, a couple of handheld sprayers, small bottles with droppers attached, and three hypodermic needles. I tried to swallow but couldn't. Maybe it was the air.

Maybe it was seeing the hypodermics. Probably, though, it was Ian Bolick. He was standing at the far end of the table reading Betty's journal pages. I wasn't at all shocked that he was in there. He most certainly would have come home to Bright Snake Farm. He couldn't go to his own home or his mother's house. The police would have already checked with them. His choices were few at this moment. He obviously hadn't slept, or if he had, had done so on the floor of one of these greenhouses. Dirt and straw covered his corduroy pants and clung to his canvas shirt. The bloodstains on his sleeve had turned black.

"Hello, Sydney." He appeared as calm as I was. "So, the Liggon goons didn't get this work after all." He leafed through the thick stack of hastily torn journal pages. "What do you think we should do with it?" Only then did he look up at me.

"She left them here for me," I said evenly.

"For you? Why you?"

"She thought I'd protect them. That Snake could somehow be saved."

His laugh was short and bitter.

"Betty killed herself, Ian. Did you know that already?"

His cool demeanor melted ever so slightly. He shook his head. "Why?"

I walked closer to him. The air was even thicker. I tried breathing deeply, coughed again when I did. "She betrayed Seth," I said between coughing. "She thought he killed himself because of it."

He stared at me.

I tried taking quick, shallow breaths. It seemed to

help. Whatever was in the air in there stopped short of my lungs.

"But we know Seth didn't kill himself, don't we, Ian?" I raised my eyebrows and nodded slowly as I spoke to him.

"Maybe he didn't," he said. He put the pages down, ran a hand through his stubby hair, and exhaled heavily. "Maybe he didn't," he repeated. "I'm sorry I scared you yesterday." His eyes were weak. He hadn't closed them in a long time.

I was now standing at one end of the table, Ian at the other. This wasn't the belligerent, confident man I'd met in the field on Tuesday. His fight was gone. He looked beaten.

I pointed to the hypodermics. "What are they for?" I asked.

"Blue mold," he said. "Trying to fight it."

"You inject the plants with something?"

"Mother does," he said softly. "She's been fighting blue mold for decades. She experiments with viruses, getting the viruses into the plant's vascular system, trying to stop the mold."

"I didn't know your mother worked with the tobacco. I thought she just dealt with the home." I heard car doors slamming, could hear distant talk. The family was arriving for the graveside service.

"She does whatever she has to do. She always has." Ian's eyes had filled with water that didn't flow over. The blue of his eyes turned pale, though, as the tears filled his sockets. "Seth got his mind as much from her as he did from Father." His voice was starting to break.

"Why didn't Seth ever talk about your mother? He

told me books' worth of details about your father. But he never talked about her. Why, Ian? Do you have any ideas?"

"She was for the land" was all he said. He tried clinching his jaw to regain the composure he was losing. A tear finally spilled to a cheekbone, ran over next to his nose.

"Do you remember the day your father died, Ian? Has she always been in charge of the greenhouses?"

He didn't answer me. I watched his eyes. He looked above my shoulders. I turned to see Tom Thurgood in the doorway. Tom's eyes spoke to me. Be calm, he was saying. He didn't know that I already was.

A sob escaped Ian's throat. "Please," he cried. "I just want to see my baby brother buried. That's why I came here. I thought I could watch, and . . . no one would know." He squeezed the high bridge of his nose with his thumb and forefinger, trying to stop his tears. Thick mucus caught in his throat. He coughed raggedly and continued to cry while he did. His pain was tremendous.

Tom still stood behind me. As Ian fought for control of himself, I turned to Tom and whispered, "Let him watch the burial, Tom. He needs to say good-bye."

He nodded once, then subconsciously pressed his hand against his chest. The moment was brief, but I knew he was instinctively checking his gun. There was always a gun strapped to his chest and another one to his calf.

The voices outside were louder now. A bagpipe started playing a mournful song, but I didn't recognize it. Tom pulled a handkerchief out of his pants pocket, held it to his nose. He walked into the greenhouse and over to Ian's side, where he took Ian's elbow and directed him toward the door. I flanked Ian's other side. He wouldn't get away from us. I didn't think he'd try.

Tom told Ian he had the guns. He warned him he'd use one if he needed to.

"You don't have to worry," Ian said. "I'm through. I don't want to fight anymore."

Before the three of us left the front of the greenhouse, Tom handed his handkerchief to Ian. When he did, the two men's eyes locked briefly. I saw something male pass between them at that moment. A pride thing. A strength thing. I'm not a man, so I don't even have the word for what it was Tom gave Ian when he handed him that handkerchief. The closest word I have for it, though, is dignity. Ian dabbed his eyes with the handkerchief, blew his nose, then dropped the soiled cloth onto the greenhouse floor. He strained to push his shoulders back. He stood proudly, his head held high, his jaws strong and firm like a Bolick.

The minister was reciting the Twenty-third Psalm as we approached the back of the group. Only a few of the mourners noticed us as we joined them. The first was the older woman I'd seen with Ian's sons at the restaurant in Bredon. She blinked and tears fell from her eyes. I knew she wasn't crying for Seth. Ian was amazing though. He gazed at her with so much love I could feel its power by merely standing next to him. He continued to hold his head high and proud. He wasn't to be pitied. Bev stopped crying as they gazed at each other across the bowed heads of the others. She wiped her eyes, held her head proudly now too.

Johnny, Sara, and Jen were close to the casket and Seth's open grave. The minister's words weren't comforting Johnny. I'm certain nothing could have. I remembered how he'd bravely fought crying at the hospital, how his tears had flowed silently, convulsing his body soundlessly in their attack. Now he cried openly, inconsolably. I was relieved that he could let himself, that he could let his grief be what it was. That he wasn't masking it in anger and resentments and his own life turned backwards. Sara had her arms around him, and he was letting her. It was a good sign for both of them.

Jen looked up at Tom, Ian, and me. I was shocked when she did, because none of us had made a sound. How could she have known we were present? The minister was commending Seth's soul to God and speaking directly to Jen as he delivered this part of the service, trying, I felt certain, to comfort the mother of the dead. His eyes followed hers briefly to us, registered us, then returned his attention to Seth's casket. Jen continued staring at us, though, especially at Ian. The corners of her mouth turned up slightly and the laugh lines edging her eyes disappeared in a smile. Out of the corner of my eye I watched Ian make eye contact with her. When he did, her smile faded. She nodded, but never let her chin drop. Ian nodded in return. Something had passed between them as well.

Two men in overalls lowered Seth's casket into the grave. I gulped back my own tears as they did it. For all the graveside services I've attended in my life, I'd never seen a casket lowered. Maybe this is a difference between city burials and country burials or public plots

and family plots. I don't know, and I've not asked anyone about it since that day. In the city the casket hovers
mechanically above its grave, and the grave itself is covered by a blanket. The mourners never see the hole, its
depth, its finality. In the city you walk away when the
service has ended. The casket remains perched, the
grave remains covered. Only after the last mourner de-
parts does the blanket come off and the body get lowered into its grave.

At first I watched in disbelief as the minister
handed Johnny the shovel. With tears still covering
his young face, he dug into the mound beside the grave.
He turned the shovel over at the grave's edge, letting
the dirt slide off and down onto the top of the casket.
The bagpipe played. It sounded to me like a battle song,
nothing close to the lonely dirge I'd heard earlier. One
by one each mourner took the shovel and spilled the
dirt back onto Seth's casket, until the only people left
were Ian, Tom, and me. I wanted to share in the ritual. I
knew Ian needed to.

Ian took the shovel from his wife, Bev. Tom stood
so close to him that his movement was awkward. He
was able to do his part though: he slid half a shovelful
over the edge, where it slipped between the casket and
the inside walls of the grave. He said simply, "I'm so
sorry, Seth." Ian remained strong as he said it, but I
didn't. I didn't wait for the shovel. I scooped up a tiny
bit of the dirt in my hand, leaned over when Ian did, and
sprinkled it on top of Seth's casket. Ian had sounded
like me at my dad's grave. I cried out loud, then wondered whom I was crying for when I heard myself. To

Seth I said three things: I loved him, but he knew that already. I told him he'd done well, because I knew it mattered to him. And finally I told him everybody, including Johnny, would be okay. I said these words hoping to make it so.

Most of us go through life without much thought to its purpose. We rally ourselves around whatever's immediate, whoever's immediate. Our kids, our jobs, our spouses, our churches, our causes. When one of our rallying points takes hold and spreads itself over life's existing landscape, it chokes the health out of everything else. Like a vine gone awry, it wraps itself around once simple pleasures, changes their character, draining their force, and eventually pulls them down. Where once you'd looked out on a varied, rich life, you now see only one thing. It happens sometimes to mothers with their children and to people with their work. It happens to religious converts and teenagers in love. But I've never seen anything take over a life with as much determination as a cause. Seth's cause had been vindication, and it had wiped out all else he might have become.

I didn't want that to happen to his son. I watched Johnny talking with the young girl I'd seen at the church service. I'd been waiting to speak to him, but I needed him alone. I was sitting on a leather sofa in the living room of his house, his grandmother's house, and nibbling at food the churchwomen had laid out. Tom had taken Ian to the car, had called for some officers and a car from Charlotte, and was waiting for them to arrive. Bev Bolick sat in a wing chair across the room.

She stared at me. Although I didn't see any anger in her eyes, the staring made me uncomfortable. I stood and walked into the large kitchen.

Sara Bolick was perched on the top rung of a short kitchen ladder, sipping something resembling gasoline from a highball glass. I think it was Scotch on the rocks.

Jen was directing the churchwomen, including Bert Keeter, as they replenished the near-empty trays. I was willing to bet Jen had been in charge of these women from the beginning—even though she was the recipient of their work. What was it Sara had said about Jen? She was naturally in charge?

I pushed at a single swinging door and found myself in a small sunroom. It held several large, old wicker chairs and a table about three feet in diameter. Sheriff Keeter was sitting in one of those chairs, his fat pressed up against its wide, substantial arms and actually hanging over them in places. His mouth was full. The two or three plates someone had placed in front of him were not.

"You should be ashamed," I said. "Eating Seth's food but not attending his services. What kind of man are you, Sheriff?"

He took his time chewing the food, swallowing bit by bit as he stared back at me. When he was through, he dabbed at his mouth. "I'm waiting for the missus," he said. "This isn't for the dead, anyway. It's for the living. I'm all for the living." He pushed himself back from the table, and I cringed for the old wicker. "About time you get on the side of the living, Miss Teague."

I walked to the window, where I could see a

Charlotte-Mecklenburg police car pulling up beside
Tom's Honda. We'd be able to leave soon. I needed to
muster the will to act.

"They taking Ian now?" Keeter said.

My back still to him, I nodded.

"We'll get him off. What's your brother's name?
Ian told me to call him." I heard an uncooked vegetable
crunch under the force of his teeth. I watched the police
car drive off with Ian in it. Tom turned and was walking
toward the house.

I turned to face Keeter. "My brother's name is Bill
Allen, but he can't help Ian now."

Keeter bit down on a delicate roast beef finger
sandwich. It disappeared. "Ian said he's the company
attorney."

"He's not a criminal attorney, Sheriff. I'm sure you
know the difference."

I left the sheriff with that thought and his dwin-
dling food supply. I walked through the kitchen and
back to the living room, where I hoped to find Johnny
alone. The girl was gone, but Johnny was greeting Tom
at the door.

"Ready to go?" Tom asked me.

"I'd like to speak with Johnny just a minute. Do you
have a few minutes, Johnny? Your dad gave me something I'd like to give to you."

He smiled at me. I led him to the far end of the
wine-colored sofa I'd been sitting on. Three or four
people still milled about the room, one of whom
was the bagpipe player, who'd unloaded his heavy
instrument on the entrance hall floor. Bev had earlier

retreated into the kitchen. Tom sat in the wing chair. He watched us.

I pulled the lapillus from my suit pocket and placed it in his hands. Somewhere along the line I'd decided to lie about the stone. I didn't want to see the boy obsessed the way two generations before him had been. I knew Seth wouldn't want it either. So I didn't tell him the stone would help him focus as his father had told me.

Instead I told him what I thought Seth would have wanted him to hear if he'd known that he would die as he had. I told him about the lapillus origins, about it being created in the center of the hottest fire on earth and then thrown clear of that fire and all its destruction.

"Wow," Johnny said. "My grandfather found it?"

"Yes," I said as I waited to see if he would glean any meaning from the stone's story.

"Why did my dad give it to you?" he asked.

I smiled at him. "Maybe he thought I needed it. You see, I've been depressed about stuff that happened a long time ago, stuff I can't do anything to change. Your dad knew that. The stone's about throwing yourself clear, getting free, getting out of the path of destruction."

He was listening intently.

"You know the source of most destruction, Johnny?"

He shook his head.

I pressed my forefinger into his chest and then my own. "Ourselves," I said as I did. "We need to get out of the way of ourselves sometimes."

I watched him thinking about what I'd said. I looked over at Tom. He moved a hand to the end of his chair arm, anticipating getting up. "Just a min-

ute," I whispered to him as I held my hand up. Tom
sat back.

God help me, I didn't want to. If I could have
thought of any other way to confirm what I'd been
thinking, I wouldn't have done what I did. There wasn't
any other way though.

"I need to ask you a question, Johnny."

"Okay." He continued studying the stone.

"It's about the morning your dad died."

His hand with the lapillus dropped to his side. He
looked at me. I saw a shade of the anger I'd seen there
two days ago.

"Did you give your dad his inhaler that morning?"
He nodded.

"Did you tell him to use it, that it was cold outside?" This was as painful for me as it was for him.

He nodded again, this time his chin trembling.

"Did someone give it to you to take to your dad?
Did someone tell you to tell him it was cold outside?"

He began to shake all over, but he was able to get
the words out. "Yes, Ms. Teague. Yes."

I held his trembling hands, looked into his frightened eyes as calmly as I could, and said, "It was your
grandmother, wasn't it, Johnny?"

He held on to me and bawled. His breakdown was
answer enough to my question. My eyes sought Tom's
as I held the broken boy.

An amazingly composed Jen Bolick rode back to
Charlotte with Tom and me that afternoon. Tom didn't
confront her outright, but he didn't give her a choice
about going either. He simply took her by the elbow

with those very large hands of his and guided her out of her kitchen.

"We have some things to discuss, Mrs. Bolick," he said. "We're going to do it in Charlotte."

She still had her apron on as the three of us got into the Honda.

26

It's exactly one week now since Seth's funeral and Jen Bolick's arrest for his murder. When Tom confronted Jen with what Johnny had told me, she confessed. Readily. Tom says she's a practical woman—above all else. She hadn't wanted to kill her son, she said. She claimed she had no choice. She'd been doing things her whole life she found distasteful, because "someone needed to step forward" and no one ever did. She professes great love for her family. Tom shakes his head whenever he talks about her. He says she'll probably spend the rest of her life in Women's Prison in Raleigh.

We still don't know if she killed her husband twenty years ago. She won't talk about him except to repeat that Seth caught his disease.

I think Ian knows though. He won't talk about it either.

The night after Tom arrested Jen, I couldn't sleep. I kept thinking about Seth and what he must have surely known. How horrible that knowing must have been, even if he hadn't let himself see the truth. Seth was the Bolick who'd found his father on that greenhouse floor, after all. And, for all our hours of soul baring, he'd never once mentioned to me the existence of his mother. Was that because he knew?

With Jen gone, I hope Johnny won't have to grow up defending his father. If he doesn't have to defend him, then he won't get caught up in vindication. And without vindication, Johnny Bolick has a shot at life.

Ian Bolick doesn't have much of a shot though. He's in the Mecklenburg County jail awaiting a trial date. He could probably be out on bail if he wanted to be. He hasn't pushed it though. He seems not to care what happens to himself. Tom says he's grown depressed. The big tobacco companies have distanced themselves from Ian. Theft, embezzlement, conspiracy, and fraud are just a few of the charges against him. Bill tells me ten years may be light in Ian's case—depending on the jury. My brother has surprised me. He's pushing the prosecution and planning civil litigation as well on behalf of the corporation. Ian may be too old to work his land when he gets out.

Joining Ian in jail is Sheriff Keeter. He'll probably get more time than Ian. Bill says he broke the public trust. The Wade County district attorney is moving both men's trials to Mecklenburg. A Wade County jury might find them innocent. Keeter is still dumbfounded by the charges. You'd think a lawman wouldn't get into such a fix, but Keeter just didn't know the law. Too many hats, none worn well, is what I say. Tom says he spread himself too thin, then chuckles with pleasure at

SMOKE SCREEN • 309

his own joke. I don't think any of it's funny. Keeter should have known better. Everybody involved should have known better.

I took a quick flight to Cleveland for Betty Zebrinski's funeral last Friday. I hadn't planned to but found I could get in and out all in an afternoon. Betty'd never been married; she had no children; she was Olaf and Miriam's only child. They were immensely proud of her. I told them how much I admired her. I was telling them the truth.

I don't know what will happen to Snake. Or to the addicting agent that is its basis. The integrity of the patents has been compromised. Bits and pieces of them are floating all over the world. Bill says it's very complicated. He told me at dinner today that tobacco companies are filing suit, actually going to court to try to block the use of the compound. Some religious groups have joined them. Addiction is, for them, a moral issue. Bill says the suit's ridiculous, nothing more than a scare tactic against Bolick Enterprises, a smoke screen for their true agenda.

"What is their agenda?" I asked Bill.

"Survival," he said blandly.

Strange as it seems, Bolick Enterprises still exists. It is now just Sara. She has met with Bill about its future and Johnny's. Bill advised her to hold tight for now, let him fight for her and Johnny. She is following his advice. I am proud of my brother.

I will stay away until I'm called back in. I may never be.

Today is Thanksgiving. Mother brought the turkey and a frozen spinach casserole. I made the dressing from a box. I made the rice from another box. I bought a Mrs. Lee's pumpkin pie and hid it until this morning. People assumed I made it. I thanked them for their compliments.

I asked Sara and Johnny for dinner, but Sara declined. They were eating with Bev Bolick and her family. The two women have vowed to keep any future court battles from tearing apart what's left of their families. I hope Ian's sons take an interest in Johnny. It could make all the difference for him. Dinner today was maybe a start.

Brother Bill was here though. He brought his wife, who didn't say more than two words throughout dinner. There was a time she tried around us. She doesn't anymore.

George junior spent much of the meal debunking the myth of the first Thanksgiving. I told him to keep it to himself. His social studies teacher had told his class the truth, he said, as he kept on. It was only some president's public relations ploy, a political move.

"If you can't say something nice about Thanksgiving," I said, paraphrasing my father's favorite expression, "don't say anything at all."

Georgie rolled his eyes.

"One more word and that food in front of you becomes a myth," I added. Only with that did I reach him. Sheesh. What does fact have to do with the truth of this day?

Joanie remained a ten-year-old throughout the meal. As I've said, she does it for Mother. And, truth be known, for some need in herself I've never been able to meet. When she was quite young, I had my problems. I've never claimed to be a perfect parent. I can only approach it as I do my sobriety: "Progress rather than perfection." Thank God for those slogans.

Mother arrived yesterday and will probably stay through the weekend. We talked last night about Dad. We shared memories of long-ago Thanksgivings. I told her I was okay now. And I really am. Something has happened for me these last couple of weeks. I see myself more clearly in relation to Dad. I don't know what did it, but no one should live with that guilt. I've forgiven myself for what I did; rather, what I didn't do. I'm sure Dad is saying it's high time.

I was late sitting down with the family. When the turkey came out of the oven, I ran two plates to Sally's house. To my surprise, Hart was there. He'd brought them a pre-cooked turkey and all that comes with it. I whispered to Sally, "Mine's better." She looked at me clearly and smiled. The old Sally smile. She's almost back to herself. She'll still be out another month according to Dr. Fritz. But that's okay. Whatever it takes. Besides, I've grown attached to Leslie. She's coming along. She's learning the world of business. I can't rationalize another administrative person at Allen Teague, but, when Sally returns, I might try Leslie in sales. That girl is so genuinely nice prospects will find it hard being mean to her.

Poor Tom couldn't make it to dinner. He'd planned to, but a South Charlotte boy shot his father last night. Tom's lead on that case. He says it's a story that will break my heart. I called at Tom's, though, to see if he was home yet. He had just arrived. He went all night with the boy, he said. Got him talking at least. Tom sounded so tired.

"Let me bring you the dinner you missed. You'll especially like my pie."

He protested, but not much.

So I climbed up into the Trooper with his meal in my backseat. I placed it on the face of my tennis racquet—for balance. I decided to serve it to him that way.

I parked next to the overgrown bushes flanking the small portion of his house that hugs the land. I retrieved the foil-covered plate perched on my racquet, deciding to cradle them close to me until the moment I would serve him. It seemed later than five o'clock. Deep shadows covered Tom's kitchen knob. The racquet wobbled as I opened the door and entered.

Tom's bedroom is in the back of his house, a house more on water than land. His window frames Lake Wylie, the South Carolina side, at a point pristine and protected. I am lying here now, looking out as Tom eats. I much prefer this to tennis with him.

The racquet I served his meal with is on the floor beside us. Tom is tickled with my effort. He calls it "a classy move."

"A classy move for a classy man," I say. I rub his thigh as I wait for him to finish his piece of pie.

He puts the plate on his bedside table. He props himself on his elbow and lowers his six-and-a-half-foot frame down to me.

"Tell me the whole world hasn't gone mad," he says. He kisses me on my lips, then on my neck. "Tell me something reassuring, Sydney."

"I am grateful for you, Tom Thurgood. I'm so very grateful."